From sadness to joy . . .

When the last tear was spent, Julianna drew back from him, at once embarrassed by her emotional display as well as her untidy appearance.

"Forgive me. I am sorry." She pressed the back of her hand to her cheek. "It seems I have nothing better to do than cry in your presence and I have undoubtedly spoiled your coat."

Nicholas bent toward her and gently cupped his hand to her cheeks, tilting her face up to him. "There is nothing to forgive, Miss Julianna."

Before she could step away, Nicholas lowered his mouth to hers and placed a soft, light kiss on her lips. Without realizing just what she was doing, Julianna ran her hands up his arms, to his shoulders and around his neck. Nicholas's kiss deepened; his arms encircled her waist, drawing her closer to him. Even within that fleeting moment, Julianna recognized Nicholas's kiss was not just a comforting gesture, but a clear indication that he wanted much more. His lips were warm and firm. A slow, sweet fire shot through her, making her weak and trembling. . . .

The Captain's Castaway

Christine Scheel

A SIGNET BOOK

SIGNET
Published by New American Library, a division of
Penguin Group (USA) Inc., 375 Hudson Street,
New York, New York 10014, USA
Penguin Group (Canada), 10 Alcorn Avenue, Toronto,
Ontario M4V 3B2, Canada (a division of Pearson Penguin Canada Inc.)
Penguin Books Ltd., 80 Strand, London WC2R 0RL, England
Penguin Ireland, 25 St. Stephen's Green, Dublin 2,
Ireland (a division of Penguin Books Ltd.)
Penguin Group (Australia), 250 Camberwell Road, Camberwell, Victoria 3124,
Australia (a division of Pearson Australia Group Pty. Ltd.)
Penguin Books India Pvt. Ltd., 11 Community Centre, Panchsheel Park,
New Delhi - 110 017, India
Penguin Group (NZ), cnr Airborne and Rosedale Roads, Albany,
Auckland 1310, New Zealand (a division of Pearson New Zealand Ltd.)
Penguin Books (South Africa) (Pty.) Ltd., 24 Sturdee Avenue,
Rosebank, Johannesburg 2196, South Africa

Penguin Books Ltd., Registered Offices:
80 Strand, London WC2R 0RL, England

First published by Signet, an imprint of New American Library,
a division of Penguin Group (USA) Inc.

First Printing, June 2005
10 9 8 7 6 5 4 3 2 1

 REGISTERED TRADEMARK—MARCA REGISTRADA

Printed in the United States of America

PUBLISHER'S NOTE
This is a work of fiction. Names, characters, places, and incidents either are
the product of the author's imagination or are used fictitiously, and any resem-
blance to actual persons, living or dead, business establishments, events, or
locales is entirely coincidental.

For Dee Hendrickson,
a mentor, a dear friend, and
a great lady.
I couldn't have done this without you.
My heartfelt thanks.

NOTE TO READER

See below for couple notes that pertain to *The Captain's Castaway*. These and other interesting facts can be found in *A Sea of Words* by Gary King (Henry Holt & Co., 1995).

In 1812 the left side of the ship was referred to as the "larboard" side, the right side as "starboard." To avoid confusion from the similarity of the words, "larboard" was officially changed in 1844 to "port," the nautical term that is still used today.

A Letter of Marque is a license granted by the sovereign entitling a ship's captain—by international law—to commit acts that might otherwise have constituted piracy. Captured ships were dealt with as *prize* cases and adjudicated in Admiralty Court.

Chapter One

Seven bells sounded in clear, sharp tones as Captain Sir Nicholas Sidney stepped out of his cabin and firmly set the black bicorne on his head, adjusting it to the correct angle. The smell of wet oak and the sound of scraping holystones against the deck assaulted his senses as he strode briskly onto the quarterdeck.

Mr. Smythe, his first lieutenant, nodded politely to him.

"Good morning, Captain."

"Good morning, Mr. Smythe."

Smythe looked toward the bow. "Seven bells and all is well, sir."

"Anything to report?" Captain Sidney turned toward the larboard rail with Smythe half a step behind him.

"Nothing of importance. Bit of a row below deck last night. Seems a couple of the lads got into it over a pint of grog. Nothing serious."

Captain Sidney snapped open his telescope and scanned the distance. The sun had just broken over the horizon sending its rays across a shimmering, calm sea.

"Disciplinary problem, Mr. Smythe?"

"No, sir. I told Mr. Collins to let 'em off with a severe reprimand—no grog for them today. The lads are keyed up, sir, being so close to port now. It has been nine months six since we've last seen land."

The captain closed the glass and eyed his lieutenant. "Nine months, eh? By God it seems like nine years. Cannot remember when I have so looked forward to going home."

"I, too, sir, am looking forward to it. I've sorely missed Mrs. Smythe and the little ones."

"You have a new addition to the family, if I am correct."

Smythe coughed and looked down. "Aye, sir. Haven't seen him yet. The missus named him Colin. She told me in her last letter. He should be gettin' his sea legs by now."

Nicholas smiled and reached across to place an affectionate hand on his lieutenant's shoulder. "Maybe not his sea legs, but your Nancy will make a sailor of him yet."

"Aye, sir. A fine sailor for His Majesty's Navy."

Turning back to the rail, Nicholas once again pulled open the telescope to scan the water. Light wind, steady seas, good sailing. They would make Portsmouth in a week. The crew was restless and tense, eager for shore leave. Aye. Eager to spend their share of the booty taken from that fat Dutch merchantman they had surprised in the West Indies not three months ago, along with the rewards from an Italian trading vessel. The pickings had been good—good enough for him to settle back into a country life free of the sea and restore Wycombe Hall to its former grandeur.

Not badly done for the son of an impoverished baronet, he thought with some satisfaction. His father had left his only son nothing but debts and a crumbling house in Hertfordshire. The only recourse left to that son was to go to sea and earn his living. With his letter of marque, Nicholas had paid off the creditors long ago, but the house would take time and attention. He looked forward to the task—he *craved* it—and by God, this *would* be his last voyage for the king and the damned Admiralty.

"Captain! Mr. Smythe! Boat off the starboard rail!"

Nicholas hastened across the deck to the rail, Mr. Smythe and a handful of sailors at his heels.

"There, sir," the midshipman said breathlessly, pointing in the direction of something that did indeed look like a small boat bobbing in the gentle swells.

Both Nicholas and Mr. Smythe trained their glasses to the object in the water.

"Captain, it looks like a launch from a ship that may've gone down," Smythe suggested.

Nicholas focused on the craft. Indeed, Smythe was correct. It was a ship's launch, in bad shape and foundering in the low waves.

"Check for survivors," he ordered crisply.

"Mr. Hatchard," Smythe barked. "Hard to starboard!"

"Hard to starboard, aye, sir!" the helmsman responded, and HMS *Gallant* promptly heeled to the wind heading for the small boat in the water.

"Mr. Smythe, lower a cutter," Nicholas snapped.

In short time, a gleaming white launch was lowered over the side of the *Gallant,* with Third Lieutenant Dain shouting orders to the six sailors pulling at the oars. Nicholas watched closely as the trim launch pulled alongside the floundering boat and the crew attached lines to its bow.

He glanced at Mr. Smythe, squinting through his own glass to make sure young Dain was following orders correctly. Nicholas eyed the unknown launch again. He could make out a rough tentlike affair, made from a scrap of sail propped over the bow as a kind of rude shelter for someone or something. They'd arrived not a moment too soon—the boat was almost filled to the gunwales with water.

Over the sound of the sea and the creak of rigging, they could hear the lieutenant giving sharp orders for the crew to pull whatever was still in the damaged boat into the cutter.

"Good Lord," Mr. Smythe exclaimed. "Captain . . . I'll be bound. Captain, I do believe one of the survivors—"

Captain Sidney's attention riveted to the form being carefully lowered into the *Gallant*'s launch. A scrap of lace, a ribbon fluttering in the cool breeze, the definite ruffling of a white flounce. He swallowed and blinked, holding the glass firmly to his eye.

"Good God, Smythe, it is a woman!"

A woman. On the *Gallant*. Something he never permitted. No women at sea. His firm, unbreakable rule—until now.

Nicholas watched, concealing his astonishment as two of the sailors lowered her to the deck alongside an older man—an old tar, by the looks of him.

"Send for the surgeon at once," he ordered and knelt next to the woman, lightly touching her sunburned cheek. Cautiously he took her hand. It was clammy and limp in his large, dry palm.

Glancing her over, he could tell she was undoubtedly a lady. Her once-trim straw bonnet was now crushed, and its bedraggled, misshapen form barely concealed her badly sunburned face. Her lips were swollen from lack of water, and her hair, a sable-colored mass, tumbled raggedly over her shoulders, covering her chest.

Her gown, salt-stained and dirty, had been torn in several places, but he could tell immediately by the cloth and the cut it was of quality workmanship.

Gently he touched the pulse point at her throat and noted a faint steady rhythm. Relieved, he brushed back some of the tangled hair from her face. Pretty girl, he thought. What could have happened?

At that moment, Mr. Philips, the ship's surgeon, elbowed his way through the crowd of curious sailors and knelt down next to the captain.

"Looks bad, sir. Sunstroke, most likely. No telling

how long they've been in that boat with no water and probably nothing to eat either. Let's get her below."

Nicholas looked up at Mr. Philips, noting the serious expression in his eyes, and nodded. "Will she die, Mr. Philips?"

The surgeon shook his head slowly. "It will be chancy, sir."

The captain stood and called for Clarke, his young steward, and ordered him to go below and clear out his quarters for the lady. He glanced at the gawking crew that had gathered about and glared at his first lieutenant.

"Mr. Smythe, have these men nothing to do?"

The lieutenant came to attention and spun on his heel. "Aye, aye, sir!" he answered and immediately ordered the crew back to their duties.

Nicholas looked down at the woman lying on the deck and then at the surgeon still kneeling by her side. He struggled with the propriety of the situation—a British naval ship's captain did not carry half-drowned young women, no matter how attractive, around his ship. Reluctantly, he gave the order: "Bring her below, Mr. Philips."

The surgeon picked her up and without a word, carried her to the captain's cabin.

Nicholas was grateful for Philips. The good surgeon was married and had daughters. He knew what to do. From a discreet distance in his cabin, Nicholas watched as Philips gently stripped the young woman of her shoes and tattered stockings. Next the gown. Philips struggled to hold her in his arms and undo the buttons at her back.

"Captain . . . sir? Would you mind? I need a bit of a hand."

Nicholas set down the hat he had been nervously fingering and approached the bunk. She looked so small, all crumpled and helpless on the expanse of linen.

"Just hold her up whilst I tug off this gown." The

surgeon clucked his tongue sympathetically. "Poor lass. I wonder what happened?"

Obliging the surgeon, Nicholas grasped her slender waist from behind to keep her from slumping on the bunk. Philips worked swiftly, almost tearing the ragged gown off her slight form.

"I think it best we leave the under . . . the . . . uh . . . her shift, Captain. When she's up and about, she can remove that herself."

Nicholas nodded with relief, not wanting to violate her privacy any further. She weighed nearly nothing. He could feel her ribs beneath his fingers. Her head fell forward, exposing the back of her neck, untouched by the merciless sun. So fair, like a flower's petal. He shook his head, uncertain where that thought had come from.

He eased her back onto the bunk, while Philips drew a blanket over her. The surgeon touched her brow. "I will need plenty of cool water to sponge her off. As soon as she's able, we need to get something down her throat."

"Of course. Any word on the old sailor?"

"McVey will look him over. He appears to be a tough old tar. He will pull through."

"Good. He can tell us what happened to the two of them."

The surgeon rose and smoothed the blanket. "Aye, sir." He nodded toward the young woman. "Such a pretty lass, but so small-like. I fear she may have a tough go of it, sir. Too many days in the sun without water. It appears the old fellow tried to make some shelter for her, however, we must consider the possibility that she may not survive."

Nicholas did not want to hear that. She would live, she must. Besides, how would he explain to the Admiralty the death of an unknown woman on board his ship? Even if she did not die, the scuttle through the fleet would be just as untenable. He could almost hear the jeering sarcasm of his fellow officers whilst they discussed him and his unexpected passenger over a convivial glass of port:

"Didja hear the one about young Sidney? Had a woman in his bunk. Claims he found her, what? Egad. I would like to find some pretty castaway and stow her in my quarters!"

"Captain Sidney claims he found a woman, lost at sea. I say, dashed amusing since Sidney has vowed never to allow a woman on board."

Nicholas signaled the surgeon to carry on. "Do your best, Mr. Philips."

If anything, Philips was diligent. For two days he sat near the young woman and sponged her hot, reddened skin and tried to get water down her throat. At night, she rested quietly, but Nicholas made a point of steering clear of his cabin. To compensate for the surgeon's absence, he ordered Philips's young assistant, McVey, to tend to any needs of the crew and to look after the old salt belowdecks.

The sailor responded quickly, taking water and eventually some gruel. Still weak, he could not speak without difficulty. Nicholas sent orders to McVey that as soon as the fellow was well enough, he was to report to him immediately.

At night, he slept in Mr. Smythe's cabin. The lieutenant cheerfully obliged his captain by sharing Second Lieutenant Lawrence's quarters.

Thank God they were so close to port. Nicholas could not imagine spending weeks or months with a woman holed up in his cabin. Too dangerous with a ship full of lonely, homesick men. He would have a riot on his hands, a full-blown mutiny.

Nicholas twisted in Smythe's too-short bunk, trying to find a comfortable position. Whom should he contact once they reached Portsmouth? The Admiralty? The Foreign Office?

What if she did not wake up by then?

What if she died?

Too many disturbing thoughts as well as the discomforts of Smythe's bunk prevented him from falling asleep. He turned again, pounding the pillow into a more cooperative shape.

It was then he heard first a low cry, followed by a terrible scream as if someone were dying or being tortured to death. He leaped from the bunk, anticipating young Clarke's anxious pounding on the cabin door. He yanked on his white breeches, shoving his bare feet into black buckled shoes, and hastily tucked in the linen shirt. He did not bother with the stock or his coat, but pulled open the door and ran in the direction of the dreadful sound.

At his own cabin door, he stopped. The sound was definitely coming from inside. Pausing only briefly, Nicholas pushed open the door.

He stared, appalled. She was on her knees, in the middle of the bunk, linens scattered and twisted all about her. Her small hands clutched the pillow to her breast as she rocked back and forth, moaning and sobbing. Her long dark hair streamed down her shoulders in stark contrast against her frightened, pale face. Enormous brown eyes, focusing on nothing, stared into the gloom of the cabin.

Nicholas stepped inside, assessing the situation. She was clearly delirious, caught in some ghastly nightmare and not even aware of his presence.

"No," she gasped. "Stop it! Stop it! Make it stop! Oh, dear God, make it stop! Save him!"

He tried to sound calm, but failed. "M-M-Miss. Ma'am. I b-b-beg you, what is the matter?" Nicholas cursed his damned, stammering tongue. Around men, or when commanding his crew, it was not so pronounced, but with women . . . "Allow me to f-f-fetch the surgeon."

His words fell on deaf ears. She neither heard nor saw him, but continued to rock back and forth, clutching the pillow. He took a step toward her, then heard Clarke's polite cough coming from behind him. Nicholas turned and saw him staring, mouth open, at the woman in his bunk.

"Fetch Mr. Philips."

Clarke blinked and continued to stare.

"Now, Mr. Clarke, or I will have you in irons!"

The lad sprang to obey. "Aye, sir. At once, sir."

As Nicholas moved closer, her soft moaning turned into helpless crying—dry, aching sobs. Cautiously, he eased himself onto the edge of the bunk and attempted an awkward pat on her back. When she did not respond, he placed an experimental arm across her shoulders.

"There n-n-now, ma'am. You must not d-d-distress yourself. All's well," he said stiffly.

Damn! What was he to do? He knew almost nothing about women and their temperaments. His mother had died when he was ten, and with no sister, he was entirely lacking in knowing how to deal with a woman—a lady—in close quarters. Well, except for the occasional liaison with certain discreet "ladies," there had been only one genuine lady in his life. He had almost succumbed to her charms, but the memory of her deceit aroused only contempt.

The door swung open and he glanced up as Mr. Philips entered the cabin.

"How is she?" the surgeon asked anxiously.

"Hysterical. A nightmare, I presume."

Philips bent down to grasp her arm and shook it gently. "Miss . . . miss? Dear lady, can you hear me?"

There was no response. Philips rubbed his jaw, appearing utterly dumbfounded. "Damned if I know what is the matter. Might be a bit off her keel. The sun may have damaged her brain." He tapped his temple with one slim finger.

Nicholas studied his perplexed surgeon and then the sobbing girl. "You mean she may be permanently d-d-demented? A lunatic?"

An unpleasant consequence, indeed. There was nothing to do but to make her comfortable until they dropped anchor, then turn her over to the care of a proper doctor on shore. There it was. Simple as that.

Nicholas patted her shoulder again, dismayed by her

obvious distress. As he did, she abruptly turned to him and pressed her forehead to his chest, still crying. Her small hands twined in the fabric of his shirt, clutching and twisting at it, while her sobs became deeper, more heartbreaking.

For a moment he sat perfectly still, unable to comprehend fully what was happening. Her hair smelled of the sea—from her skin, a trace of lavender. Warm tears soaked through the fine fabric of his shirt, wetting his skin—a disturbingly erotic sensation.

"There now," he murmured. Without considering what he was doing, he put his arms around her shoulders, pulling her closer to him.

"Looks like all she needs is a good cry, sir. Many's the time I've comforted my own girls—let 'em weep till they're dry." He nodded approvingly. "That's what's needed, sir."

Nicholas returned the nod. "I think you are right. You can go, Mr. Philips. I will see she gets back to sleep."

"Very good, sir. I'll check on her in the morning. Good night." Philips saluted him smartly and left the cabin.

Nicholas was not sure how long he held her—sometimes she gasped and sometimes she seemed to scream, but in the end he felt her body go limp and her crying subsided to a soft hiccupping. Finally, she lay quietly against him, asleep.

Nicholas looked down and noticed her hands had stopped their desperate clutching at his shirt, lying peacefully in her lap. Her breathing became deep and steady. Inexplicably, he could not let her go. He sat there on the bunk, holding the girl in his arms, breathing in the hint of lavender.

It had been so long. Long years at sea had almost obliterated his memories of pretty girls and flowers. He could scarcely recall the fine parties his mother had held, being too young to attend them, but he had managed to watch from a favorite hiding place on the staircase. Beautiful gowns, feminine laughter, and the scent of fine perfume had filled the rooms and hallways of Wycombe Hall. A gentler, happier time, until his mother died. And then, with his father's despair, came the drinking.

Nicholas shut his eyes against the memories and pressed the frail girl closer to him, like a broken doll clutched in the arms of a heartsick child.

She must not die. *Must not.*

At last he reluctantly eased her down onto the bunk. The ribbon holding her shift over her left shoulder slipped, exposing the creamy expanse of her shoulder. Nicholas managed to suppress a gasp of surprise. He leaned forward and touched the mark exposed on her back just below her shoulder blade. He had seen it before many times, the ugly scarring from a wound having been cauterized with a hot iron. It was not large, about two inches in length, but so ghastly he could not imagine how she had endured it. It stood out in horrible contrast against the petal whiteness of the rest of her back. Many a stout seaman had died of such wounds.

How had she received such a scar? By what, or more distressing to ponder, by whom? Sickened by such thoughts, he stood and tugged the covers over her. Her tears were encouraging; she would come round soon. What sort of monster could have done this to her?

By God, the bastard should be flogged for it.

Chapter Two

The thought of the young woman never regaining consciousness prompted Nicholas to do what he could only describe as despicable. He would have to go through the small bag that had been found in the doomed launch in order to discover her identity. Clarke brought the soft leather satchel to his cabin and set it on the chart table. Nicholas decided it would be best to ask Mr. Philips to witness the proceedings.

At first, there wasn't much in the satchel to be of any help. Nicholas pawed clumsily through the fragrant jumble of delicate underthings, a fringed shawl, hairbrush, and a small jewel case containing a string of pearls, until his fingers touched a packet. Pulling it out he realized it was a letter, slightly damp and dog-eared. The wax seal had been damaged so badly, the letter fell open naturally. He flipped it over and scanned the address.

"Mademoiselle Lysette Corbeil, London," he muttered.

"Maybe our guest is a French girl?" Philips offered.

"I doubt that. Last night . . . that is, she did not *sound* French at all. Indeed, I daresay, she sounded American."

He glanced at Philips, who had raised a questioning brow.

"An American? How, in heaven's name, did a young American woman come to be shipwrecked off the coast of France?"

"Obviously her ship went down." Nicholas turned the letter over, loath to invade someone's most private thoughts, but he had to find out who their guest was and from where she had come.

It was a brief note scribbled down as if written in haste, like a reminder for some task.

Nicholas cleared his throat and read,

Dear Friend:
  All has been set in train. The dimensions have been obtained and the plans secured. Anticipated arrival in August. Watch for the empress. E.A.

Unease fluttered in his belly. *E.A.* He ought to know what those initials meant. It was something he recalled from a dispatch sent by the Admiralty—a command or a warning.

"Curious wording, but of little help," Philips said. "Perhaps this Lysette Corbeil is a relation."

Nicholas refolded the letter and tucked it inside his coat.

"I am not so certain. If my memory serves me well, I seem to recall that 'E.A.' has serious implications. Besides, the note is quite vague, but I am sure has significant meaning with perhaps dangerous ramifications. What do 'dimensions obtained,' and 'plans secured' mean? It has the suspicious ring of espionage, Mr. Philips, and I do not like it."

Philips looked slightly aghast. "Captain, you cannot mean that the young lady is a . . . *spy*?"

Irritated, Nicholas closed the satchel. "I did not say that. But the letter disturbs me."

"Sir, I suggest you query her when she wakes. I am

certain she will readily explain its meaning, considering the situation."

"I hope you are right, Mr. Philips."

To Nicholas's relief, their passenger awoke the next morning, however, she was still very weak and pale. Mr. Philips provided her first meal of broth and tea. The tea, as well as a remaining bit of bread to make toast, came from the captain's own private stores. There was not much left. That the ship's supplies were low had been the most urgent reason why the *Gallant* needed to return to Portsmouth, but the needs of the young woman in Nicholas's cabin now took precedence.

Philips had promised an early report on the lady's health and, like a nervous suitor, Nicholas stood outside the cabin awaiting the surgeon's prognosis. When he emerged, Nicholas was relieved by Philips's reassuring expression.

"She will pull through, Captain. She is sitting up and eating, but still very weak. Seems to be in her right mind, too. She has no recollection of last night, but did ask about the old fellow—Jacko, she called him."

Nicholas nodded. It was probably for the best. However, *he* would never forget the previous night. After leaving her, he had hurried back to Smythe's cabin, where he removed the tearstained shirt, but the memory of her pale, lovely shoulders and the hint of lavender stayed very much in his thoughts.

"Did you discover her name, Mr. Philips?"

The surgeon nodded. "Aye, Captain. Her name's Julianna Adams. But bless me, Captain, I believe the lass is a widow—lost her husband and now her father. Cannot be more than two and twenty if she is a day. Poor girl!"

A widow. With that scar? Good God, what if a blackguard of a husband had done it? Nicholas fervently hoped the coward was burning in hell for such a crime.

"Is she strong enough for questioning?" he asked cautiously.

"Aye, but not too long, sir. She tires quickly."

Clearing his throat, Nicholas tugged down on the edge of his spotless blue coat making sure there were no creases across the flat of his belly. He nodded to Philips, who stood aside and let him pass into the cabin.

He was not sure what he expected to see, but he certainly did not expect such maturity in one so young. Her sweet, heart-shaped face held all the melancholy of someone who had lost everything. Wrapped in a shawl taken from the satchel, she sat upright in the bunk, her sable-colored hair brushed off her face in some semblance of order. Dark circles beneath her eyes emphasized the thick, nearly black lashes. Her skin was still bright pink, but now there was more of a healthy glow to it instead of the alarming redness.

Nicholas offered her a short bow and again cleared his throat. "Allow m-m-me to introduce myself, ma'am. I am Captain Sir Nicholas Sidney of His Majesty's Ship *Gallant*. I am at your service, Mrs. Adams."

"Yes. Dr. Philips told me." She looked down, plucking the fringe on her shawl. "I am so sorry to be such a burden, Captain. I know I am keeping you from your quarters and—"

"It is a t-t-trifle, ma'am," he said shortly. "Please do not discomfit yourself. We will anchor in P-P-Portsmouth three days hence and I will see to it that you are taken ashore and receive proper care."

"You are kind, sir." She looked up at him, a slight smile touching her lips. "I do not know how I can thank you enough."

"Not at all. However, perhaps you could enlighten us as to how you came to be set adrift and so far from any shore of c-c-consequence."

She nodded and gestured for him to sit down. Nicholas dragged a dining chair in from the main cabin and sat down gingerly, his hat balanced carefully on his knees.

"As you may have guessed, I am an American— from Baltimore. My father and I were aboard the *Hart,* a merchant ship bound for England. It had taken on a cargo of tobacco from Charleston, then sailed to Baltimore, where we secured our passage along with four others. My father and I were on our way to London to meet my great-aunt and uncle, my mother's relatives.

"About a week ago, we encountered a storm which blew us off course. I believe it was near the coast of France. The ship struck some rocks and we began to take on water. Captain Denton ordered the small boat lowered over the side, and we—another woman and I—were to be rowed to shore."

"Captain Horace Denton?" Nicholas asked sharply. She nodded. "You know him?"

"Aye." Nicholas felt himself bristle with ill-concealed rage. Denton had captained the *Hart*? That filthy scoundrel?

"Only I and that dear sailor, Mr. Jacko, managed to get into the boat before the rope snapped and we were set adrift." She paused and passed a tired hand across her brow.

"You are t-t-too ill to go on, Mrs. Adams. Allow me to return later today," he murmured politely.

"No. Oh, no. I am quite well enough to continue. Please allow me." She drew a deep breath and tugged the shawl tightly across her shoulders. "Mr. Jacko tried to care for me. We had little to eat and only a small amount of water. He found a piece of sail and tried to make a shelter for me. He even managed to catch a fish by striking it with an oar."

She suddenly looked away. "I am afraid I could not keep down such a dearly bought supper."

"Raw fish is not pleasant to eat, even when in g-g-good health," Nicholas consoled her.

She sighed and closed her eyes a moment. "I do not know how long we were in that boat, but I do recall seeing . . . sails. Great white sails, and I thought I was in heaven at last." She smiled then looked down again, twisting the fringe of the shawl.

Nicholas paused a moment, absorbing her pitiful story. Adrift at sea with only a swallow of water and scarcely any food. It was a miracle she had survived.

"And the *Hart*? Did it break up?"

She shrugged. "I do not know. I . . . we presumed so. My father was still on board with the lady and three other gentlemen and, of course, the crew. We must assume they were all lost."

He watched her swallow quickly, forcing back her tears. Her chin lifted.

"I am sorry for your loss, Mrs. Adams. My s-s-surgeon tells me you are also a widow. A double tragedy, to be sure."

"Dr. Philips is a bit muddled. I *was* to be married, Captain, but—" She pressed her fingers to her eyes. "Forgive me."

Embarrassed, Nicholas stood, clutching his hat. All thoughts of questioning her about the letter had flown. "I beg your pardon, ma'am. I will not d-d-distress you any longer. Please make yourself comfortable. I will ensure no one else disturbs you." He bowed and backed to the door.

She did not look at him, but did speak. "Thank you, Captain Sidney. I will try to remember more tomorrow."

Within minutes he issued terse orders to have two marines posted at the door. No one was to enter the cabin except for Mr. Philips, Mr. Smythe, or himself. And young Clarke, if necessary. One stern look reminded the boy to keep his mouth shut concerning the lady. Nicholas would not tolerate the lad prattling to his mates about a rather lovely half-dressed woman in the captain's sleeping cabin.

After summoning Mr. Smythe to assist him, Nicholas began the painstaking task of sorting through some of the earlier dispatches he had received from the Admiralty concerning covert activities against the Crown, particularly those mentioning the initials *E.A.*

"Aha," Smythe announced triumphantly, holding up a piece of paper heavy with wax seals and ribbons. "Here it is."

Nicholas took the paper from him and scanned its contents. The dispatch was a year old, but he remembered it. The letters *E* and *A* were said to be the initials of a secret French operative whose contact in England was supposedly selling naval secrets to the French government. Neither the Foreign Office nor the Admiralty had identified them yet. The fact that Captain Horace Denton was somehow mixed into this clandestine brew troubled Nicholas greatly, especially since the matter somehow touched on Miss Adams.

Adams and the letter *A*. Surely, not . . . her?

By midday he received word that the rescued sailor, Jacko, was well enough to report to him. Standing firmly on the quarterdeck, hands clasped behind him, Nicholas assessed the old fellow, from the fringe of his silver hair to his bare feet. Sharp blue eyes set in a mass of mahogany-colored skin, creased and lined from decades of living at sea, looked up at him. The old salt knuckled his forelock, waiting permission to speak.

"How many days were you adrift, sailor?"

"Well, sir, nigh onto five days it were. The young miss didna do so well. Had a drop o' water in a flask I keep wi' me, but no food atall, sir. But she were a brave lass, she were."

"Who was your captain, again?" Nicholas asked sharply.

"Cap'n 'orace Denton. Fine cap'n he were. Takin' a cargo of tobaccy from Charlest'n, y'see. All's well till we ran into the storm. Nor'wester it were. Blew us straight into the Frenchies. Struck some rocks near shore and we took on water fast."

"You went aground?"

"Aye, sir. Cap'n Denton, he's thinkin' fast and orders the launch away. Me and another lad were to take the two ladies ashore. Risky it were, with the *Hart* bound to break up. But the lines ran afoul—snapped they did—and we was set adrift." Jacko looked down. "Never saw the other lady, I'm sorry to say."

Nicholas stroked his jaw, perplexed. Denton had ordered a launch ashore during a storm with women aboard? What was that fool thinking?

"You have done your duty well, sailor. You saved the lady's life. Quick thinking, there. A pity the others were lost, but you did all you could. You may go now. Have Mr. Talbot get you something hot to eat and there will be an extra tot of grog for you tonight."

Jacko bobbed his head and again tugged his forelock. "Aye, sir, thankee, sir. Beggin' the cap'n's pardon, but might I be so bold as to ask about the young miss, sir?"

Nicholas clasped his hands more firmly behind his back.

"She is awake and well. She will recover. That is all." He dismissed the old tar with a curt nod of his head.

Jacko tugged at his forelock one last time and hurriedly hobbled away to rejoin the rest of the crew.

"Can we believe him?" Smythe asked, keeping his voice low. "How do we know he is not a deserter?"

"Why should we not? Miss Adams confirms the account. I do not believe she is capable of concocting such a tale. The woman was barely alive, Mr. Smythe, hardly in any condition to consider consorting with an old seaman who fancies desertion."

Smythe nodded. "Aye, you are quite right, sir. And one thing is verifiable: we caught the edge of a storm about six, seven days ago. The log confirms it."

"I do recall it." Nicholas paused, pondering the situation, then squinted up at the towering, swaying masts, the rigging creaking and humming in the wind. "Send a man aloft, Mr. Smythe. I will have those t'gallants trimmed properly."

"Aye, aye, sir."

The letter still troubled Nicholas. He could not dismiss the unpleasant possibility that Miss Adams was somehow involved, perhaps innocently, with the likes of that blackguard Denton, or the mysterious *E.A.* Duty reminded him that everyone and everything on his ship was not above his scrutiny, especially if it involved treachery against the king.

The next morning he resolved to ask Miss Adams about the letter. He braced himself with a splash of brandy in anticipation of her tears and outrage. He had, after all, gone through her personal effects. She had every right to be angry.

At the cabin door, he knocked, then waited for her polite permission to let him enter. This time, he felt his pulse quicken, blood beating heavily through his veins. An unaccountable sense of excitement flitted through his belly.

"Come in."

Nicholas ducked inside and stopped. The change was astonishing. While still sitting in the bunk, she was awake and alert. Somehow she had managed to wash the unruly mass of sea-soaked hair and had brushed it into dark supple waves that fell to her waist. Her skin glowed with health; nearly all the redness was gone. Someone, probably Mr. Philips, had given her a linen shirt which covered her from neck to midthigh—a charming picture of dishabille.

She hastily rearranged the blanket to cover a fleeting glimpse of an alabaster ankle. Embarrassment rather than sunburn flooded her cheeks. "Excuse me, Captain. I did not realize. . . ."

Nicholas kept his face expressionless, determined not to let her see how she affected him. Damnation! This was not the way he had anticipated conducting an interview—her half-reclining in a disarray of bedclothes and a tangle of lustrous dark hair, the soft, compelling scent of lavender wreaking havoc with his senses.

Maybe this was the way of it, he thought, annoyed. A lovely young chit, an American at that, using her feminine wiles to throw him off guard.

"Miss Adams, I must speak with you concerning a

personal m-m-matter that may have serious implications."

She pulled the blanket a bit higher. "I see. Very well."

Her expression revealed that he had her complete attention. Nicholas detected no coyness in her demeanor, nor the merest trace of flirtation in her eyes.

"Regretfully, I must advise you that while you were so ill, I was obliged to search through your satchel to f-f-find some sort of identification. Mr. Philips expressed concern that you might not . . . that is to say, he thought you might—"

"Die?" Her mouth tightened slightly. "Yes, I believe he could have come to that assumption."

"While examining the articles, I found this." He drew the letter from inside his coat.

Her eyes widened. "Mr. Rameau's letter!"

"Rameau?" Nicholas asked, trying to keep the suspicious tone out of his voice.

"Yes, Monsieur Edmund Rameau. I met him at a soiree in Baltimore just before my father and I embarked for England."

"You are friends with him?"

She shrugged slightly. "Not exactly. He was a pleasant acquaintance. He asked that I have his letter posted when I arrived in London. I believe it was for a lady who happens to be his sweetheart."

"Did you ever happen to read its contents?"

Miss Adams's brows drew together in a frown. "No. Why would I? I am certain it is of the utmost personal in nature and besides, the letter was sealed." Her frown deepened, a note of rebuke entering her voice. "Did *you* open it, sir?"

"It was already open, Miss Adams. The dampness and so forth had damaged the seal."

"So you did read it?"

He nodded. "In an attempt to d-d-discover your identity. Unfortunately, the contents of this letter do not read like correspondence to one's ladylove."

Her chin went up again. A touch of defiance entered

her dark eyes. In spite of her weakened condition, Nicholas detected a thread of steel in her, which he could not help admiring.

"Perhaps Monsieur Rameau was corresponding with a family member. In which case, Captain, you have violated his privacy as well as mine."

Nicholas felt his skin prickle at her reprimand, but bit back an angry retort. Instead, he tempered his tone to cool severity.

"I must remind you, Miss Adams, that it was for your benefit I committed such a heinous crime. However, as I am the single authority aboard this ship, I am responsible for the *Gallant* and the welfare of my officers and crew. I am also a captain in His Britannic Majesty's Navy and if I discover information which I deem threatening to the Crown, then it is my duty to take appropriate action."

He saw her face flush again, embarrassed, and he immediately regretted his rather imperious little lecture. She looked away and swallowed—tears? He could not be sure.

"Forgive me, Miss Adams. I spoke too harshly."

She said nothing, but bit at the full softness of her lower lip.

"The contents of this letter," he went on in a more moderate tone, "suggest circumstances and events of a suspicious nature." He read the letter to her and watched for any further signs of offense. Then he said, "It is signed 'E.A.' "

As if reading his mind, Miss Adams looked up at him. A new wariness clouded her gaze. "My father's name is—" She choked on her words. "His name was Edward Adams. Are you suggesting, Captain, that my father was a *spy*?"

"I am suggesting nothing of the kind, but it does seem curious that you carried the l-l-letter from a Monsieur *Rameau*." He paused and went on in a more conciliatory voice. "I assume the gentleman is French. You must realize, Miss Adams, that we are at war with the French."

She nodded. "Yes, I know. It does seem a bit odd, but I assure you, sir, I have no explanation for the contents of this letter, nor can I give you any other information concerning Monsieur Rameau except that he was a gentleman visiting Baltimore on business."

"I see."

Nicholas noted her color had turned a distinct shade paler and the eager luster was gone from her eyes. Illness and fatigue made her weary of his relentless questioning.

"Forgive me, Miss Adams, I shall be b-b-brief. I have come to ask if I may take this letter to the Admiralty. Rest assured, after it has been examined, it shall be posted to the addressee. You have my word on this."

She nodded. "Very well, Captain. I shall take you at your word." Her shoulders slumped as she turned her gaze away from him. "I have no choice but to trust you."

Nicholas rose and bowed. "Good day, Miss Adams. I thank you. I pray you will be feeling better soon."

He did not hear her thank you, but swiftly turned and left the cabin. In his larger day cabin, he tossed the letter on top of a pile of nautical charts stacked on his work desk, then dropped wearily into the chair. He ran a tired hand through his short, cropped hair.

The interview left him drained and feeling like a cad. The woman had suffered the loss of her father and barely survived a shipwreck. And he had just given her a thumping-great dressing-down fit only for the lowliest of miscreants aboard his ship. Duty and humanity warred miserably within him.

He supposed he would have to think of some way to make amends. Perhaps dinner? No, it was too late for that, and besides, there were no stores left aboard ship for a fine dinner.

Nicholas sighed and reached for the brandy. He would think of *something*—something to win back approval from those lovely dark eyes.

*   *   *

In three days the *Gallant* anchored in Portsmouth Harbor. Across from them lay the HMS *Arrow,* a first rater, with Admiral Walter Howard commanding her.

It took a little maneuvering in Smythe's tiny cabin, but with Clarke's assistance, Nicholas managed to dress. Clarke had carefully brushed his best blue coat and passed a cloth over the heavy gold epaulets. They were real bullion, Nicholas could boast, having been purchased with the winnings the *Gallant* had nabbed from a French merchantman off Antigua. Taken right underneath the Little Corporal's nose.

Clarke helped him into his last pair of silk stockings and the black buckled shoes. The tip of the gold-hilted sword clanked noisily against the bulkhead, but it could not be helped. A body could scarcely turn around in such a small space, much less dress with any decorum.

"Should be only a day or two before I am back in my quarters, Clarke," he apologized gruffly.

Tucking his hat under his arm, Nicholas ducked out of Smythe's cabin and hastened up the ladder to the quarterdeck. Bosun pipes twittered as he made his way to the rail where he turned and climbed down to the awaiting longboat bobbing gently against the side of the ship.

"Mr. Smythe," he called up. "Make sure all is in order. No shore leave until I return. See to it."

"Aye, aye, sir," Smythe responded with a sharp salute.

Nicholas dreaded visiting Admiral Howard. Two hours at least of sitting in bored silence while the old admiral relived Trafalgar and his fond memories of Nelson. Not that accounts of Trafalgar were tedious, but Admiral Howard had the uncanny knack of making such a momentous naval battle sound about as exciting as taking tea with an elderly, deaf auntie.

However, *Mrs.* Howard, the admiral's wife, was charming and thoughtful. Though he needed to report to the admiral, it was she who Nicholas really wanted to see.

When the launch came alongside the *Arrow,* the pipes shrilled above, announcing his arrival. Once on deck, the crew snapped to attention and Nicholas allowed himself a brief surge of pride. He was a post captain in His Majesty's navy.

"Captain Sidney, what a pleasure it is, man!" Admiral Howard boomed. "Come below, we will share a bottle of port and talk about the loot y' nabbed and the action. The scuttle is you have an Indian princess aboard. Good God, man! A native. You will never get her into society. Won't do, won't do at all, my dear fellow."

It took half an hour and two glasses of port before Admiral Howard understood the exact circumstances surrounding Miss Adams.

"And she is still quite frail, sir," Nicholas went on. "Lack of nourishment and water."

"Of course. What are you going to do with her?"

"I thought it best to put her up in a room in Portsmouth then get word to her relations in London."

"Capital thinking, Sidney. Capital. No need to cause a fuss. Perhaps we could have the lady on board for supper. Mrs. Howard would find it a charming diversion."

"With all respect, sir, Miss Adams cannot. She can barely take anything but broth and a bit of bread. And there is the delicate problem of . . . well, her *attire,* sir."

"Good Lord, was she completely unclothed? That really won't do, man." The admiral's face was a picture of shock and disbelief.

"No, sir. She was decently clothed, but poorly. Her gown was in tatters and she—"

"Well, that settles it. I will see to it that Mrs. Howard finds some gewgaws and fripperies and sends them over. We cannot have this young gel parading about Portsmouth in her shift! Won't do, won't do at all."

Nicholas smiled, relieved. Mrs. Howard was one of the few naval wives permitted to live on board with her husband and she was also as diminutive as Miss

Adams—a coincidence he had hoped would work toward the young lady's benefit.

That settled, Nicholas drew a deep breath. "Sir, there is another matter, concerning the lady." In the most succinct terms, Nicholas read the letter and explained the subsequent actions he felt needed to be taken.

Admiral Howard nodded his approval. "Well done, sir. I shall draft a letter for you to take to Lord Yorke at the Admiralty."

Mission successfully completed, Nicholas proceeded to report on his recent ventures, relaying the details of his encounters with the French.

Upon his return to the *Gallant,* Smythe announced all was in order. Nicholas reluctantly gave his consent to allow the crew off the ship, but only after Miss Adams was taken ashore. He would lose nearly half the crew to desertion, but there it was. They had been at sea for almost a year. He simply could not bring himself to hold any man from his wife and children, regardless of the Admiralty.

The next afternoon, Nicholas personally assisted Miss Adams into the trim longboat that conveyed them to shore.

"You say we are in Portsmouth?" Miss Adams asked, her soft voice almost drowned out by the sound of the oars cutting the water.

"Yes. I have made arrangements for you to stay in the Red Anchor—a respectable inn. Once settled, I shall write to your relatives in London."

"I am sure my aunt and uncle will be most happy to reimburse you for all your expenses, sir. You have been more than generous."

Nicholas said nothing for a moment, but became acutely conscious of her slight form pressed innocently against him. Damn and blast! He had been too long at sea—could not keep his head clear to save his soul. In spite of her modest appearance, the faint scent of lavender again filled his senses—a scent he would forever associate with her.

"I have been only too happy to be of assistance," he murmured, so the men at the oars would not hear him.

At dockside he was relieved to see Lieutenant Dain at the ready. With a sharp word, Nicholas instructed the crew to keep the launch steady as he handed Miss Adams up to Mr. Dain. Once he set foot on the dock himself, Nicholas noticed her color go a bit paler.

"You are not well, Miss Adams. Are you f-f-faint?"

"No. No. Just a little weary."

He looked about anxiously. It would be disastrous if Miss Adams decided to collapse here on the dock amidst the rough sailors and teeming squalor.

"Mr. Dain, did you procure a conveyance?"

"Aye, sir." He pointed in the direction of a trim carriage drawn by a pair of well-groomed bays. "I sent the trunks ahead."

Nicholas glanced down at his charge and caught her elbow.

"Can you walk, Miss Adams?"

"I believe so." She took a cautious step forward and stopped. Passing an absent hand across her brow, she murmured, "Captain Sidney, I fear I *am* light-headed. If I could just sit down for a moment."

He held back an angry oath directed at Captain Horace Denton, whose poor navigational skills had landed Miss Adams in this predicament. Clearly she was still too ill to be out of her sickbed, much less strolling about the dockyards of Portsmouth.

Jamming his hat more firmly across his brow, he bent over and lifted Miss Adams up into his arms. She weighed next to nothing and did not struggle against the shocking impropriety of the situation, but seemed almost complacent, agreeable.

"Captain," she murmured, her head drooping against his shoulder. Her free hand clutched at the gold-trimmed edge of his coat lapel, trying to hold herself more closely to him.

"Hush now, ma'am," he admonished sternly, while taking rapid strides toward the carriage. "You will only tire yourself even more." Gently he set her on the cushions then stepped in and sat next to her, his arm about her shoulders. "Mr. Dain, get in, man."

Dain scrambled in and sat across from them, deep concern etching his fair features. "She looks quite ill, Captain."

Nicholas lightly touched her chin with a tentative finger. "Miss Adams?"

There was no answer. He searched her pale face, noting her eyes were closed, then glanced back at the young lieutenant, who looked positively ashen.

"Mr. Dain, we must get her a doctor at once."

Chapter Three

Julianna did not know how long she had slept, nor did she care. It simply felt wonderful to sleep on something that did not move, creak, or smell of the sea. When she finally awoke, the first thing she noted was the play of the pale golden rays casting soft, dancing patterns across the quilts. She sat up and pushed back her hair.

Her stomach growled ominously, reminding her that she had not eaten anything substantial in nearly two weeks. The poor broth and bits of bread she had eaten aboard the *Gallant* scarcely counted as a meal. Not that she did not appreciate it. The captain and his men had been most kind, but clearly at a loss as to how they should care for her. Well, they had done their best considering the circumstances. She only hoped Uncle Fairchild would be able to repay the good captain for his many services on her behalf.

Julianna thrust back the covers and eased from the bed, placing her toes on the polished wood floor. It felt slightly damp attesting to the fact that the inn was quite near the sea. Across the room, a bright fire burned in the hearth. Her shawl had been draped neatly over a chair near the bed and, to her surprise, her leather satchel had been placed in the seat.

She stood, legs trembling, then abruptly sat back on the bed. The room began to spin in mad circles and she hastily retrenched by lying down.

Frustrated, Julianna could only manage to sit up and fume. How would she manage to get dressed? As if she had spoken out loud, there was a soft knock at the door. It opened a crack and the cheeriest, roundest face peered in on her.

"Yer awake, miss! Can I come in?"

At her nod, a girl in a fresh white apron and cap slipped in and dropped a quick curtsey.

"We was so worried about you, miss. The doctor said you was so bad, he feared for your life. An' the captain frettin' an' pacin'. Worryin' himself into a state."

"I am a little confused. Who are you?"

"Margaret, miss. Captain Sidney, he asked me to look after you. You've been sleeping all day an' night for two days now."

"I see. Where is Captain Sidney?"

"He's in his rooms, miss. He's been writin' an' worryin', worryin' an' writin'." Margaret looked at her anxiously. "How do you feel, miss? Can I fetch the doctor again?"

"I am much better, Margaret, but I *am* very hungry. Perhaps a bit—?"

"At once, miss. I'll fetch a tray this minute." The girl turned and hurried out of the room, her freshly starched apron rustling about her ankles.

Julianna settled back into the pillows and sighed. At least eating would ease her angry stomach and lightheadedness, but not the deep sorrow she felt in her heart. The terrifying memories of that day aboard the *Hart* were still fresh and painful, as were those long miserable days in that wretched little boat, nearly demented by hunger and thirst. Poor Mr. Jacko had tried to make her comfortable, but she had scarcely been able to appreciate all his efforts. She had been too ill and too weak to do anything but lie in the bottom of that boat and suffer. Even now, she would not allow herself to think about her father. To do so would be too painful.

Looking out the window, she spotted several ships anchored in the harbor and her thoughts turned abruptly from her father to Captain Sidney. The maid said he had been locked up in his rooms writing and worrying about . . . her? She had to admit she was deeply touched by his concern, but still allowed herself to be a bit cross with him over the matter of the letter.

Mr. Rameau had entrusted her with his letter and expected her to make sure it was delivered. Still, the captain's brusque words forced her to realize that perhaps the charming Monsieur Rameau was not at all what he had appeared to be. Perhaps he was, indeed, some kind of political agent.

Julianna rubbed her temple. Politics made her head ache and Papa had always loved to discuss politics. . . .

Margaret's sudden knock made her hastily rearrange herself against the pillows and tug the blanket higher.

"Come in."

The cheerful girl bustled into the room and placed the tray across Julianna's lap. The aroma of tea and toast tickled her nose and filled her with a contented warmth.

"There now, miss. You'll feel much better after you've had a bite of something."

"Thank you, Margaret."

"Will there be anything else, miss?"

Julianna swallowed her first sip of tea and nodded. "Can you tell me where I am, exactly?"

"In Portsmouth, in the Red Anchor. Mr. Perkins, he's the proprietor here."

"Well, it is a start. I wish I could remember more. Sometimes I am so muddled. So much has happened."

The serving girl hesitated a moment before turning to leave. "If you don't mind me asking, miss, but they say you're an American lady. Is it true?"

Julianna smiled. "Yes, I am from Baltimore—that is a city in Maryland. I was . . . that is, *we,* my father

and I, were on our way to England when a storm
came up and wrecked our ship. I am afraid he did
not survive."

"I'm ever so sorry, miss."

"Yes, well, thank you."

Margaret bobbed her head. "If that is all . . . ?"

"Yes, Margaret. Oh, and Margaret, please convey
my regards to the captain. Tell him I am doing quite
well and perhaps he would be so good as to see me
later this afternoon. If it is acceptable to him, of
course."

"I will, miss. I'll tell him straight away."

The captain was much taller than she recalled. His
shoulders nearly filled the doorway as he ducked to
enter her tiny sitting room. Julianna made a deliberate
effort to hide her admiration for the imposing figure
he cut in his blue-and-gold uniform.

Unlike Captain Denton's hair caught in an old-
fashioned queue, Captain Sidney's dark, almost black
hair had been brushed forward in a more modern style
and clipped neatly above his collar.

She did not attempt to rise from her chair, but
smiled and held out her hand to him. "Thank you,
Captain Sidney, for coming. I am much obliged."

"Not at all." He took her fingers lightly in his own
and bowed over her hand. "You are l-l-looking
stronger, Miss Adams. A healthy color has returned
to your cheeks."

"Yes, thanks to you and Margaret." She smiled at
Margaret, standing close to the door. Julianna gestured for the captain to be seated in the chair across
from her.

Captain Sidney cleared his throat and eased into the
chair. "It has been my duty to write to the Admiralty
and explain to them the circumstances concerning the
Hart," he began without preamble. "I am uncertain if
they know of the incident already. However, I have
also asked them to write to your aunt and uncle and

tell them of your whereabouts and that I have made arrangements to escort you to London."

"Oh, no, Captain, but I thank you. I simply could not impose. I am sure Uncle Fairchild will come for me. If not, I am sure he will send someone."

The captain frowned. "But you know no one in England, Miss Adams, not even your own relatives. You do not know where they live, and the j-j-journey to London is long and tiresome. You cannot travel there alone. It would be . . . unseemly."

Julianna studied the captain's stern expression, noting the determined set of his square jaw and the firm line of his mouth. No tenderness etched his strong features. Fierce black brows swept over intense, dark blue eyes, and no humor glinted within their cool, shadowed depths. His nose was quite straight, his mouth perfectly chiseled in uncompromising curves. Though undeniably attractive, it was the face of a man unaccustomed to having anyone question his authority, particularly ignorant American girls.

She nodded. "You make my situation sound quite desperate."

"I am thinking only of your safety. Besides, you are unwell. I have thought about this very carefully and I m-m-must insist."

Abruptly Captain Sidney stood and bowed. "It is a matter you need not trouble yourself about, Miss Adams. I have procured the services of a post chaise and we leave tomorrow at seven. Will that be too early?"

She shook her head. "I will be ready. I promise."

"Very well. Then I bid you good day." He bowed again and turned to leave.

"Captain?"

"Yes?"

"Is there any chance my father could have survived?"

The captain hesitated, obviously distressed by her question.

"I w-w-would not want to give you false hopes, Miss Adams. The sea is quite unforgiving. I am sorry."

Julianna looked down. "Yes, I see. Thank you."

"If it is any consolation to you, I am sure your father did not suffer long. The cold, it is . . . well, I have said too much to cause you greater distress. If you will excuse me?"

This time, he left the room quickly, shutting the door behind him with a decisive click.

The remainder of the day was spent packing the few clothes given to her by Mrs. Howard. Julianna had not met the kind lady who had so generously supplied her new wardrobe, but she made a mental note to write a proper thank you letter once she reached London.

Even the simple task of folding clothes made Julianna light-headed. As she rested on the bed, she watched Margaret bustle about the room, packing a stout-looking trunk presumably donated by the estimable Mrs. Howard. The trunk held the gowns she had provided, together with a shawl or two and another bonnet. All of Julianna's remaining garments, mostly underclothing freshly laundered and pressed, went back into the satchel that had survived the shipwreck.

While Margaret worked, she entertained Julianna with her cheerful patter about everything in general and nothing in particular: the weather, life in Portsmouth, her family. Julianna noted that Margaret avoided any mention of the captain—which she found rather odd. Perhaps the girl was frightened of him, or merely being polite.

Promptly at six forty-five, Julianna made her way downstairs to the waiting coach. The captain stood nearby, imposing in a black hat and great cape covering his uniform.

"Miss Adams?" The captain bowed slightly.

"Captain Sidney."

"A fine morning." He attempted a smile, but it dissolved into a disapproving frown as she approached him. "You look unwell, Miss Adams. Perhaps it is too early?"

"Oh, no, Captain. Please do not worry yourself. I am quite sure once we are under way the fresh air will be invigorating."

His reproving look told her he was not at all convinced.

"I hope you do not mind, but I have procured the services of Miss Chetley to attend to you. Mr. Perkins has consented to part with her for a few days until you are settled in London."

From behind him, Julianna watched Margaret hurry out of the Red Anchor, a small bundle clutched tightly in her work-roughened hands. She made a timorous curtsy to Captain Sidney, then bobbed her head to Julianna.

"Beggin' your pardon, miss. I needed to fetch me things."

"Yes, of course. I am glad you will be coming along, Margaret."

"Well, then, we have a l-l-long journey ahead of us. We should be getting under way." The captain gestured to the open door of the coach.

Julianna accepted his proffered hand and stepped into the dark interior. Margaret followed her, making herself as unobtrusive as possible in the far corner. The entire frame of the coach shifted under his greater weight as Captain Sidney climbed in and sat opposite the two women. He rapped on the roof. The coachman called to the team and they were off.

For the first few miles, Julianna kept her gaze firmly directed on the scenery, ostensibly to enjoy the early morning and the English countryside, but in actuality it was to avoid Captain Sidney's intense scrutiny.

It may have been her imagination running wild, but after several minutes, she began to feel acutely uncomfortable. He was not being rude . . . exactly. He was just so *earnest,* intent. And disturbingly attractive, with those intense eyes the color of indigo, and his wide-set, straight shoulders. Julianna was suddenly glad the dark interior of the post chaise hid the flush creeping into her cheeks as she recalled that morning on the dock when he had swept her into his arms and carried her to the awaiting coach.

She told herself she ought not to be thinking of the captain in such a way. She was, after all, in mourning, but each time she allowed her gaze to stray from the scenery outside the coach, she found herself locked in his unwavering stare. She tried unsuccessfully to make polite small talk, but eventually gave up. The captain appeared uninterested in idle chatter. Perhaps it had to do with his soft stammer, or because he simply did not wish to converse with a slightly disheveled, sickly American girl.

It was possible he had never seen an American before, or more precisely, an American *woman*. Julianna could not imagine English women being so terribly different, but then, she had only known one—her mother.

Pretty Caroline Fairchild had voyaged to America after being swept off her feet by the dashing Colonel Edward Adams, who had come to London with his cousin, John Adams, after the colonial wars to renew diplomatic relations between England's Parliament and the newly created United States. The gentle Caroline and the wildly handsome American colonel were married by special license, much to everyone's dismay, but later the match proved solid.

Colonel Adams was no scapegrace upstart, but a gentleman, well landed, offering Caroline Fairchild a gracious home in Maryland with a more luxurious lifestyle than she could have ever hoped for in England.

While their marriage had been a happy one, it did not last many years. The birth of their first child, Benjamin, weakened the already delicate Caroline. When Julianna was born, Caroline did not fully recover, but went into a slow decline. By the time Julianna was twelve, Caroline was laid to rest under the flowering cherry trees planted in the small graveyard behind the plantation house.

It was from her mother Julianna had learned proper

manners. From Caroline, she had also acquired the slight English accent that gave her speech a charming lilt.

Julianna sighed and tore her gaze away from the rolling hillside and neat hedgerows. And now her darling papa was gone, too. Papa and dearest Michael. She caught her lower lip between her teeth and looked down. It would not look well to weep in front of the stern-faced captain.

"Miss Adams? You look quite pale. Shall I s-s-stop the coach?" The captain's eyes seemed to penetrate right through her, scrutinizing her very soul.

"I was just thinking how much my father would have enjoyed this part of our journey. He so wanted to see England again and my mother's family."

"A bitter loss for you, I am sure. But your family will be happy to see you and comfort you during this d-d-difficult time."

"Yes, I am sure they will be most considerate."

She looked away from the captain, again to gaze out the window. A sharp morning breeze stung against her cheeks and eyes, bringing unwanted tears.

For some unaccountable reason, Julianna had no desire to see the family she had never met, but wanted only to feel the warmth of the captain's arms about her again. The notion surprised her, and, as she happened to glance at the captain, she had the distinct feeling he was thinking something quite similar. His gaze held hers—intense and ardent.

Scarcely ten words passed between them during the rest of their journey to Town. Tongue-tied and ill at ease, Captain Sidney sat in silence, cursing his inability to converse properly and angry with himself for having no words to offer Miss Adams as any real consolation. Her struggles to keep from weeping disturbed him greatly. Against his better judgment, he found himself wanting to take her into his arms and comfort her. Rigorous discipline finally won out. He decided he would be only too glad to surrender Miss Adams to her awaiting aunt and uncle, thereby releasing him from this distressing and frustrating duty.

After eight exhausting hours, the coach finally stopped in front of the Fairchild residence in Hanover Square. Nicholas rose, stiff-kneed, and stepped down. He then helped Miss Adams alight, keenly aware of her slight form stooped with fatigue and grief. Even in the dusky light, he noted her color was not good.

Before young Margaret had managed to descend from the coach, the front door was flung open and two liveried servants rushed out.

"Upon my word, make haste, Crawford! And you, Hodges, assist the young lady at once!" A commanding feminine voice filtered out from the interior of the house. A flurry of activity swirled about them as the Fairchild servants helped take down Miss Adams's trunks and carried them into the house, with Margaret trailing behind.

Once inside, Captain Sidney thought he had entered the home of a cheerful, round-faced pixie—a grandmotherly sprite. Miss Adams's Aunt Fairchild enveloped her great-niece in a loving embrace, her soft blue eyes aglow with compassion and relief.

"Dear child, dear child! How you have suffered! Come in, come in. Hodges, take her wrap and the good captain's things. Mr. Fairchild, you must attend to Captain Sidney. Dear me, Captain, you are done in. You must stay for a bit of supper."

Somehow Miss Adams made the introductions, but fatigue made her accidentally mix his name and titles, making him "Captain Nicholas Sir Sidney." To add to the confusion of servants and trunks a scrappy little terrier scurried about, barking at everyone's feet.

"Hush, Toby! You are upsetting everyone," Mr. Fairchild chided. "Come here and sit like a good fellow."

The obedient dog trotted over to his master and sat down, his tail thumping happily against the polished floor.

"You must excuse Toby, Sir Nicholas. He becomes quite excited when visitors arrive," Mr. Fairchild apologized.

Relieved, Nicholas observed his hosts with an exacting eye and decided he could, in all conscience, relinquish Miss Adams into their charge. Mrs. Fairchild was precisely as he had hoped—a pink-cheeked matron who would take Miss Adams under her wing and see that she was properly cared for. Her uncle appeared to be a congenial gentleman, not easily ruffled by Mrs. Fairchild's flutterings.

"Allow me to offer you a brandy while the ladies get settled." Mr. Fairchild gestured upstairs, toward the drawing room.

Nicholas hesitated, suddenly loath to leave Miss Adams's side. The servants had dispensed with her wrap and bonnet, leaving her standing in the entryway still under Mrs. Fairchild's scrutiny. Her aunt clucked disapprovingly over her attire.

"Dear me, child. Where did you manage to procure such garments?"

Julianna glanced across at him and blushed slightly. "The good captain . . . that is, it was Sir Nicholas who managed to acquire some suitable apparel, as my own were lost."

Mrs. Fairchild's eyes grew round with astonishment. "My dear Sir Nicholas, you are too amiable. How can we ever thank you enough?"

Nicholas bowed to the older woman. "I thank you, ma'am, but compliments should be d-d-directed to Mrs. Howard, Admiral Howard's wife. It was she who provided the extra garments."

"But it was you who saw to it," Miss Adams reminded him. "I am sure I do not know what I would have done if not for your good offices. I am greatly obliged."

Again, tongue-tied, Nicholas struggled not to stammer a response. Instead, he only managed a formal "It was n-n-nothing, ma'am."

But Mrs. Fairchild would hear none of it. "Indeed,

I shall write Mrs. Howard in the morning. And the Admiralty. Such heroics must not go unmentioned. You are far too modest, Sir Nicholas." The ruffle of her lace cap fairly quivered with her emotion.

"I thank you, Mrs. Fairchild," he murmured and bowed again. "And now I must take my leave."

Miss Adams took a hurried step toward him and stopped, struggling against propriety. "Will you not stay, Captain? You must be greatly fatigued. Please? I am certain—"

"No, thank you. I must away. Please do not concern yourselves. I have rooms awaiting me."

Mr. Fairchild shook his head. "My dear fellow, how can we thank you properly? What you have undertaken the past few days . . . really, sir, you must allow us some sort of recompense."

If he stayed another minute, Nicholas knew he would not have the resolve to leave at all. Miss Adams's pleading dark eyes would haunt him forever if he did not make a quick escape.

"Only doing my duty . . . what is to be expected. Good-bye Mrs. Fairchild, Mr. Fairchild." He glanced at Miss Adams, her sweet face weary and downcast.

"Good-bye, Captain. Thank you for everything you have done, for saving my life. I simply cannot thank you enough."

"Good-bye, Miss Adams. It has indeed been a pleasure. Perhaps we shall meet again, under . . . different circumstances."

For the last time, Nicholas bowed, a tight nervous bow, then hurriedly backed out of the Fairchild residence, turned, and raced down the steps into the waiting coach.

The coachman called to the tired horses and they set out once more, heading for Nicholas's London residence.

Chapter Four

A good night's sleep did wonders for Julianna, but could not dispel her sorrow or the heavy feeling of loss that was not entirely for her father, but also for the captain. She blushed recalling her blundering introductions, particularly after her mother had instructed her on the proper manner in which to address those with titles.

Of course, her dearest papa thought it all twaddle. Why should Julianna concern oneself with English titles, especially when she lived in America? But her mother had insisted on this particular facet of her upbringing, one which Julianna had studied with great enthusiasm.

As she peered through the curtains at the rain, the gloomy day only heightened the feeling that she had somehow let her mother down. It gave her scant comfort to recall that Sir Nicholas had appeared completely unperturbed by her mistake.

A light tap on the door caused her to turn suddenly. She tugged at the edge of her night-robe. "Come in."

"Why, Miss Julianna, you're up!" Margaret bustled in, bearing a tray laden with a delicious-smelling breakfast.

"Yes, Margaret, I am. Thank you. Please, just set it on the table. Is my aunt awake?"

"Oh, yes, ages ago. I heard the housekeeper say Mrs. Fairchild was making arrangements to have new gowns made for you. That is, mourning gowns, miss." The maid looked down. "I'm ever so sorry."

"Do not fret yourself, Margaret. I have been through mourning several times: first for my mother, then for Mich— Well, for several others besides my father." She shrugged dejectedly. "I am somewhat used to it."

"Such a pity, bein' as how you've just come to England." Margaret placed the tray on the table and fussed with the tea things, aligning the silver next to the plate. "Would you like me to set out your attire for the day, miss?"

"Yes, please." Julianna sat down at the table and forced herself to eat. She scarcely tasted the delicious scones and fresh jam, having become so absorbed in her own thoughts. She did not want to contemplate wearing mourning since it would remind her of Papa. Somehow, it did not seem right to wear mourning for him. He certainly would not have wanted it, regardless of what propriety dictated.

Edward Adams was too fine a man to die, especially in a shipwreck. He *ought* to have died in battle, sword in one hand, pistol in the other, urging his favorite horse, Hotspur, into the fray. But Captain Sidney had advised her that no one could have survived the cruelties of an Atlantic storm, especially if the *Hart* had broken up.

Julianna ate the last bite of scone as she watched Margaret lay out the last hand-me-down frock of Mrs. Howard's. While a newly made mourning gown would fit properly, she could not be ungracious toward Mrs. Howard's generosity, particularly where Captain Sidney was concerned. He had gone out of his way to make her comfortable and must have risked his own reputation by trying to find her presentable clothing,

securing rooms for her in Portsmouth, and then escorting her all the way to London. He had even found
Margaret for her.

After breakfast, Margaret helped her get dressed.
Examining her reflection in the glass, she still looked
too pale. Julianna smoothed the biscuit-colored gown,
which did not complement her fair skin and dark hair.
She longed for her trunks filled with gowns and frocks
of azure blue, bottle green, and amaranthus. Too soon,
even the drab little frock she now wore would be considered lively next to black bombazine.

"That will be all, Margaret. Thank you." She gave
her hair a last pat and hurried out to meet her aunt.

Emily Fairchild sat at her breakfast table almost
obscured by fabric remnants, bits of lace, boxes of
buttons, and assorted trinkets. Her own lace cap sat a
trifle askew over her graying curls as she rummaged
through a small bandbox stuffed with ribbons and
other gewgaws.

"I *know* it is here," she fumed, not yet seeing or
hearing Julianna.

"What do you know, Aunt?"

"Ah, Julianna. Do sit down, my dear. You look well
today. The color is returning to your cheeks."

"Do you think so? I am not so certain." She sat
down next to her aunt and fingered a bit of cambric
stuck between two scraps of challis.

"Of course you do. Dearest, you were at death's
doorstep not a week ago and you have made a remarkable recovery—thanks, of course, to the estimable Sir Nicholas and your natural youthful strength."
Aunt Emily resumed her rummaging in the bandbox.
"By the bye, I have already written the Admiralty,
commending the captain for his actions, and will write
Mrs. Howard this afternoon . . . after I find . . . gracious, wherever is that lace?"

"Aunt Emily, whatever *are* you looking for?"

"I know I have a pretty bit of black alençon that
will do well on a gown for you. Such a pity. I had so

many lovely plans for you." A handful of ribbons landed on the table in a colorful jumble. "Dear me, how thoughtless I am."

Julianna looked down. Already her aunt was preparing her for wearing black, as Margaret had warned. Had not she worn enough black? Enough for two lifetimes.

Her aunt stopped her search and looked up, noticing her downcast expression. "My dear Julianna, are you unwell again?"

"No, only disheartened." She pulled a handkerchief from her sleeve, preparing for the storm of tears gathering in her eyes and at the back of her throat. "To wear mourning again, so soon after grieving for Michael. Now Papa." At last the tears came, long held back, she having not wanted to upset Mr. Jacko or the captain.

Aunt Emily rose from her chair and came around, placing a comforting arm across Julianna's shoulders. "You have had a frightful shock and a terrible loss. I confess I have been dreadfully thoughtless. We will not press the matter of mourning just yet."

Julianna's weeping quieted. "I am sorry, but it has been too much. It simply is not right that Papa is gone. What am I to do, Aunt? I will only be a burden for you and Uncle Fairchild."

"Nonsense! We are only too delighted to have you. These sad times will pass. Now then, we shall go out. Perhaps a drive about town will cheer you up. And not another word about mourning!"

The drive did help cheer her heart as Aunt Emily made certain they passed notable sights: Westminster Abbey and then through Hyde Park. The clouds had broken up and the raindrops clung to the leaves and flowers, sparkling like jewels in the warm spring sun.

Her aunt chattered on about trifles: a forthcoming dinner party, an assembly, then later on in the month, a private ball at Lady Elwood's. Occasionally she would nod and bow to passersby, an acquaintance, or friend. Tiring, Julianna found herself sinking deeper into the cushions, her eyelids impossibly heavy.

"Dear me, I have worn you out. We will return home at once." Aunt Emily gave instructions to the coachman, and the horses were turned about smartly and driven straight back to Hanover Square.

Once home, Julianna gladly handed over her bonnet and cloak to Margaret and followed her aunt into the drawing room. They were both surprised to find Uncle Fairchild sitting near the fire, absorbed in a newspaper.

He looked up. "Ah, my dears, you are returned."

Julianna sat down wearily on a nearby settee, grateful to be resting on something that did not jolt or sway.

Her uncle rose from his chair and approached Julianna, taking one of her hands in his. "A letter has come, Julianna. One of utmost importance to you." He let go of her hand and plucked a folded piece of paper from inside his breast pocket.

Julianna's heart bumped within her chest; her hand went to her throat. Who would send a letter? She knew no one in London, except perhaps the captain . . . ? Her pulse began to pound in anticipation until a second thought struck her. Perhaps it was news of her father. Dreadful news.

Her uncle adjusted his spectacles and cleared his throat.

Dear Sir:
   I am sending this message to you under the gravest of circumstances. Suffice it to say, I cannot divulge my whereabouts, however, I hope to advise you soon of all information pertaining to this matter. I am writing to ask you to convey this message to my daughter, Julianna. I pray she survived the storm and shipwreck and has somehow managed to find you. Please let her know I am well and am attempting everything in my power to be rejoined with her.
   E.A.

Julianna felt the blood leave her face. Her dearest papa was alive? She stood, trembling, and swayed against Uncle Fairchild. Her head felt impossibly light and she scarcely heard Aunt Emily's cry of alarm or felt her uncle's hands attempting to grasp her shoulders, her elbows. The floor seemed so far away and yet, too soon, she felt the thick carpet against her cheek and saw the curious outline of a chair leg, mere inches away. A soft blackness descended.

"You are sure this is in his hand?" Uncle Fairchild asked.

"Oh, yes, I am sure of it. Papa has a dreadful hand—so careless and illegible," Julianna answered after examining the short letter.

"Hmmm. Odd." Her uncle tapped the paper. "Good quality paper. I collect he may be staying someplace nearby, perhaps an excellent hotel here in London. I could make inquires there."

Her aunt became frantic to make inquires of her own, and quickly invited her cousin, Lady Elwood, to take tea so that she could apprise her of the situation. Julianna had been two days in bed recovering from the shock of her father's letter, then endured another three days of anxious waiting for responses from her uncle's inquiries, when the handsome barouche stopped in front of the Fairchild residence. Julianna watched in astonishment as the lady fairly stormed into the house, sweeping into the drawing room.

"I came at once, Emily, and I shall not leave until you tell me every particle of information."

"And not a moment too soon." Aunt Emily stepped forward, embracing the tall, elegantly dressed woman, then introduced Julianna to her cousin, Charlotte, Lady Elwood, widow of the late Marquess of Elwood.

Glad for the new blue gown instead of the drab borrowed frocks, Julianna made her curtsy. "Lady Elwood, a great honor."

A quizzing glass appeared from nowhere. "Well, she looks nothing like Caroline, I will say that, but a prettyish sort of girl. A bit small. Not too colonial, nor the rustic I had feared."

Emily Fairchild bristled. "Charlotte, I shall not tolerate one unkind word about Caroline's child. Miss Adams has experienced the most frightful of circumstances—a dreadful voyage, ill health, the near loss of her father. On top of all this misfortune, she has recently lost her intended to a ghastly fire. She is family and will be treated accordingly." Her usually warm, blue eyes flashed her indignation.

Unperturbed, Lady Elwood raised a questioning brow. "You are quite impertinent today, Emily. But I perceive you are excessively distraught or would not behave so . . ." She turned to Julianna. "You are well, Miss Adams?"

"I am improving, ma'am, and shall be completely well in a very short time."

"You have manners, I see." She sniffed, a trifle haughtily. "At least Caroline taught you something in that wilderness. Do you play or draw?"

Julianna looked down, hiding a smile. "I play the harp tolerably well. And I can even read."

An ominous pause hovered between them, until Lady Elwood smiled a taut, pleased smile. "The child has wit! There are possibilities here. Come, Emily, I will take tea."

It was only later Julianna learned that Lady Elwood and her Aunt Emily were cousins through their mothers, and close friends. Once the prickly introductions were over, Lady Elwood revealed a sympathetic and generous character, immersing herself in Julianna's unhappy story.

"Most extraordinary!" The Dowager Marchioness of Elwood finished stirring her tea and set the spoon down with a thoughtless rattle. "I declare, a complete mystery." The tassel dangling from her turban quivered, matching the excited tone in her voice. "And you say you know nothing of his whereabouts?"

Julianna shook her head. "He only said he would write again, soon. I am so thankful he is alive, I find myself not worried *when* he will write again, but only concerned for his safety."

Aunt Emily's guest nodded enthusiastically and sipped her tea. "To be sure, but most curious circumstances."

"I have been in an utter state of confusion as to what should be done," said Aunt Emily. "My nerves are in rags. Dear me, and poor Julianna still not completely well." She shook her head. "Mr. Fairchild *has* made inquiries, I have made certain of that."

"Of course, he did write to the Admiralty?" Lady Elwood asked. "They certainly would have information concerning the ship and possibly Miss Adams's papa."

Aunt Emily pressed a hand to her ample bosom. "He has, indeed, but no news as yet. We are all on pins and needles."

Julianna sipped her own tea, absorbing her aunt's comments and Lady Elwood's contribution.

Uncle Fairchild had investigated all the fine hotels, but to no avail. No one seemed to know or had heard anything of a visiting American, either injured or in dire straits. Julianna felt at odds with herself. She was impatient for news of her father, but relieved he was alive. Wherever he was, Julianna was certain he would write soon and then they would be reunited.

"There is nothing more to be said about it. We shall have to take charge of the situation. Tongues will wag, I daresay. First, Miss Adams must have new attire."

"Agreed." Aunt Fairchild nodded happily. "If she is to step foot into society, she must have the proper clothes. Gracious, Charlotte, she arrived in near tatters. Scandalous! Except for the generosity of Sir Nicholas Sidney, poor Julianna might have arrived on my doorstep in her—"

Julianna suddenly looked up at her aunt. "The captain. Of course."

Aunt Emily blinked and shook her head, bewildered. "I do not understand, my dear. 'Of course' what?"

"Aunt, the captain . . . I mean that Sir Nicholas may have heard something of my father. Perhaps he has been in touch with the navy or his officers. He may have news."

Lady Elwood started so abruptly, she almost upset her teacup. "*Sir* Nicholas Sidney, son of the late baronet Sir Edmund Sidney?"

"Yes, Lady Elwood. He is also the captain of the *Gallant*; he was the gentleman who rescued me."

Her aunt leaned forward, eager for gossip. "You know something, Charlotte, I daresay. Now tell."

The grand lady pulled herself into a more regal posture. "It is no secret. Sir Edmund was something of a rake until he married Helena Collins; then he became quite settled. They had one son, who is now, of course, Sir Nicholas. Lady Sidney died many years ago—I collect over twenty years now. It was rumored that Sir Edmund went to pieces afer she was killed in a dreadful carriage accident. The poor man turned to drink and became utterly ruined."

"How do you know this?" Aunt Emily demanded.

"It is common knowledge, cousin. Wycombe Hall is not five miles from Malthorpe. I have been by it on numerous occasions. It has gone through some renovations, I believe."

"Then the captain has known great loss, too," Julianna murmured, recalling his long silences and the deep sadness in his eyes.

Her aunt Emily appeared not to have heard her. "Then we *must* write to him immediately and invite him to dine. I am certain he will have news."

"Excellent idea, Emily! Where is he staying—at Fladong's on Oxford Street? Navy men seem to always congregate there."

"If he is still in Town. Mr. Fairchild would know. Gracious, this is exciting. My dear Julianna, you will see the good captain again!"

The Admiralty Office loomed gray and bleak in the relentless afternoon downpour. Nicholas descended the carriage, snapped open his umbrella, and moved briskly across the courtyard to the main entrance. The

First Lord of the Admiralty, Charles Yorke, had re-
quested this meeting, and a mere post captain dared
not be a moment late.

Once inside, relieved of his greatcoat, hat, and umbrella, Nicholas made his way up to the grand oak-
lined boardroom, trying to keep the anxious beating
of his heart in check. He knew the letter tucked inside
his coat was the main focus of the interview. The First
Lord's response to Nicholas's initial letter had been
surprisingly quick. It was clear the Admiralty had a
keen interest in anything marked or signed "E.A."

He was ushered into the room without ceremony.
Both Lord Yorke and the First Secretary awaited him.

"Ah, Sir Nicholas. Good of you to come." His lord-
ship gestured to the gentleman standing next to him.
"I believe you have met our First Secretary, Mr.
Andrews."

"I have, indeed." Nicholas bowed politely. "It is an
honor, sir."

"And now, to business." Lord Yorke indicated a
chair where Nicholas should sit. "We have read your
letter with great interest, as well as the report from
Admiral Howard. I might add, he rates your handling
of these matters quite highly, sir. However, it is this
particular letter you mention that we wish to discuss.
Please proceed, Captain."

Nicholas drew out the water-stained letter and set
it before him so both the First Lord and Secretary
could see it. He read the terse note, then continued
with a detailed explanation of Miss Adams's rescue,
the sinking of the *Hart,* and the pertinent details con-
nected with the letter.

Lord Yorke shook his head slowly. "Extraordinary.
Lost at sea for a week, eh? A miraculous rescue. And
Miss Adams? Is she well?"

"When I left her with her relatives, she was on her
way to a complete recovery." Nicholas touched the
note. "She has no explanation for the contents of this
letter, nor the coincidence concerning these initials
matching those of her father."

The First Secretary, a neat little man with crisp white hair, reached for the letter and examined it closely through a gold-rimmed glass suspended around his neck by a fine chain. "You must know, Sir Nicholas, that this January past, a small French ship was captured off Ramsgate. Not only was the captain smuggling illegal goods, but several papers were discovered, encoded, and all signed by 'E.A.' The captain claimed he knew nothing of what these papers meant—he was just going to have them delivered."

Lord Yorke continued. "The papers were addressed to Lysette Corbeil, just like the one you have brought to us. Through the Foreign Office, we have also learned that this Lysette Corbeil is a French émigré and a known courier—for whom, we do not know yet."

Mr. Andrews tapped the letter with his glass. "However, a maid has been placed within the household where Mlle Corbeil resides and has been instructed to report anything of consequence, particularly anyone who pays a call or picks up these letters. So far, no one has come for the letters."

Nicholas heard the spring rain rattle against the window. Somewhere a clock chimed two. "Sir," he said slowly, "are you suggesting that Miss Adams's father may be the signer of these letters?"

"It is entirely possible," Lord Yorke said. "And it is imperative we find out this man's identity. Military information, particularly naval intelligence, is being passed to him—probably sold by an operative here in England. I must tell you, Sir Nicholas, this letter and the information you have obtained is our first crack in the case."

Nicholas frowned, troubled. "Mr. Adams went down with the *Hart,* sir. Have you received no other reports of any shipwrecks? Besides, Miss Adams stated that the man who handed her this letter was a Frenchman by the name of Edmund Rameau. It is hardly likely—"

"The Foreign Office will look into finding out Rameau's identity, Captain. In the meantime, we ask that you keep this information in absolute confidence."

"Of course, my lord."

"There is one other thing, Captain Sidney," Mr. Andrews said. "We must also ask that you keep an eye on Miss Adams. Discreetly, of course. She is probably quite innocent, but we cannot be too sure."

Nicholas heard himself make the appropriate responses. Of course. Duty above personal interests—but he didn't like it. Julianna was innocent of any wrongdoing and knew nothing about spying or . . . espionage. *Espionage.* Even the word left a foul taste in his mouth.

He scarcely heard his lordship assure him that the letter would be carefully copied, resealed, and sent on its way to Mlle Corbeil's address. After bidding goodbye to Mr. Andrews and the esteemed First Lord of the Admiralty, Nicholas hurried to the awaiting carriage, almost forgetting his hat and coat.

He stared out the carriage window, the tiresome rain only adding to his gloomy state of mind. He really did not want to spend his brief shore leave overseeing the activities of a sick, grieving, American girl. He would take his half-pay, gladly, together with the hard-won prize money, and go home to Wycombe. He had plenty to do there.

Duty battered at him once again. Suppose Lord Yorke was right? What *if* Julianna were involved in some kind of clandestine activities against the Crown? Her tears and grief a well-rehearsed act? It was possible, but in his heart, Nicholas knew it was not true. The woman he had held in his arms that night in his cabin wept heartbroken tears of pain, terror, and bitter loss. It had not been an act.

Duty and honor came to a mutual agreement. Captain Sir Nicholas Sidney would watch and report on the activities of the American, Miss Adams, but Nicholas would help Julianna find out what happened to her father.

Chapter Five

Captain Sidney was *not* staying at Fladong's, and, much to Julianna's dismay, the Admiralty knew nothing about the *Hart* or the fate of its passengers and crew. It was as if both the captain and her father had simply disappeared.

Lady Elwood remained optimistic—Sir Nicholas was probably staying at his residence in the country, Wycombe Hall. A tactful letter would surely bring a response.

Aunt Emily had a more ready answer—the good captain was probably still occupied with navy matters and not attending to his personal correspondence.

Julianna held back her disappointment and allowed herself to be caught up in her aunt's plans. Two weeks of dressmakers, fittings, and countless decisions as to colors and fabrics absorbed her time. Short carriage rides refreshed her spirits. A regular walk with her uncle strengthened her limbs. She even found herself gazing longingly at the fashionable equestriennes riding through the park, cutting elegant figures in their stylish habits. Their splendid horses reminded her of her father's fine animals and of her own mare, Minuet. However, riding was out of the question, at least for a time. She still tired easily and avoided activities requiring too much exertion.

An invitation to a card party and supper came just as Julianna thought she would go wild with boredom. Her aunt was jubilant.

"Mrs. Heldon's parties are quite the rage. She always invites the best society. You shall be in good company, my dear."

Standing before the cheval glass, Julianna smoothed a wrinkle from the creamy white silk of her gown. Gone was the haunted look, as was the sunburned skin. Her complexion had taken on a healthy pink hue. A far cry from the girl who had been pulled from a floundering boat in the middle of the ocean, starving, crazed with thirst and grief.

She turned to the sound of a now-comforting voice. Margaret had agreed to stay on as her abigail. Aside from her aunt, Julianna found Margaret's company a source of consolation and understanding.

"Will you be wantin' your wrap, miss?"

"Yes, I am ready."

Margaret placed the matching wrap over her shoulders and handed her a little reticule.

"You look lovely, miss. You'll have gentlemen callers by the dozen."

"I doubt that very much. I do not think English gentlemen are interested in American girls, particularly those who have been shipwrecked!"

Margaret only shrugged and stepped aside, allowing Julianna to pass.

Once in the carriage she felt her palms go damp and was immediately grateful for the long white gloves hiding the signs of her nervousness. Her aunt and uncle complimented her on her attire, raising her confidence and hopes.

At Mrs. Heldon's, Julianna found herself moving through beautifully furnished rooms lit to golden softness by dozens of candles. She remained firmly attached to her aunt's side, not daring to venture beyond her protection. Only Lady Elwood was a familiar face. The great lady moved regally through the salons wearing a glittering gown of silver tissue, diamonds encircling her throat and wrists.

"My dear Miss Adams, you are a picture."

Julianna curtseyed. "Thank you, Lady Elwood."

"Come, I would have you meet a few of my friends." She nodded to Aunt Emily. "I shall return her to you, I promise."

Taking her elbow, Lady Elwood guided Julianna through the sea of elegantly attired men and women— some were courteous, a few only politely curious.

"Egad!" one gentleman exclaimed. "To go down with a ship. Extraordinary."

And another: "I must commend you, Miss Adams, for your courage under the most fearsome circumstances. Remarkable."

In a music room, Lady Elwood stopped before a gathering of two ladies and three gentlemen. The first, a woman in apricot silk, sat before a pianoforte. A slender gentleman wearing a striped waistcoat stood at her side, poised to turn the pages of her music.

Across the room, another gentleman—immaculate in a coat of black superfine, his neckcloth of flawless white linen—peered at Julianna through a quizzing glass, taking in every detail of her attire from the top of her head to the soles of her satin shoes.

"Ladies and gentlemen," Lady Elwood announced, "allow me to introduce to you Miss Julianna Adams from Baltimore." She gestured to the lady seated before the pianoforte. "Miss Adams, Mrs. Haworth and Mr. Tanner."

The lady nodded graciously and the gentleman made a short bow.

"And Mr. Thorneloe." Lady Elwood indicated the tall, elegant man standing near the window.

A third gentleman, sprawled on a gold brocade chair placed next to the matching divan, snored softly.

"Mr. Haworth . . . ?" Lady Elwood questioned delicately.

The gentleman grunted, cleared his throat, and rose

on unsteady feet to perform a slightly clumsy bow. "The American gel! I say, how quaint. Nothing like a colonial to liven things up a bit."

Julianna made her curtseys. Embarrassment flooded her cheeks. She sensed Lady Elwood's well-concealed outrage and wondered how she was going to extricate the two of them from this dreadful situation.

"La, Mr. Haworth," a cool feminine voice scolded him gently. "You are shockingly wicked. Cannot you see you have vexed the poor girl?"

Mr. Haworth made a nondescript noise in his throat then resettled himself into the chair, bored, having lost all interest in the events at hand. He poured himself a glass of port from a half-empty decanter and settled himself to resume his nap.

Julianna glanced at the source of that shimmering voice and caught herself in time so as not to stare. The young woman who spoke was by far the loveliest creature she had ever seen. Honey blond hair had been caught up in blue silk ribbons, with a charming array of curls tumbling about her forehead and at the nape of her neck. The color of the ribbons matched her exquisite eyes—the exact shade of sapphires.

She rose from the divan, her watered-silk moire gown rustling softly, and closed the lace fan she carried with a decisive flick. "Lady Elwood." She curtseyed to the older woman.

"Miss Landon, allow me to introduce you to Miss Adams."

The lovely blonde turned her serene gaze on Julianna and offered a condescending smile. "Miss Adams. You must forgive Mr. Haworth. He is indeed out of sorts this evening. Although I must confess none of us had any idea of what to expect. I am quite sure we envisioned someone not nearly as . . . refined?"

Mrs. Haworth tittered, trying to hide her smile behind a gloved hand.

The other gentleman, Mr. Tanner, made a sniggering noise, then said, "Indeed, Miss Olivia, I daresay

I half expected some kind of charming rustic. One can never know with these Yankees. In one moment, fire a shot at you from behind a tree like some wild Indian, and in the next, dance an allemande pretty as you please, what?"

"Really, Mr. Tanner, you exaggerate. Cannot you see that Miss Adams would do neither?" Miss Landon turned to her and smiled—a poorly disguised attempt at an apology. "It seems I must excuse the gentleman. Mr. Tanner, I fear, was ill used by some of your countrymen not long ago. However, you are quite a surprise. I had no idea Americans had such a fine eye for style."

Miss Landon glanced over the new white silk gown as if viewing an oddity in a traveling circus. Hot blood rushed to Julianna's face, scalding her cheeks. She forced herself to remain calm, but the furious pounding of her heart almost betrayed her. Her right palm itched to slap the arrogant, disdainful look from Miss Landon's face.

"Regretfully, Miss Landon, my buckskins sank in the Atlantic along with the ship. I fear I must disappoint you. However, perhaps you would care to witness a display of my marksmanship. I *am* an excellent shot with a musket and have been known to shoot at least a dozen wild bears in a single day." Her voice cool, she kept her anger under control.

She glanced at Lady Elwood's grim expression and at Mrs. Haworth's rouged mouth developing into a perfect little circle of complete astonishment.

Miss Landon's delicate brows rose in pale twin arches. "Oh."

Julianna was certain she heard a soft laugh from the back of the room, from Mr. Thorneloe—not a derisive laugh, but more like polite approval.

"Pray, excuse me. Lady Elwood." Julianna spun on her heel and hurried out of the room, convinced she heard their mocking laughter. All she could think about was getting away from this dreadful situation.

The rooms suddenly became unbearably hot—there

were far too many people. Her aunt and uncle were
lost amidst the frightful crush, and Julianna dreaded
meeting Lady Elwood again. Anger and embarrassment scalded her cheeks as she hurried down a
short hallway hoping to find a room where she could
have a moment to think clearly, but found herself in
a small library lined with bookshelves and dark heavy
furniture. The only occupant was an elderly, old-
fashioned gentleman—his white periwig perched
askew over a pink bald pate as he snored peacefully
in one of the armchairs.

Sinking into one of the nearby chairs, Julianna
clenched her hands in her lap, struggling to control
her anger. How dare that . . . creature! Papa had been
right when he had counseled her about the British and
their opinion of Americans. In their eyes she would
always be a country bumpkin, a hopeless provincial
with no manners or refinements. It was all too
infuriating.

"I must commend you for the extraordinary manner
in which you put Miss Landon in her place."

Julianna jumped to her feet and whirled toward the
sound of that bemused masculine voice. Mr. Thorneloe stood just inside the room, one hand braced
against the doorway.

"May I come in?" he asked politely. Noticing the
old fellow in his chair, he smiled. "I believe your reputation is quite safe even though Mr. Brockhurst sleeps
through all the better soirees. However, I shall leave
the door open, just in case."

"Yes, please do."

Julianna stepped away from the chair into the
deeper shadows closer to Mr. Brockhurst, hoping Mr.
Thorneloe would not notice her shaking hands or
flushed cheeks.

"I came to offer an apology for Miss Landon's behavior. She is quite spoilt and cares nothing for another's feelings. It is not often someone, anyone, puts
the leash to her collar. I must say, you did it quite

thoroughly." A slow smile touched his mouth, a rather beautifully shaped mouth, Julianna noted.

"I did not mean to insult her."

"And why not? She insulted you. No, it was commendable. Miss Landon deserved every word."

Julianna turned away and looked down. "Yes, well, I am afraid I have sealed my fate by my hasty words. News of this will be about London in no time. I have embarrassed my relatives and perhaps ruined their standing in Society."

Mr. Thorneloe made a disparaging noise in his throat. "Your fears are unfounded, Miss Adams. It was Miss Landon who was rude, not you. Do not worry yourself."

She glanced at him, noting the veiled humor in his eyes.

"You are quite reassuring, sir."

"I had hoped so. Now perhaps you will allow me to escort you back to the card rooms? You do play whist?"

"Yes, a little."

"Young ladies always do something 'a little.' They play the pianoforte *a little*, sing *a little*, draw *a little*. I hope you are accomplished in something more than just 'a little.' "

Julianna could not resist. She took his offered arm. "Yes, I can *shoot* quite well."

A warm laugh escaped his lips. He glanced down at her, clearly delighted with her rejoinder. "I would wager you have already proven yourself this night, bringing down one bird, eh?"

"Perhaps. But I would also wager that most of the coveys have already taken flight, they not being willing to be brought down by an upstart colonial."

Mr. Thorneloe's smile matched his warm laugh. "You are a wit, Miss Adams, and I vow I will not surrender you for another partner!"

Throughout the rest of the evening Julianna remained in the attentive presence of Mr. Thorneloe.

After she won several rubbers, he declared humorously that Miss Adams played tolerably well—the little joke being missed by everyone at their table.

She avoided any further unpleasant confrontations by seating herself with her back to Miss Landon and her insufferable table partners. Julianna also noted that the estimable Lady Elwood kept a watchful eye on Miss Landon, obviously to make certain there would be no more embarrassing conversations.

After playing several hands, Mr. Thorneloe announced he had played quite enough whist and wished only to spend the rest of the evening in quiet conversation with Julianna. To her surprise, he proved equally skilled in stimulating conversation as well as playing cards. He listened with keen attention as she explained the details of her perilous voyage across the Atlantic, the sinking of the *Hart,* and her near brush with death. In spite of herself, Julianna even shared with him the contents of her father's letter—how it was signed with only the initials "E.A."

He stroked his chin, perplexed. "Hmmm. Curious, indeed. Why would he not reveal his name?"

She shrugged, defeated by the dilemma. "I do not know, unless he is in some dire danger."

"Have you made inquiries?"

"Oh, yes. My uncle has written the Admiralty and the Home Office. Even the American consul here in London."

"What do they say?"

"We have not heard anything yet. We are hoping Captain Sidney will have some information soon."

"Ah, yes. The good captain," Mr. Thorneloe murmured. "A paragon of duty and responsibility."

Julianna was not entirely clear what he meant by that comment. She did not inquire any further into the matter, now suddenly weary of the conversation and longing to return home.

By two A.M. the Fairchild party took their leave of Mrs. Heldon and headed for home. Aunt Emily kept silent for a long time until at last she spoke her

thoughts. "Lady Elwood is utterly enraged by what
transpired between you that dreadful Miss Landon.
Dear child, she is quite overset by the whole
business."

"I am not angry with Lady Elwood, Aunt."

"Olivia Landon is above herself! I have always said
so." Aunt Emily began working herself into a fine
mettle. "It is insupportable. The chit is in need of a
proper setdown. Mark my words, I shall see to it. I
will speak to Lady Jersey."

"Aunt, you must not!"

"Dearest Julianna, Miss Landon insulted you, before the entire *ton*. It was disgraceful. Such impu-
dence. Well, what can one expect from a fortune
seeker? I have heard scandalous talk about her and
her mother. Miss Landon's mother is the *second* Mrs.
Thorneloe. She married Mr. Thorneloe's father a few
years ago—they say only for the title."

Confused, Julianna shook her head. "Title? I do
not understand."

"Mr. Thorneloe's father, who met his reward several years ago, was brother to Earl Desmond. The earl
has no children. When he passes away, the younger
Mr. Thorneloe, his nephew, will inherit the title, and
Miss Landon will be quite satisfied with that arrangement to be sure!"

"So Miss Landon is Mr. Thorneloe's stepsister?"

"Indeed she is, and a more spoilt creature cannot
be found."

Uncle Fairchild cleared his throat. "My dear, you
will overset *yourself* if you continue in this manner. I
suggest prudence. Let us remain calm. Tomorrow we
will decide if the willful Miss Landon is in need of a
'setdown.' Perhaps she will apologize and then all will
be agreeable again."

Aunt Emily cooled her temper. "Of course, you are
quite right, Mr. Fairchild. I shall consider the matter
in the morning. But I still contend Miss Landon was
insufferable."

The carriage swayed and Julianna grabbed for the

strap. "However, the remainder of the evening passed well," she observed.

"Indeed it did! Mr. Thorneloe is such a fine gentleman and paid you a very high compliment," Aunt Emily agreed. "Mrs. Heldon did advise me, in the most confidential of terms, that Mr. Thorneloe *is* a bit of a rake, so you must take heed, dear girl."

Julianna said nothing. Mr. Thorneloe had been charming, with easy manners, and he paid her the most thoughtful compliments. But for all his appeal she could not quite trust this perception of him.

She willed herself to put the curious thought behind her and think about other, more significant things, particularly the difficulty in trying to find her father. Why had he not written her again? And for pity's sake, why had he been so evasive? Julianna simply had to have more answers.

Sighing, she sank against the squabs. In the darkness of the coach she caught the faint glint from one of the buttons on her uncle's coat, reminding her of another—blue, with gleaming braid at the collar and heavy gold epaulets emphasizing wide, straight shoulders. She remembered his keen attentiveness and concern for her as they journeyed from Portsmouth to London.

Each time they had stopped to change horses or to take tea, Sir Nicholas stayed close to her side, protecting her from any unpleasantness—a rude hostler, the odd beggar, or a light-fingered pickpocket. And always he had watched her with those intense eyes, looking for the slightest sign of illness or an indication she might faint. Her dearest Michael had never looked at her that way making her feel at once helpless and . . . desired.

But Sir Nicholas was as elusive as her father. It did occur to her that perhaps the captain did not want to be found or contacted—which led her to another astonishing thought. Perhaps her father did not want to be found either.

Chapter Six

"The post has arrived! Dear me, Julianna, do come down."

Her aunt's frantic cries sent Julianna racing from her bedroom to the drawing room in a most inappropriate manner. She stopped herself in time, making sure her aunt saw nothing but serene composure as she took the thick cream-colored letter from the salver set on the table near the door.

Trembling, she sat down next to her aunt and broke the seal, scanning the firm, bold handwriting. A thread of disappointment shot through her as she realized the letter was not from her father, but quickly gave way to quiet pleasure. "It is from Captain Sidney."

"Oh, my dear, Lady Elwood *did* write to the captain." Aunt Emily beamed at her, delighted by the outcome of her cousin's intervention.

Julianna cleared her throat and began to read:

Dear Miss Adams:
I apologize for my tardiness in writing to you, however, business has kept me from keeping abreast with my correspondence.

"You see," Aunt Emily exclaimed, "I was right. The

good captain has not been avoiding you, only preoccupied. And I think there is something to be said for his attentions to you, my dear." Her eyes twinkled mischievously.

Julianna nodded, determined not to encourage her aunt's blatant insinuation, and continued reading Captain Sidney's letter.

Lady Elwood's intervention on your behalf has prompted me to write the Admiralty again in regards to the fate of the Hart. *I have been awaiting their response and only today did I receive word. There have been no reports of any ship, either a private vessel or of commerce, going down within the last few weeks. I must confess, it is an astonishing piece of information. Nonetheless, I will pursue all avenues at my disposal to discover the ultimate fate of the* Hart *and perhaps the whereabouts of your father. I rejoice in learning that your father did not perish in the storm and will continue to make inquiries on your behalf.*

My best wishes for your continued good health.
Yours etc.,
Nicholas Sidney, Bt.

Julianna refolded the letter and glanced at her anxious aunt, whose lace cap was fairly atremble.

"The captain seems equally perplexed as I. Still, it was thoughtful of him to look into this matter." She rose, uncertain exactly how she would respond to the captain. Thanking him for his efforts was certainly in order, but to expect him to continue searching for her father seemed somewhat presumptuous on her part. And yet, he had offered.

"My dear Julianna, the captain has been a positive *saint* in the matter. We must invite him to dine with us, or at least to tea. What do you think?"

"I think it would be entirely appropriate. Then I

can thank him properly. Pray, excuse me, Aunt. I will write him immediately."

However, once seated at her writing desk, Julianna found it impossible to put her thoughts to paper. How could she find the right words to convey her gratitude when all she could think about was . . . was . . . ? She blushed at the memory of his arms about her, carrying her across the pier at Portsmouth to the waiting carriage. Or the recollection of his intent gaze upon her as they traveled to London, watching for the slightest indication she might become ill again.

Somewhere in the deepest recesses of her mind, Julianna seemed to recall being held firmly against him while she clutched at his shirt and sobbed out the horror of her nightmares, of shipwreck and fire. He had been a solid bulwark against the terrors of the darkness.

Julianna sighed and put her quill down, unable to continue. Perhaps it would be easier if she spoke to him face-to-face at dinner. It *ought* to be easier. Seated across from him at a dining table, she could hide her shaking hands in her lap, as well as keep her gaze firmly attached to her plate and not on those intense, dark eyes examining her every move.

An invitation to dine with the Fairchilds proved to be both a pleasant and disturbing occasion for Sir Nicholas. While he enjoyed the company, listening to the stimulating conversation and sampling the culinary talents of the Fairchild cook, he was not pleased with the new and bewildering sensations warring within him, all centered upon seeing Miss Adams again.

He dressed with care, making sure every button gleamed, but still felt like a green midshipman on his first voyage—awkward, clumsy, and unable to put two consecutive words together without sounding like an imbecile.

The very fact that Mrs. Fairchild had invited him to dinner was enough of a surprise. He knew he had

received the invitation simply because he had assisted
her niece and it was her way of thanking him, but he
did not expect the small, intimate gathering of close
friends and family.

He knew the widowed marchioness, Lady Elwood.
The great lady's country estate was not five miles from
his own. She greeted him cordially, making him recall
the happier days of his youth when his mother still
graced Wycombe Hall and had received Lady Elwood
into their home.

"Sir Nicholas, how good to see you again. It has
been several years, I collect, since I last spoke with
you, is it not?"

"Indeed, madam. In truth, I cannot recall the exact
time. I trust you are in good health?"

"Excellent, I thank you. And you, sir? The sea
agrees with you?"

"It is not the sea that is hazardous to one's health,
but the food. The Admiralty finds it amusing to supply
the n-n-navy with whatever is at hand no matter how
bad. That is why I am looking forward to d-d-dining
with you this evening."

To this, there was polite laughter from everyone
present.

"But surely, Sir Nicholas, you jest," Mrs. Fairchild
said.

"I am afraid not, but for now, I shall not think of
the navy and its provisioning practices."

"Here, here," Mr. Fairchild said with good humor.

Sir James Edlington and his wife, Nicholas did not
know. The other gentleman, a Mr. Powell, was a relation of Mr. Fairchild.

Sir James was a genial sort with an easy manner
and had the uncanny knack of making Nicholas feel
comfortable at once in his surroundings. After introductions, Sir James walked with him into the drawing room.

"My brother is in the navy, Sir Nicholas. Perhaps
you know him? Lieutenant Christopher Edlington?"

"Ah, um, n-n-no, sir. I regret I have not made his acquaintance."

"Good fellow, young Chris," Sir James continued amiably. "Smart chap, too."

Nicholas soon lost interest in Sir James's mindless nattering.

It was Miss Adams who completely arrested his attention. He could scarcely prevent himself from staring at her. In the few short weeks since he had last seen her, the change had been nothing short of remarkable. All traces of her ordeal had vanished. Except for the somewhat anxious look in her eyes, she had transformed from a sunburned, delirious invalid to a lovely, poised young woman. Her amethyst-colored gown complemented her soft dark eyes. The upswept hair had been caught in a matching amethyst ribbon accentuating the few stray tendrils caressing the nape of her neck. Her greeting had been cordial, her manner, serene—and yet, she seemed strained and tense. Nicholas sensed this was due to her worries about her father.

The seating arrangements at the table placed Nicholas at Mrs. Fairchild's right, which afforded him the perfect opportunity to observe Miss Adams, seated diagonally across from him, without appearing ill mannered or too forward.

Lady Elwood was seated next to Mr. Fairchild, who presided at his end of the table with bemused detachment, while the grand lady and Mrs. Fairchild kept the conversation spinning along with endless anecdotes, advice, and gossip. When they faltered, the charming Lady Edlington carried on with unfailing enthusiasm.

Sir James said little until the ladies were forced to partake of their soup, leaving the conversation open. Quick to take the advantage, Sir James said, "I say, how many men do you command, Sir Nicholas? I have never been aboard a frigate."

On familiar ground, Nicholas averted his attention from Miss Adams to the affable Sir James. "The *Gal-*

lant is manned by a crew of two hundred and fifty-six—no finer c-c-crew in His Majesty's navy."

"Indeed sir, I daresay they have a high regard for their captain, too. And I am quite certain Miss Adams would agree." He turned toward her and gave a reassuring smile.

Nicholas saw Miss Adams look up from her own soup and blush, realizing that she was now the center of attention.

"I do, Sir James. I owe my life to Sir Nicholas. If it had not been for him and an old sailor, Mr. Jacko, I might not be—"

"—dining with us this very moment!" Mrs. Fairchild exclaimed, reasserting her position in the conversation. "The captain has been too kind. Upon this we are all agreed, and I am sure when we locate Julianna's dear papa, we will have greater reason to rejoice. Do not you agree, Lady Elwood?"

Lady Elwood drew herself up even taller. "A day that cannot come too soon. I, for one, find it most mysterious why we cannot locate Miss Adams's father. We have attempted by every means at our disposal, but to no avail. And you, Sir Nicholas, despite all your connections in the navy, have not been successful either. It is a positive riddle. I am excessively diverted by the whole matter."

Nicholas drew a deep breath, taking deliberate care with each word. "It d-d-does seem odd, ma'am. Even I find it strange that the Admiralty does not have any information, particularly concerning the *Hart*. It was too large a ship to disappear completely. There would have been wreckage, and those who did not—Well, l-l-let us say there would have been sufficient evidence."

"Unless it did not actually go down," Mr. Fairchild interjected. His statement caused everyone to become silent for a long moment.

"What can you mean, Mr. Fairchild?" Lady Elwood asked.

"I mean, what if the *Hart* did not go down at all? What if it simply went adrift, lost at sea?"

Nicholas pondered Mr. Fairchild's comment. It was a serious and important suggestion. "That is possible, sir. Not probable, but possible."

"Yes, but what of the letter? Why was he so secretive? Why did my father not reveal his whereabouts?"

Miss Adams's former anxious look had become one of unfeigned anguish, the distress in her voice impossible to hide.

"I do not know, Miss Adams. I am sorry."

Nicholas tried to sound reasonable, but he did not like giving her such an empty answer. He truly did not understand how her father had survived the wreck, then sent a letter and specifically not mentioned where he was staying. If he did not go down with the *Hart,* then where was he? And what about the crew? Captain Denton? All lost to a raging storm off the coast of France?

There was the other disturbing fact that the letter had been signed with the initials E and A, not Adams's full name, and there was no mention of the French émigré Lysette Corbeil.

Nicholas poked idly at his soup, swirling little bits of vegetables around in a miniature sea of broth. Tiny ships bobbing about in a soup bowl storm. The *Hart.* The *Gallant.*

Raising a steaming spoonful to his lips, he happened to look across the table at Miss Adams. Her silent torment nearly broke his heart.

He tried to assemble the facts into some kind of logical order. There had been two ships returning to England. The *Hart* and the *Gallant.* One caught in the storm, the other just skirting it. How many other ships had managed either to outrun the storm or had survived it and navigated to a safe port?

Two tiny pieces of carrot, sailing about bravely in his soup, bumped into each other. Nicholas almost choked. Of course! Why had not he thought of it before? There had to have been another ship, larger no doubt and more seaworthy than the *Hart,* but also caught in the storm. Seeing the *Hart* in distress, it had probably sent out longboats to try to rescue those still on board the doomed ship. Cast adrift in their own launch, Miss Adams and the old salt, Jacko, never saw them and never knew those aboard the *Hart* had survived.

As tempting as it was, Nicholas decided to keep this startling conjecture to himself. There would only be more speculation and unanswerable questions, especially from Miss Adams. A vague idea began to form in his mind as to how he should proceed, and it took firmer shape as dinner progressed with each of the following courses. Later, when Mrs. Fairchild at last rose from the table, his plan had become quite clear. It would take a little traveling. . . .

"Sir Nicholas, do you think there is any possibility my father is here in England?"

By some extraordinary luck, the Fairchilds, Sir James, and Lady Elwood had moved ahead into the drawing room, leaving him quite alone with Miss Adams for a few moments. The scent of lavender filled Nicholas's senses, and his heart began to drum in slow, heavy beats, making it increasingly difficult to speak.

"It is a possibility, but I would n-n-not want to raise your hopes too high. There is always the chance he is . . . perhaps on the C-C-Continent."

Her eyes widened in astonishment. "You mean, in France?"

"Yes."

"Do you truly believe this? Sir Nicholas, please, do not assume my character is too delicate to hear the truth. I am made of sturdier stuff, I assure you. If you think there is the slightest chance my father is alive and well in France, I shall go there at once to find him."

Nicholas stopped himself in time before catching her arm in a cautioning grasp. "I beg you, Miss Adams, do not be so hasty. Allow me to investigate— make a few inquiries on your behalf. I will be d-d-discreet, but I believe I can obtain information in a

prudent manner without either endangering him or
putting you in an awkward position."

She nodded. "Very well, sir. I am in your hands,
but you must promise me you will advise me the instant you—"

"Julianna!"

They both turned toward the drawing room, where
Mrs. Fairchild was gesturing frantically to them. Reluctant to surrender her so quickly, Nicholas hesitated,
hoping she would afford him a few more moments of
her company.

"We are all waiting, dearest, for you to delight us
with your musical talents."

"Coming, Aunt."

Miss Adams afforded him one last imploring, almost
desperate glance. Had it been any other place than
Mrs. Fairchild's elegant drawing room, Nicholas would
have given in for the second time to the unaccountable
urge to catch her in his arms, then and there, and kiss
away the torment in her eyes. Instead, he offered her
his arm and escorted her into the drawing room. The
warmth of her small hand pressed to his sleeve only
added to his rising heartbeat and his baffling inability
to speak with any coherence.

He led her to a beautifully crafted and very new-
looking harp, where she took her place behind it and
began arranging the music on the nearby stand.

"Do join us, Sir Nicholas. I am quite certain you
will enjoy Julianna's performance. She is most accomplished. And I venture to add that the instrument is
a splendid one. Mr. Fairchild has recently acquired it
for her."

Seated next to Sir James, Nicholas focused his entire
attention on Julianna. She made a pretty picture with
the graceful, upward curve of the harp resting against
her right shoulder.

Having no real ear for music, Nicholas had no notion if she was accomplished or not, but the lovely
tone of the instrument was pleasant enough and some-

what eased the disturbing emotions beating within him. He was in uncharted waters here, with no compass or sextant to guide him.

Later, after the thank-yous and good-byes, Nicholas found himself at home staring moodily into the fire while downing the last of a cognac. The nightcap did nothing to ease the growing and certain sensation that he was becoming hopelessly lost to the effects of beseeching, dark eyes and the captivating, fragrant scent of lavender.

Chapter Seven

The spring warmed rapidly into early summer, making Aunt Emily frantic to get out of London and into the country. The city was so dreadful in the summer: the heat, the smells, and of course, the distinct lack of society. It was no surprise when Julianna's aunt and uncle eagerly accepted Lady Elwood's invitation to her country estate, Malthorpe Park.

The traveling arrangements sent Aunt Emily into near apoplexy, her already pink face flushed scarlet with anxiety. Only when the last hatbox had been packed, the last trunk strapped to the carriage, did she finally compose herself.

For Julianna the trip was enjoyable enough, though much different from her first journey, when the captain had escorted her from Portsmouth to London. This time the air was warm and pleasant and the flowers along the way were in full bloom.

As the carriage swept up the drive to Malthorpe Park, Julianna found herself greatly impressed by the beauty of Lady Elwood's home. It was not quite as large as she had expected, but once inside, it was apparent the marchioness had perfect taste in furniture and appointments.

Situated near a pond encircled with willows, Malthorpe also boasted a large park, where Julianna knew she would be able to take several long walks.

The estate delighted her, reminding her of home. Margaret, too, fell to its charms, and soon Julianna was aware that her maid had caught the eye of one of the young grooms who cared for Lady Elwood's horses.

Scarcely a week had gone by before Lady Elwood announced to her guests she would begin making plans for a ball in order to acquaint Miss Adams with the local society and the finer aspects of country living. Julianna had no interest in a ball or any other social occasion planned by her hostess. What she really wanted was more information concerning her father— and there was scarcely any of that since she had received no further communications from Sir Nicholas. That in itself was cause enough for her to be worried.

In spite of her concerns, Julianna found herself curious to see Sir Nicholas's residence, Wycombe Hall, as it was situated not far from Malthorpe. The latest news was that he still remained in London and not likely to visit the country for some time.

Lady Elwood's second item on her social agenda was for Julianna to call upon and meet the "better families" in the neighborhood. There was no way around it. Aunt Emily thought it an excellent idea. For three consecutive afternoons, they visited Lady Elwood's neighbors, took tea, gossiped, and discussed at length the dernier cri in fashion.

At first, Julianna did not mind the diversion. The countryside was beautiful, and for the most part, the people she visited were congenial and gracious. No one made the slightest disparaging comment about the fact that she was an American. But after three days, Julianna's patience began to fray. There had been no word from the captain. She wanted desperately to talk to him, to learn the slightest bit of news no matter how trivial.

During their return to Malthorpe, Julianna suddenly could not contain herself any longer. "Lady Elwood, might we pay a call on Sir Nicholas? I understand we are not far from his estate."

"Quite true, my dear, but Sir Nicholas is in London."

"I know, ma'am, but could we not pay a short visit? Perhaps he has sent some kind of communication, a message or something of that nature?"

The grand lady eyed her sharply. "And if there is no message for you, what then? Miss Adams, we certainly do not want to give the captain reason to believe that you are becoming *fast*." She leaned forward. "To visit a gentleman just for that purpose? Well!"

Aunt Emily began to ruffle. "Now, Charlotte, you are being quite unreasonable. Poor Julianna simply wishes to find out any information she can concerning her dear papa, and Sir Nicholas is the only one who can provide it. I say we turn the carriage at once and make straight for Wycombe Hall."

"Very well," Lady Elwood said stiffly, clearly not convinced or pleased with Aunt Emily's unexpected outburst.

The coachman was promptly redirected, and in only a few minutes they passed through the gates to Sir Nicholas's estate.

Unlike the stately redbrick Malthorpe, Wycombe Hall sat at the top of a hill, built entirely of weathered, ancient stone. Ivy twined its west wall; a peak-roofed conservatory graced the east side. The lawns and walkways spilled over with flowers, lush shrubbery, and clipped yew.

"A Tudor folly." Lady Elwood sniffed disdainfully. "Fortunately, Sir Nicholas has saved it from complete ruin. His father, the late baronet, had let the place fall to pieces."

"Sir Nicholas must be commended for his remarkable job in restoration," Aunt Emily observed.

"Indeed, but such a huge, wild place for a single gentleman, especially for a man who spends most of his time at sea."

"I am sure the captain finds great peace here—a sanctuary," Julianna murmured, staring in awe at the place. She loved it on sight—rough-hewn, strong, and a bit austere, much like the captain himself.

The moment they stopped at the front door, two liveried footmen appeared, one to hold the horses' heads and the other to help the three ladies alight from the carriage.

"If Sir Nicholas is not at home, we must make our inquiry brief and leave at once," Lady Elwood stated firmly.

Once inside, the butler bowed and said, "If you will wait here, my lady, I shall announce you at once to Sir Nicholas."

"Sir Nicholas is here?" Aunt Emily asked, surprised.

"Yes, madam. He has been here but two days."

In moments, they were ushered into a large, airy room lined with massive mahogany bookcases. A masculine room, heavy with the aroma of wood and leather, it was filled with the exotic and sometimes curious mementoes of someone who had seen much of the world—mysterious weapons, a skull of some rare beast, and various nautical instruments.

At the far end of the room, near the window, stood Sir Nicholas. His splendid captain's uniform had been exchanged for a plain coat of deep green, riding breeches, and polished boots to the knee. Afternoon sunlight streamed over his dark hair and shoulders. Absorbed in a book, he did not hear them at first, but the moment he sensed their presence, he spun about, snapping the book shut.

"Sir Nicholas . . . Lady Elwood, Mrs. Fairchild, and Miss Adams," the butler intoned solemnly.

The captain's serious expression at once transformed to astonishment. "L-L-Lady Elwood? Mrs. Fairchild, Miss Adams. This is an unexpected surprise."

Lady Elwood was all smiles and courtesy. "Sir Nicholas, how good to see you! We thought you in Town."

"No. That is to say, I *was* in Town, but I have been granted a few weeks to stay in the country." He gestured for them to sit down.

"Captain . . . Sir Nicholas," Aunt Emily began breathlessly. "Miss Julianna has been beside herself with worry and all of us are desperate for news of Mr. Adams. Are you able to tell us anything?"

"I am expecting a communication from the Admiralty at any moment. They are investigating the entire incident and I am hoping they will shed some light as to what happened to the *Hart* and her crew. Unfortunately, the gathering of this intelligence takes time."

Julianna could contain herself no longer. "But you *will* inform me the minute you hear anything of consequence."

Nicholas inclined his head slightly. "That very moment, Miss Adams." After a slight awkward pause, he continued. "Shall I ring for tea, ladies?"

"Thank you, no, Sir Nicholas—" Lady Elwood began, her words smothered by Aunt Emily's simultaneous exclaim, "That would be lovely!"

The two ladies eyed each other, as close to glaring as could be considered just short of unladylike, until Julianna intervened.

"It is very late, Captain, and Uncle Fairchild will become worried about us. Perhaps we could see some of the restorative work on Wycombe, or the gardens?"

"I would be delighted," he said, clearly pleased at having something to do other than make small talk over tea and cakes with three fluttering women.

Once outside, they walked along the wide pathway through the garden, to the outer edge of Wycombe's park. Aunt Emily had somehow managed to make sure they walked two by two—Julianna and Sir Nicholas leading while the older ladies brought up the rear.

"I am glad to see you again, Miss Adams," Nicholas said, just above a murmur so Lady Elwood and Aunt Emily would not be able to hear exactly the content of his conversation.

"I, too, am glad to see you. You are well?" Julianna asked.

"Quite well, thank you. And you?"

"Very well, indeed."

Julianna sensed his difficulty in making small talk and said the first thing that popped into her mind. "Will you attend Lady Elwood's ball?"

"I am uncertain, as I have not yet received an invitation."

"Then, I will make sure you receive one. I am told it will be quite the *thing*." She smiled. "I have never referred to a ball as a 'thing' before."

"Not in the American vocabulary, I assume? I would wager to say 'a smashing do' is not a part of the American language, either."

She glanced up at him and saw the merest gleam of humor in his eyes. It suddenly occurred to her that he had barely stammered at all since their arrival.

"I find myself having to learn how to speak English all over again. So many different phrases and words."

He looked at her archly, a smile just touching his lips. "So, in America, what would one call Lady Elwood's 'smashing do'?"

"A ball, Captain."

At that, Sir Nicholas laughed—a full-throated, pleased laugh. "You are quite the wit, Miss Adams. I shall remember that rejoinder." He looked down, shaking his head, and murmured, amused. "A ball. . . ."

"Well, I have attended several. At home, that is. My father enjoyed dancing very much. Sometimes we would have garden parties, or perhaps a hunt party."

"Do you ride, Miss Adams?" he asked, surprised.

"Yes, but not lately."

"Perhaps I can arrange an afternoon ride."

"Or perhaps a ball?"

Nicholas's tone took a sudden harder edge. "No, I think not. Wycombe is not ready for that kind of festivity yet. Wycombe needs . . ."

He clasped his hands behind his back, a captainlike, dismissive gesture Julianna did not miss. He looked up and beyond the far ridge of the trees. "More restoration is needed to Wycombe Hall before any kind of large party can be considered."

The quiet longing in his voice intimated that Nicho-

las was not referring to restoration, but something—
someone—else was needed? A wife? Julianna briefly
tried to imagine what it would be like to be his wife,
a captain's wife, traveling the great, wide world and
seeing exotic places and acquiring wondrous things,
like the objects in his house.

There was something else that troubled her. Finding
Papa. She certainly could not allow her muddled feelings for the captain to get in the way of finding her
father.

Or forgetting Michael.

Julianna unconsciously bit her lower lip. She could
think of nothing to say to Nicholas, however, she was
spared any further conversation when she heard her
aunt call out.

"Dearest, I think it is time for us to leave now. Mr.
Fairchild will be worried."

Lady Elwood added, "I am certain Sir Nicholas has
had quite enough of three bothersome females. We
shall take our leave, Sir Nicholas, and not infringe
upon your hospitality any longer."

Nicholas stopped and turned around to face the two
older women. "You have not bothered me in the least,
Lady Elwood. It has been a pleasure seeing you, Mrs.
Fairchild, and Miss Adams."

Julianna was certain she heard Nicholas place a distinct emphasis on the word "pleasure," but quickly
dismissed it as fancy. Cool, sensible reasoning told her
that Sir Nicholas was only being polite as he had been
on his ship and at the inn while they were in Portsmouth.

The curious pleasurable feeling, however, did not
go away. It remained long after they had arrived back
at Malthorpe. Was it her imagining that she still felt
the warm pressure of his fingers when he handed her
up into the carriage, or heard the hollow ache in his
voice when bidding her good-bye?

Lady Elwood's enthusiasm for a country ball remained undaunted by Julianna's lack of outward inter-

est. Preparations were made and invitations delivered, including one sent to Sir Nicholas. Lady Elwood reasoned that one never knew about sea captains.

"I have always suspected officers in the navy to be somewhat *changeable,* since life upon the sea demands of one the ability to make sudden decisions."

Julianna could only smile at such an assumption. In truth, she suspected the invitation had been sent to reciprocate for their surprise visit to Wycombe and a grand gesture to make certain Sir Nicholas had been included in the festivities since he was Lady Elwood's neighbor and a baronet.

Every notable family within ten miles had been invited, including the Earl and Countess Desmond, whose estate was next to Lady Elwood's. Even though Lord Desmond was quite ill, Lady Elwood made the point of inviting him, because, as she was fond of saying, "one never knew."

Aunt Emily enthusiastically supported her cousin's determination to hold the event. She fluttered over Julianna like a mother hen with only one chick. "Dearest, you will find those of Lady Elwood's acquaintance quite fine. I am certain you will have a delightful time, and please try not to worry about your papa. He is bound to write soon."

Julianna tried to take her aunt's advice to heart. Even though she had only known her aunt for a few weeks, she had come to love her dearly. Aunt Emily and Uncle Fairchild had accepted her completely and gone to great lengths to make sure she was happy and comfortable. Worries about Papa would have to wait.

Standing before the cheval glass, she examined her attire; she had taken great pains to dress with care. The new gown of white moire with the violet trim set off Julianna's eyes to perfection. Matching violet ribbons caught up her hair in a soft mass of dark curls.

Michael had loved her hair, and at one time been bold enough to demand the single curl he had twined about his little finger for a keepsake. He had made a great commotion about locating her embroidery scissors in order to cut the lock of hair himself, and he had kept it with him always . . . until the end.

Julianna's attention shifted as Margaret entered the room carrying her gloves. The girl had not left her side since Portsmouth and was now a constant in her life. Julianna could not do without her. Margaret's loyalty and simple friendship were more valuable than all of Lady Elwood's considerations or her aunt's generosity. For some reason, Margaret reminded Julianna of home and of her special, quiet friendship with Cassie. Whereas Margaret was as fair and pale-skinned as milk, Cassie had been dusky—dark as the night, solemn-eyed, gentle—blessed with endless patience and a dignity far beyond her years.

Julianna studied her reflection while watching Margaret kneel before her to straighten the hem of her new gown and tug at a wayward crease—just as Cassie had done, but Cassie was dead. The fire and Michael—

"There! You'll be turnin' every gentleman's head. Mark my words, miss."

"You make me sound like . . . how did Lady Elwood put it? Like a 'diamond of the first water.' I am uncertain what that means." She twisted and turned before the mirror, making sure everything was fastened properly. "But I think a pebble in pond water would be more appropriate."

Margaret grinned and got to her feet. "Yer sharp-witted, miss."

Julianna sighed. "Perhaps too sharp-witted. My tongue will be the death of me yet." She reached for her gloves. "I only hope I have the good sense not to say anything foolish."

Once downstairs, however, she found introductions easier than expected. As Lady Elwood promised, her guests filled the salons and ballroom, the cacophony of their conversation smothering any chance for Julianna to say something the least bit awkward.

Recalling names left her somewhat befuddled— there were so many of Lady Elwood's guests Julianna lost track, but greeting one particular gentleman made her smile. A very elegant Mr. Thorneloe stepped forward and bowed, his own delighted smile lighting up his handsome face.

"Miss Adams. What a pleasant surprise. I had heard rumor you were in the country with Lady Elwood, but one can never be certain of what the prattle-boxes will devise these days." He raised his quizzing glass, inspecting her from top to toe with mock severity. "I trust you are in excellent health? You have not been *shooting* anyone yet, I daresay."

Julianna afforded him a pleased smile. "I am very well, Mr. Thorneloe. And you?"

"Capital. And I trust you have good news to report concerning your father?"

"Nothing more than a rather cryptic letter to my uncle. I am at a loss as to where my father could be. However, I am pleased to report Captain Sidney— that is, Sir Nicholas—has been making inquiries for me."

Mr. Thorneloe's eyes narrowed slightly, his beautifully shaped mouth pressed in a firm, disapproving line. "Hmmm. And has he been at all successful?" he asked, his tone suddenly disdainful, cold.

The abrupt change in his voice made Julianna look up at him. Gone was the former warmth in his eyes, now replaced with a disturbing remoteness. She dismissed it as fancy but could not escape the faint prickles of alarm dancing under her skin.

"Well, he thinks there might have been another ship that rescued my father and the others still on board the *Hart*."

"Indeed." One slim, black brow lifted. "Might I caution you, Miss Adams, that the sea is a harsh taskmaster. I would not want anyone to give you false hopes. However, I yield to the captain's better judgment, he being more knowledgeable on the subject."

Julianna felt the blood leave her face. What could

Mr. Thorneloe possibly mean? Was he suggesting Sir Nicholas had deliberately deceived her—told her lies to salve his conscience as well as to ease her fears? She did not know what to think, but her distress must have been obvious to Mr. Thorneloe. He at once reverted to his former self—all cynicism dissolved like clouds on a summer day.

"But I have upset you. I beg your pardon, Miss Adams. Please forgive me. Perhaps I can make amends for my bad manners by asking you to dance this first set with me?"

"Why . . . yes, of course."

Julianna allowed him to lead her across the floor. The first dance was a cotillion, which she managed easily and kept the conversation to a minimum. As when she had first met him, Mr. Thorneloe was attentive and courteous. The fact that he was an accomplished dancer only added to her growing esteem for him. She made a pointed effort to dismiss their earlier conversation, pushing it firmly to the back of her mind.

When the dance concluded, he bent close to her and managed a conspiring whisper. "I fully intend on claiming a second dance, Miss Adams. I will not yield on this matter."

"I shall be happy to oblige, sir." She took his offered hand as they moved back to where her aunt and uncle waited. Aunt Emily's face was flushed with excitement. She gestured frantically for Julianna to come closer.

"My dear, you will never guess who just arrived!"

"No, I am sure—"

"Of course you cannot possibly guess. Look over there."

Julianna looked where Aunt Emily was indicating and quite suddenly felt her own face grow warm. Just inside the entrance to the ballroom, resplendent in his blue and gold uniform, ramrod straight and decidedly ill at ease, stood Captain Sir Nicholas Sidney.

She sensed Mr. Thorneloe's mood again turning aloof and remote. "So the famous Captain Sidney— Sir Nicholas—has arrived," he said coolly.

"He has. I am surprised to see him. Both Lady Elwood and I thought he might have returned to London. I do hope the Admiralty has sent him news of my father."

Before Julianna could say another word, the captain spotted her and began moving in her direction. Taller than most of the men in the room, Sir Nicholas shouldered his way through the crowd, forcing those in his path to part like a respectful crew on a ship.

"Mrs. Fairchild, Mr. Fairchild." He bowed stiffly to them. "Miss Adams, I am pleased to see you again."

"Sir Nicholas, how delightful!" Aunt Emily was almost gushing and Julianna felt herself inwardly cringing. She did not want her aunt to make such a scene in front of the captain or Mr. Thorneloe.

She made her curtsy to him. "It *is* a surprise to see you, Captain, since we all thought you might return to Town."

"I was planning to. However, I find I am obliged to stay for a while."

Recalling her manners, Julianna completed the introductions.

"Sir Nicholas, are you acquainted with Mr. Thorneloe?"

The captain's voice was cold, remote. "We are acquainted."

The two men eyed each other, offering only polite, formal bows. Their chill demeanor surprised Julianna, but was entirely overlooked by her aunt.

"And you have found Julianna's papa, Sir Nicholas." Aunt Emily beamed at him. "I knew it. I knew you would come the instant you had good news!"

The captain's face remained stern. He held up a cautioning hand. "Regretfully, ma'am, I have not yet found Mr. Adams, but I have received some news."

"You have heard something?" Julianna interjected eagerly.

"I have *some* news." The captain paused.

An awkward silence rose among the party, until Mr. Thorneloe spoke. "Pray, forgive me, but I must speak with Lady Desmond. She and Lord Desmond are my hosts while I am in the country. Perhaps you will excuse me?" He bowed and moved away without another word.

"How odd," Aunt Emily commented while watching him disappear into the crush of guests. "Did you notice his expression? I daresay, he looked . . . well, quite *overset* by something or other. Did you notice it, Mr. Fairchild?"

"No, in point of fact, I did not."

But Julianna did. The change in Mr. Thorneloe had been nothing short of startling—his manner bordering on rude the moment Sir Nicholas arrived. The captain, however, appeared unchanged, but then, he had always presented himself as a serious, austere man.

She ventured to look at him. His keen gaze still followed Mr. Thorneloe's retreating form.

"Sir Nicholas?"

His attention turned back to her at once. "I beg your pardon, Miss Adams. I fear I am the victim of an old habit of mine—hard to b-break. I . . . I, that is, would you do me the honor of this next set?"

Julianna accepted his arm and proceeded onto the dance floor. While not as refined in his movements as Mr. Thorneloe, the captain executed the allemande with perfect ease.

"Miss Adams, I could not speak openly in front of the others, but I must tell you, I have more information c-c-concerning your father."

She almost stopped in the middle of her step. "You have? I beg you, sir, please tell me."

"It will take longer to explain than these few moments allowed to us."

"I see. What do you suggest? I am desperate to hear your news."

"It is imperative I s-s-speak with you."

The captain had not said the word "alone," but Julianna knew what he meant. She turned under his arm, then moved back to prepare for the next step.

"But how? I am scarcely out of my aunt's sight. She is constantly worried about my health."

The design of the dance forced them apart for a moment. When she faced him again, Sir Nicholas spoke rapidly. "You told me not long ago that you do ride?"

"Yes, but it has been a while."

"Good. Perhaps a short outing could be arranged." He smiled—a sudden, all-too-wicked smile for an officer in His Majesty's navy. "For your health, of course."

She returned the smile. "Of course."

The dance finally ended and Sir Nicholas took her hand, leading her into the adjacent room, where several tables had been laid out with a large selection of choice dishes to tempt the guests and an enormous silver bowl filled with punch. He offered her a glass, then took one for himself.

With so many people nearby, Julianna felt reasonably safe in continuing their conversation. To the casual eye they appeared to be two friends engaged in a harmless tête-à-tête

"So can you tell me nothing else?" she asked lightly, hoping she sounded more like a young lady attempting a mild flirtation than a half-sick daughter consumed with worry.

Sir Nicholas tilted his head back to finish the punch, exposing the firm column of his throat above the high collar of his uniform and black stock. He had nicked himself shaving and for some reason it caused Julianna a twinge of distress.

"Now is certainly not the time, Miss Adams, but I have good reason to believe your father is not only alive and well, but actively employed—in a manner of speaking."

Julianna felt the blood drain from her face. Sir Nicholas's alarming tone, concealed by a forced smile, chilled her heart. But she had to find out what he had discovered.

"Please, Captain, what do you know?" she whispered through smiling lips.

"I believe, Miss Adams, that your father has been impressed into service, along with the rest of the *Hart*'s crew, aboard a British man-of-war."

Chapter Eight

It took all her self-control to remain unmoved by the shocking news Sir Nicholas had given her. Impressment! How many times had her father gone into a rage over this perfidious practice by the British navy— their deliberate capture of American vessels and impressing the crew to man their own ships. It had been a hotly debated issue at many dinner parties and made her father so furious he would often toss down his napkin and leave the room.

Edward Adams, condemned to the hardships aboard a British warship, never to see his home or family again? She wanted to weep or scream. For one irrational moment, she almost hated the captain. He was one of them, part of a powerful navy that took what it wanted with no apology or sympathy for its victims.

But seeing the stricken expression on his face made her relent. He had, after all, discovered what had happened to her father. It was not his fault her father had been captured.

"Miss Adams, I d-d-deeply regret alarming you in this manner," he said softly.

Julianna did not know what to say. The strength of the captain's remorse matched the depths of her own despair. She could not be angry with him even if she wanted to be; he had done too much for her already.

"Well, what must be done now?"

"Can you arrange for us to have a private discussion? Perhaps a walk or r-r-ride through Malthorpe's park?"

She nodded. "I am sure Aunt Emily will understand."

"May I call—?"

"Miss Adams?" The intruding voice caused both of them to turn toward its source. "I have come to claim my second dance. With the captain's permission, of course." Mr. Thorneloe inclined his head toward Sir Nicholas, the gesture just short of being uncivil, his tone edged with sarcasm.

Flustered, Julianna glanced first at Sir Nicholas then at Mr. Thorneloe. "I . . . that is to say . . ."

Sir Nicholas spared her any further embarrassment. "I would not wish to spoil your evening, Miss Adams." He bowed politely to her, but his address was clearly aimed at Mr. Thorneloe. Their constrained hostility had become almost palpable. The captain's eyes had darkened with ill-concealed contempt. Mr. Thorneloe's gray gaze was as cold and hard as winter ice.

Julianna sensed the jealousy between these two men was so strong, it bordered on murderous—the kind of unfathomable masculine hatred that women spoke about only in secret whispers, behind closed doors. Vengeance and honor. Blood and death.

She curtseyed to Sir Nicholas. "Please excuse me." Julianna could not bring herself to look at him directly, but instead turned and took Mr. Thorneloe's offered hand. Once on the dance floor she found she had nothing to say to her partner. He was as considerate and refined as ever, but a new, uncomfortable barrier had sprung up between them.

When the dance was over, she looked frantically about the ballroom trying to locate Sir Nicholas, but as she suspected, he was gone.

                        *   *   *

"Do you not think Mr. Thorneloe's behavior was rather curious last night?" Aunt Emily buttered a morsel of breakfast scone and popped it into her mouth.

"Hmmmm?"

"Well, it is obvious he is quite taken with you, dearest. Perhaps he holds a *tendre* for you?" Aunt Emily suggested.

Julianna snapped out of her reverie. "No. That is to say, I do not believe so. He was merely being polite."

Lady Elwood made a discreet disparaging sound. "Oh, fiddlesticks! My dear Julianna, the man is *besotted* with you. You could do far worse. He *is*, of course, a bit wild, but then he is young. I knew his mother. Excellent connections."

"But, Charlotte, Julianna is not of a mind or disposition to consider a gentleman's attentions. Her papa—"

"Nonsense." Lady Elwood sniffed disdainfully. "A young woman of Julianna's age must seize every opportunity if she is to secure a proper alliance. Mr. Thorneloe would be an excellent match. She could hardly do better."

Julianna bristled at Lady Elwood's callous assessment. She felt like a commodity, a shipload of tobacco or a mare placed up for auction. Monetary worthiness was Lady Elwood's entire basis for a marriage. She knew Aunt Emily had advised Lady Elwood, in the strictest confidence, of her inheritance. Even though her brother, Benjamin, would receive the bulk of the estate, she would never be in want. None of that mattered if her father were discovered dead in the hold of some filthy ship, beaten or starved to death by a cruel captain.

Would Captain Sidney ever do such a thing? *Had* he ever committed such a heinous crime? How many American sailors had lived out their lives in misery serving aboard his ship?

"Mr. Thorneloe is very kind but I am afraid I could not accept him, or any gentleman's offer, Lady Elwood, not until Papa is found."

"Of course. He shall be found, I am sure of it. I was merely suggesting that Mr. Thorneloe would be quite suitable." Lady Elwood took a sip of her coffee. "A handsome young man, too."

"Indeed he is," Aunt Emily agreed. "Though not as *imposing* as Sir Nicholas, but he commands a navy frigate, whereas Mr. Thorneloe is a gentleman."

"And Sir Nicholas is not?" Julianna asked, a little too sharply.

"Of course," Lady Elwood interjected. "However, he is not as refined in his manner as Mr. Thorneloe. Still, Sir Nicholas has made quite a fortune at sea." She leaned forward so the servants would not overhear. "Thirty thousand pounds! Can you imagine? He has certainly made good use of it. Wycombe Hall was practically a ruin until he had it restored."

Thirty thousand pounds. The spoils of war to rebuild his house. Well, at least he had not gambled it away or spent it on drink. Confused and irritable, Julianna folded her napkin and placed it next to her plate.

"I fear I am somewhat out of sorts. Will you excuse me? I believe I shall take a walk."

She rose and slipped out of the dining room, heading straight for the front entrance. She would take the air and clear her mind of disturbing thoughts. It was going to be a fine day and she might as well enjoy it.

The park surrounding Malthorpe's main building was at least ten acres of woods and fields. Once out of sight of the house, she tugged off her bonnet and yanked the pins from her hair. This was the way she liked to walk at home in Maryland. She could be Julie Adams again, sunburned and freckled, climbing trees in the orchard or splashing barefoot in the stream down behind the great barn. Her mother had been shocked with dismay; her father only laughed. When she was older, her mother gave her lessons in decorum; her father taught her to ride and shoot like a boy. But that all ended when Mama died.

Sobered by her death, Papa at once decided Julie must become Julianna. Shooting muskets and riding horses were replaced with dancing and deportment. Skipping stones in the stream gave way to French lessons and music.

Julianna kicked at some loose leaves. Someday she would go home and be that carefree girl again.

Thudding hoofbeats made her stop her daydreaming. Ahead she could make out the form of a horse and rider coming her way. As they drew closer, Julianna realized it was Mr. Thorneloe mounted on a handsome chestnut. Seeing her, he reined in and touched his hat brim.

"Good morning, Miss Adams. What a surprise. I had no notion you would be walking out this far. Lady Elwood's park just touches Lord Desmond's estate."

Blushing furiously, Julianna tried to make some semblance of order out of her disarrayed hair. "Forgive me, Mr. Thorneloe, but I thought I would not be seen."

He smiled and dismounted. "It is charming. Your secret is safe. I shall not tell a soul."

Julianna pulled on her bonnet and hastily did up the ribbons. "Do you often ride this way?"

"Sometimes, when I stay with Lord and Lady Desmond. However, I do not come here as often as I would like. I have little family and I enjoy their company very much."

"Lord and Lady Desmond are your relations?"

"Indeed. I am their nephew." He squinted up at the sun just edging the top of the trees. "It is past the noon hour. Perhaps you will allow me to walk you back."

"Very well." They turned and headed back to Malthorpe, the horse clopping along amiably at Mr. Thorneloe's side.

"You must forgive me for my behavior at the ball. I fear I embarrassed you in front of Sir Nicholas. The truth is, I found myself having a difficult time trying to conceal my jealousy."

Julianna looked up at him, startled. "Jealousy?" So perhaps she had guessed right.

"Indeed. I am thoroughly jealous." He grinned at her. Again, impossibly appealing. "And he has the advantage: he knew you first. Dashed unlucky for me. Still, I have my work before me if I am to win your affections." Mr. Thorneloe's eyes danced with high humor. He was teasing her.

"Mr. Thorneloe!"

"I am determined. You cannot dissuade me."

"How can I take you seriously? You are outrageous, sir."

He stopped and faced her, his expression sober. "But, you see, I am not. I find myself quite captivated by charming American girls who can shoot muskets and dare to run wild without their bonnets."

Astonished, Julianna could not speak.

Mr. Thorneloe only smiled. "Do I surprise you by my frankness? In truth, Miss Adams, I am rarely so unconstrained with my declarations, but I find I am unable to stop myself where you are concerned."

"I do not know what to say. . . ."

"Then, say nothing. I shall not pursue this conversation, seeing that it makes you ill at ease."

They proceeded on, down the wide pathway leading back to Malthorpe without conversing for some time. Julianna struggled to find something to say, but Mr. Thorneloe appeared unconcerned by the interval of silence. She had never engaged in such an unsettling conversation in all her life, not even with Michael.

She allowed herself a furtive glance at the man walking beside her. Certainly handsome and well-spoken—a model gentleman with perfect manners. He seemed to know everyone of importance and was at ease with them, and he clearly admired her. Lady Elwood was right, Mr. Thorneloe would be an excellent match. She really could not do better.

Except. Except. Julianna tried to shrug off the niggling idea that something was not quite right. She could not place it. Maybe it had to do with the way the captain had looked at Mr. Thorneloe at the ball.

It was probably the same manner in which he assessed the character of his officers or of his crew. What did Sir Nicholas find so loathsome in Mr. Thorneloe?

The horse suddenly lifted its head, ears pricked forward. Both Julianna and Mr. Thorneloe heard the sound of approaching horses and a vehicle. A smart-looking phaeton drawn by a pair of sleek grays rounded the bend in the road. Upon seeing them, the driver deftly halted the team.

"Sir Nicholas?" It still surprised Julianna to see the captain wearing civilian attire—a claret-colored coat, buff breeches, and riding boots.

Her hands flew to her hair, tucking the straggling ends that had fallen from beneath her bonnet. What would he think of her—so unkempt and common-looking?

"Miss Adams, Mr. Thorneloe." He touched the brim of his hat. "I am glad I caught up with you. Your aunt asked that I drive out to see if you had become lost. She was somewhat worried."

"As you can see, she has been found, quite safe." Mr. Thorneloe took her elbow and guided her to the phaeton. "It would seem she now has a much speedier conveyance to carry her home. I would be much obliged, Sir Nicholas . . . ?"

Mr. Thorneloe handed her up to the captain, who assisted her settling in the seat next to him.

"Thank you, Mr. Thorneloe, for seeing me this far."

"My pleasure, Miss Adams. I will enjoy recalling our walk and conversation."

He swung onto the chestnut. With a light touch of the crop to his hat brim, he spun the horse about and trotted off into the woods.

"Good-bye," she called, but she could see it went unheard.

Sir Nicholas chirruped to the team, turning them back toward Malthorpe. Julianna clutched the edge of the seat as the horses picked up a brisk canter, the rush of air pushing against her cheeks making them sting a little. It was evident the captain wanted to put as much distance between her and Mr. Thorneloe as possible, but after a few moments he drew the team into a sedate walk.

"Forgive me, Miss Adams, but I could not resist letting them have a bit of a run."

"It was very exciting. My brother Benjamin has often taken me for rides in his gig, which he drives like a madman I might add. Be assured, I feel much safer with you at the reins, than with him."

Sir Nicholas chuckled, the second time she had heard him laugh, but it was the first time she had heard him speak so easily without the soft stammer.

"I am not so sure of that, Miss Adams. It has been a long time since I have driven these fellows. My coachman likes to take them out. Sometimes I have them stabled at Lord and Lady Desmond's. Lord Desmond enjoys a bit of driving now and again."

"You know Lord and Lady Desmond?"

"They are old friends—I have known them since I was a child."

"What an amazing coincidence. Then you must know Mr. Thorneloe well. He is Lord and Lady Desmond's nephew."

Sir Nicholas snapped a rein over the right gray's back. "Yes, we are acquainted," he said shortly.

"I see." It was on her lips to ask him what it was about Mr. Thorneloe that caused such coldness, such outward resentment. She could not flatter herself into thinking it was something so obvious as jealousy.

For several minutes, they said nothing, but their silence made Julianna increasingly uncomfortable. She became acutely aware of Sir Nicholas's right thigh pressed firmly against her own limb—an unavoidable contact since the seat of the phaeton was just wide enough for the two of them.

When Sir Nicholas finally spoke, his tone was bitter, cold with anger. "Mr. Thorneloe and I met over a year ago, under somewhat unpleasant circumstances. We are *not* at all friends."

Bright sunshine filtered through the trees, deepening the dappling on the horses' coats; their hoofbeats thudded heavily on the damp earth. The creak and sway of the phaeton only emphasized another profound silence between them.

Julianna did not want to press the issue by asking why the captain and Mr. Thorneloe seemed to be such enemies, but she could not remain silent for long. "I am sorry you think so ill of him. Surely, he cannot be as despicable as you seem to think."

"Perhaps not."

"He has been very kind to me, Captain. When others treated me rather abominably, Mr. Thorneloe was most considerate. I cannot think so ill of him in spite of what you say."

Sir Nicholas again said nothing more about Mr. Thorneloe, but she could tell he was only being polite. Perhaps there was some merit to his opinion, but she was determined to set aside such unpleasant thoughts and enjoy the afternoon.

Their journey continued until they came closer to a small lake not far from Malthorpe. Sir Nicholas turned the team and drove to a grassy open space then halted them just under a great willow near the water's edge. Julianna shaded her eyes from the bright afternoon sun, taking in the breathtaking view.

Swans glided across the lake, dipping and bobbing their long necks into the still water. In the distance, she could make out the great house, perched on a knoll overlooking the lake.

"Beautiful," she exclaimed.

"It is. I hope to renovate Wycombe Hall to some semblance of beauty as to what Lady Elwood has done with Malthorpe."

"I am certain you will, Captain. Wycombe is a magnificent structure."

"Thank you, but I still have much to do. My father allowed it to fall into such a state of disrepair it has taken several years to complete the basic restoration."

Sir Nicholas climbed down from the phaeton. "Would

you like to make a closer inspection of the lake?" He held up his hands, offering to help her down.

Julianna allowed him to swing her down until she stood directly in front of him, almost too close for propriety. She kept her gaze firmly fixed on the folds of his cravat, not daring to look up. Certainly Mr. Thorneloe had never caused such an alarming reaction within her as did the captain—feelings that left her wanting something she could not describe. His hands were suddenly too firm upon her waist, too warm, encouraging her to abandon all decorum.

"Perhaps if you let me go, Sir Nicholas, I might be able to see the lake."

"Would it not be acceptable, Miss Adams, for me to call you by your given name? At this d-distance, the gossips will hardly be able to hear us." A light, wry smile touched his lips.

Julianna's own smile returned the little jest. "Very well, but far from the gossips, of course."

"Of course, Miss Julianna."

A light thrill raced through her at the sound of her name on his lips. She suddenly longed to hear her name repeated again and again.

Nicholas took her elbow and guided her to the shoreline.

"Needs a boat, I daresay," he said, gazing across the water.

"I perceive you would have every expanse of water filled with boats and ships at your command—even in a duck pond."

He looked at her apologetically. "I meant a small boat, so that one could go fishing. Have you ever gone fishing, Miss Julianna?"

"Oh, yes, when I was a girl. My brother and I used to fish nearly every day in the creek down behind the barn. I was quite a naughty child."

"I do not believe you," he said firmly.

"But it is true. Until I was twelve, I ran wild like my brother. My father taught me to ride and shoot."

She glanced at him mischievously. "I can bring down a pheasant at fifty yards."

Nicholas's black-winged brows shot up. "Indeed? You are full of surprises."

"Well, my father had some rather curious notions about how girls should be raised. He and Mama were at odds many times, but when she died, Papa became . . . changed. I was not allowed to fish or shoot again. I was to become a refined young lady so that I might marry."

"But you d-d-did not. Marry, that is."

"No." An overwhelming sadness filled Julianna's heart, but she forced herself to continue. "Michael and I were to be married last year, in the summer. But—"

She sensed Nicholas bending toward her.

"Please, do not continue, if this is too painful a memory."

Julianna shook her head. "For some curious reason, I am glad to speak of it." She turned away to collect her thoughts, amazed with herself for speaking so intimately to him. "Michael had just seen to the completion of what would have been our new home. We were so happy. Last spring, Michael and I toured the house, looking at every room, making plans. He was very excited. He wanted everything to be just perfect. It was late in the day and my maid, Cassie, was following us through the upper rooms, holding up a candlestick to light the way. Then, suddenly, she somehow dropped the candlestick. The fire caught the curtains, then her dress. She screamed and screamed. We tried to put it out. Michael had to use his coat to smother the flames. I remember running to the stairway—the whole upstairs was burning. Michael was right behind me, carrying Cassie. I heard him shouting for me to hurry, to get down the stairs and outside, but once I was outside, I could not find him. He was still in the house. So I went back in. And then, a beam fell, pinning me to the floor. I tried to push it off, but it was too heavy. I tried and tried." Julianna's voice began to crack at the memory, but she was determined to finish.

"Is that how you received that terrible burn on your back?"

Startled, she looked up at him. "Yes. How did you know?"

"When my surgeon, Mr. Philips, brought you down to my cabin, I saw . . . that is to say, your gown was badly torn. One could not help noticing."

She nodded. "Yes, the beam that held me to the floor was still burning. If it had not been for Big Moses, I would have died. He brought me back outside. I remember lying on the grass, choking, watching the house burn and the servants trying to put out the fire, but it was too late."

"Did they find Michael and the girl?"

Julianna gulped. Her tears could not be contained. They slid down her cheeks, scalding her with the terrible memory. "Yes, they found him, but he did not die from the fire. He was untouched—not even one hair was singed. No, he broke his neck from falling down the stairs trying to reach me."

Grief welled up within her. So much loss: first her mother, then Cassie and Michael, a beautiful home, then the shipwreck, and now her father's disappearance. Julianna reached for the trunk of the great willow to steady herself, head down, sobbing heartbroken, painful tears. It did not matter if the captain was watching—she did not care.

Quite suddenly, Nicholas's hands were on her shoulders, turning her, pulling her into his arms against him, against the same solid strength she had felt while in his cabin aboard the *Gallant*.

He said nothing but allowed her to cry out her grief. Only for a moment did she speculate upon the scandalous picture they made: embracing in full view of Malthorpe. What if Lady Elwood or Aunt Emily just happened to be looking out the window onto such a shocking scene? However, she sensed the captain was not the least bit concerned what anyone might think.

When the last tear was spent, Julianna drew back

from him, at once embarrassed by her emotional display as well as her untidy appearance.

"Forgive me. I am sorry." She pressed the back of her hand to her cheek. "It seems I have nothing better to do than cry in your presence, and I have undoubtedly spoiled your coat."

Nicholas bent toward her and gently cupped his hands to her cheeks, tilting her face up to him. "There is nothing to forgive, Miss Julianna."

Before she could step away, Nicholas lowered his mouth to hers and placed a soft, light kiss on her lips. Without realizing just what she was doing, Julianna ran her hands up his arms, to his shoulders and around his neck. Nicholas's kiss deepened; his arms encircled her waist, drawing her closer to him. Even within that fleeting moment, Julianna recognized Nicholas's kiss was not just a comforting gesture, but a clear indication that he wanted much more. His lips were warm and firm. A slow, sweet fire shot through her, making her weak and trembling.

He drew back, releasing her. His breath came in short rasps. "I beg your pardon, Miss Adams. I should not have—" A dark flush suffused his tanned face. Now it was he asking for forgiveness.

She stepped away from him and lowered her arms, reluctantly.

"Oh, no. I believe it was something we both wanted."

Nicholas said nothing, but she sensed that his silence only confirmed her words.

"Since we both have each other's apology . . ." he said while reaching into the breast pocket of his coat to remove a handkerchief, which he handed to her.

The sweet moment had vanished.

"You have had some nasty shocks and I daresay there are not many ladies who could boast your c-courage under the same circumstances."

Julianna could think of no reply, but silently dabbed at her eyes and nose. She did not feel courageous, only disheartened and now, bewildered. What must he think of her, she thought miserably. An American girl, given to reckless tears, then throwing herself into his arms? However, it was he who kissed her, she reminded herself. And, yet he did not seem put off by her tears, or embarrassed. He stood, like a rock on the shore, unmoved by the waves or the winds.

"Perhaps I should return you to the house?" His voice was soft, but she noted he seemed completely recovered from their brief moment of passion.

"I thought you wanted to see me, to tell me what you discovered about my father?"

"Ah, yes . . . ah-hmm." At once all seriousness, Nicholas turned away from her toward the lake as if to shake off the last of their former intimacy and collect his thoughts. "After making several inquiries, I recently received a letter from an Admiral Dell, who advised me that two ships in his squadron had been returning to Portsmouth for provisioning, when they ran afoul in that storm. They made harbor, but whether or not your father is on board one of them is hard to say. I know both captains and their ships, at least by reputation. One is the *Cassandra.* She is commanded by Captain Needham. I know him. Excellent man, tough but fair. I do not think your father would have been treated badly if he has not created too much of a disruption."

"What does that mean?" Julianna felt herself go a little weak as she was almost afraid to hear his response.

Nicholas took a deep breath. "If he caused trouble, that is, openly defied orders, Captain Needham would be obliged to act accordingly. Discipline must be kept at all costs and sometimes it is quite harsh."

Julianna did not really want to know what he meant by that, but she could guess. Her father was a proud man. She seriously doubted he took impressment without a fight.

The captain went on. "If he is aboard the *Dagger,* then he may not have been treated so well. Captain Pittman is not so . . . fair."

"Then, how can we find out which ship he is on?"

"In a few days I return to L-L-London. I am to meet with a few officers I know. They will most likely have the information we seek. When I discover which ship he is on, then I will leave immediately for Portsmouth. I will send word, but you must remain ready to come to London at a moment's notice."

"Of course. I shall be ready."

"If your father is on the *Cassandra,* then I know Captain Needham will readily discharge him into my custody. But if he is on the *Dagger,* Captain Pittman will demand official orders to release him. That is where you come in."

"What am I to do?"

"If Pittman has your father, then we must visit the American consul in London and get the proper protection paper to discharge him into my custody. Since you are the closest living relation to Mr. Adams, you must vouch for him."

Julianna's former grief vanished with the captain's brisk instructions. She tugged off her bonnet and made quick reparations to her hair. It was not the most tidy effort, but it would have to do.

Her chin went up. "Very well. I will be ready."

"You must not hesitate. Your aunt m-m-must understand the urgency of the situation. If either ship sets sail within a fortnight, I will be hard-pressed to catch up to either of them."

"What if this Captain Pittman decides not to surrender my father?"

"Be assured, Julianna, I shall speak with Admiral Dell."

She almost could not bring herself to ask the next question. "And if he is not aboard either ship?"

"Then we must assume he was rescued." He took a step closer to her, his eyes filled with foreboding. "Miss Adams, he may be on a French ship. If that is so, then our task becomes infinitely more difficult."

Chapter Nine

Nicholas did not like leaving Julianna with such unpleasant news, particularly the possibility that her father might be in the hands of the French, but there was no other way to tell her. It was simply another difficulty they might have to face. Getting Edward Adams off a French ship would be impossible. The consequences were staggering and the worst of it was, Julianna's father might truly be dead. Life for a sailor aboard a ship of the line was just as harsh, if not worse in the French navy as it was in the British.

Their drive back to Malthorpe was heavy with silence. In truth, he could not voice his own concerns or bring himself to face the idea that Edward Adams might be under Pittman's command. Those who had survived service aboard the *Dagger* did so either by luck or by the protection of Providence. Of the twenty-three crewmen now on board the *Gallant* who had previously served on the *Dagger,* only one did not bear the marks of the lash. Captain Pittman was known throughout the fleet for his brutal treatment of his crew; he was neither liked nor respected.

Once at Malthorpe's door, Nicholas made certain Julianna was safely inside with her aunt and Lady Elwood. He declined the offer to take tea knowing if he stayed, he would have to answer awkward questions as to why he and Julianna had been gone so long and why she looked somewhat disheveled.

Nicholas climbed into the phaeton and, without looking back, called to the team and drove away.

The letter came two days later while Nicholas was overseeing the construction of a new portion of stable roofing. There was a serious structural problem that demanded his immediate attention. He stood, hands to his hips, as he watched the final placement of the roof-framing erected into position. From behind him, he heard a polite cough.

"Captain Sidney, sir."

Nicholas spun about and stared at the man before him, astonished. "Lieutenant Dain! Good God, what brings you here?"

The young man shifted uncomfortably. He looked decidedly ill at ease—a naval lieutenant standing amidst a stable yard, taking scrupulous care to avoid stepping into any suspicious-looking dark mounds.

"I have just come straight from London. I have a letter from Lord Yorke. I was ordered to hand it to you personally, Captain."

Dain held out a thick, heavily sealed letter. Nicholas took it and examined the seals and the handwriting. It was from the Admiralty. He tapped it against his thumb. This was what he had been waiting for: the news concerning the fate of the *Hart* and quite possibly the information about Adams.

He cracked the seals and scanned the letter. The contents revealed much more than he had anticipated.

. . . *regretfully, wreckage of the* Hart *has not been recovered, however, it has been confirmed that two other British naval ships, the* Cassandra *and the* Dagger, *were in the same approximate area during the storm. At present, both ships are harbored in Portsmouth for repairs and provisioning. We are endeavoring to discover more details concerning the* Hart.

The most decisive intelligence ascertained to date is that Miss Julianna Adams's father, Edward Adams, is not E.A. We have been informed through agents that the French contact is Edmund Rameau, the Marquis d'Avergne, using the initials E.A. as a code for specific correspondence. We have strong reason to believe Rameau may be making contact soon with his English counterpart. You are to report to the Admiralty at once for further orders.

Relieved, Nicholas refolded the letter and tucked it inside his coat. At least Julianna's father had no part in this ugly business of espionage. But where the devil was he? Could Admiral Dell's information be of any help? The *Cassandra* and *Dagger* were in Portsmouth. What if Adams were aboard either one of those ships and held, like Nicholas's own crew, from going ashore to avoid the opportunity for desertion? Or escape?

"Lieutenant Dain, have you a conveyance?"

"Aye, sir, but 'tis only a pony cart from the inn. One of the village lads there brought me—"

"Send it back and have your things brought to the house. I would impose upon you to ask my man, Peters, to pack for me."

"Aye, sir, I will."

Nicholas turned and hurried toward the main part of the stable. "Hollis! My horse! Hurry!"

Lieutenant Dain followed close at his heels. "Captain, what should I do?"

"Wait here until I return. I have an important message to deliver."

The head groom led out a tall, fidgeting bay that eyed Lieutenant Dain's fluttering cloak suspiciously. Nicholas took the reins and swung onto the saddle. He looked down at the bewildered-looking officer.

"I should be back before dark. We leave the moment I return."

Nicholas put heels to the ardent horse and headed straight for Malthorpe.

Aunt Emily at last permitted Julianna the opportunity to ride—but slowly, on a safe, reliable mount. Lady Elwood boasted a small but excellent stable of riding horses, and with Mr. Thorneloe's expert advice, a suitable animal was saddled and led out for Julianna's inspection.

Although the day was partially overcast, nothing could have diminished her excitement. To be riding again! She was even pleased with her mount, a large dappled-gray pony named Sterling. Julianna patted his velvet muzzle and offered him a slice of sweet apple, which Sterling accepted with gentle dignity.

"He is a darling. I love him."

"I knew we could find the appropriate mount for you. Lady Elwood claims she has ridden him herself and finds his manners faultless."

Mr. Thorneloe led the gelding alongside the mounting block and waited while Julianna climbed the short two steps, then settled herself onto Sterling's back.

"I am sure he is a perfect gentleman."

"Make sure he does not go too fast, Julianna," Aunt Emily called out.

She glanced back at her aunt perched next to Uncle Fairchild on the seat of a high-wheeled gig. The two had decided to accompany her as chaperones on the morning outing and it pleased Julianna to see her uncle handling the reins.

Mr. Thorneloe mounted his splendid chestnut and proceeded to lead the little party down the drive and out onto the road. Julianna kept Sterling moving at a smart trot to keep up with Mr. Thorneloe's taller horse.

"Sterling seems to be living up to his name," he observed, reining in the chestnut to a slower pace.

"I could not have asked for a better mount, Mr. Thorneloe. Sterling is perfect."

"I daresay, you and he will have many outings together."

They spent the next several minutes in amiable conversation, which only deepened Julianna's sense of puzzlement concerning the captain's feelings toward Mr. Thorneloe. Why did Nicholas detest him so? She could not believe his resentment was merely due to jealousy. Besides, she reasoned, jealousy did not suit Nicholas's character.

She cast a surreptitious glance at Mr. Thorneloe. He sat well, handling the keen chestnut with ease—certainly better than Michael. But then, dear Michael disliked riding. He claimed that driving was the true skill, not bouncing about on the back of some headstrong, jaded nag. Julianna smiled at the memory. Michael had driven his splendid matched blacks with the same style and finesse as Nicholas drove his grays.

Her rambling thoughts had again turned her to the captain. Mr. Thorneloe was, indeed, far handsomer and possessed such manners as to turn any young woman's head, but Nicholas had saved her life. Now he was her ally and friend. He was something more, too. Julianna recalled his kiss and felt a hot blush creep up her throat. She bent over Sterling's mane and patted his neck.

"Are you quite all right, Miss Adams?"

Julianna kept her face averted so he would not see her scalding cheeks. "I am quite fine. I just thought of my father."

"Ah, I see. May I offer the reassurance that you should not be too disheartened. He will be found soon. I am sure of it."

"Yes, I have been encouraged to believe he will be discovered quite soon. Captain Sidney feels certain he has been impressed aboard a British naval vessel, or possibly a French ship."

"Impressed? Deuced unpleasant situation, to be sure. But that would explain why you received the letter. Obviously, your father was permitted to write to your uncle."

"Yes, but why did Papa not sign his name?"

"It must have been a matter of safeguarding the

whereabouts of the ship, should his letter have fallen into the wrong hands."

"I suppose. . . ." Julianna did not quite agree with him. It still made no sense. Even if the letter had fallen into the wrong hands, why would it make any difference? Papa had not mentioned the ship nor where it was located. His signature, his name, would mean nothing to the French or the English—just another luckless American impressed into service aboard a naval vessel.

"You must remember, we are at war with them, Miss Adams, and Mr. Adams's presence may have forced the captain to take certain precautions."

"Perhaps," she murmured, still unconvinced and strangely unsettled by the conversation.

Their ride continued through the countryside. The air turned warm and fragrant. The scattering of clouds vanished, leaving a brilliant blue sky crowned by the sun.

Sometimes they trotted briskly and later Julianna gave in to Mr. Thorneloe's invitation, urging Sterling into a steady gallop until she grew short of breath and had to stop.

"Well, done!" Mr. Thorneloe beamed at her.

From behind, they both heard the gig catching up.

"My, my, that was quite exciting," Aunt Emily exclaimed. "Perhaps we could stop a moment and just catch our breath."

"Of course, and Mrs. Fairchild, I would not worry about Miss Adams. She is a capital horsewoman." Mr. Thorneloe circled the excited chestnut in tight circles, trying to calm the horse down. "Better than I, what? Perhaps we should consider entering her into the Derby."

Both Uncle Fairchild and Aunt Emily chuckled at such a proposal. Even Julianna had to smile. Apparently, when it suited his purposes, Mr. Thorneloe could be a charming rogue.

When the horses had cooled down, they turned and

began a quiet walk back to Malthorpe. Nothing more was said about Edward Adams or naval vessels.

Once at Malthorpe, servants hurried out to hold the horses' heads, while the Fairchilds descended the gig and Julianna prepared to dismount. But Mr. Thorneloe would have none of it. Ignoring the mounting block, he raised his hands to lift her down from the saddle. She stood much too close to him, and, as she had done with Nicholas, kept her gaze firmly fixed on his cravat.

"Miss Julianna," he murmured so that Aunt Emily would not hear. "Surely, you must realize I—"

The sudden staccato clatter of hoofbeats on the drive made them both look up. A lathered bay horse approached at full gallop—Julianna could even hear its labored breathing.

"Upon my soul, 'tis Sir Nicholas," Uncle Fairchild exclaimed. "What would bring him out here in such a hurry?"

The captain brought the bay to a skidding halt, almost causing the animal to rear upon its hind legs.

"Miss Adams! Forgive this abrupt intrusion, but I must speak with you this instant." He dismounted and shoved the reins into a servant's hands.

"My dear Sir Nicholas, you are in a state. Do come inside and we can discuss this over tea."

"Regretfully, Mrs. Fairchild, I do not have much time. I must away to London this very night."

"You have news of Papa?" Julianna asked.

"Yes, but I must speak with you privately."

Nicholas removed his hat and approached her. Stark lines etched his tired face. His gaze took in Mr. Thorneloe's hand, still grasping her arm. It was then Julianna realized that the sentiment between these two men was far deeper than jealousy—it was cold hatred. Mr. Thorneloe and Sir Nicholas detested each other for reasons far beyond simple rivalry.

"If you would not mind, sir, I would speak to the lady in private."

Mr. Thorneloe let go of her arm and bowed. "Your servant, sir," he answered formally and moved away.

"Miss Adams, I have just received word from the Admiralty advising me that Mr. Adams is *not* 'E.A.' "

She closed her eyes, almost weeping with relief. "Thank God."

"However, they have also discovered the true identity of this man. Regretfully, I must inform you that the writer of that letter you carried from Baltimore is indeed, Edmund Rameau, the Marquis d'Avergne. It is now certain that the marquis is a spy for the French. That letter was intended for his English counterpart."

"That woman, Lysette?"

"Lysette Corbeil is merely a courier. She is being watched, at present."

"Good heavens," Julianna breathed. "Then, my father—"

". . . is exonerated of any implication in the matter, which leaves us free to find him."

She looked up at Nicholas. "What must be done?"

"I leave for London immediately. Wait here. When I find out for certain on which ship Mr. Adams is being held, I will notify you at once."

"Then I, too, shall leave at once."

"Miss Adams, I beg you to wait. Allow me to find out more information. This may take time and there is no need for you to travel until I know the exact circumstances."

"Very well."

He started to turn, then stopped. "And Miss Adams, you are not to divulge what I have just told you to anyone, only that you must leave for London the moment I advise you."

Julianna nodded. "Of course, Captain."

His gaze, now cold with the seriousness of the matter, swept over the nearby Mr. Thorneloe, then her, chilling her to the bone. "Good day, Miss Adams."

He bowed and nodded shortly to the Fairchilds. He turned and strode to his horse—a short, sharp acknowledgment of Thorneloe on his lips. "Sir."

Nicholas mounted the mettlesome bay, spun him about, and was down the drive in a flurry of hooves and rattling gravel.

"Gracious! What on earth did he say to you, child?" Aunt Emily shaded her eyes against the afternoon sun. "I declare, the dear man was in a positive *rage*."

Julianna watched the captain go, the bright dot of horse and rider growing smaller and smaller with each passing moment.

"Only that I must be ready to return to London at a moment's notice."

Mr. Thorneloe moved next to her. "When the time comes, you must allow me the honor of escorting you to Town," he said warmly, even eagerly.

Only when Julianna happened to glance up did she notice that Mr. Thorneloe was not looking at her, but at the diminishing figure of the captain. There was no warmth in his gaze. None.

Thorneloe handed the reins of his tired horse to the groom and mounted the stairs to Greystone Priory, thoroughly exhausted and irritated. Events were not proceeding as planned, particularly his ongoing pursuit of Julianna Adams. The chit was *not* cooperating.

Gloves, hat, and riding crop were shoved into the hands of Barton, Lord Desmond's ancient butler. "Where is his lordship, Barton?"

"Asleep, sir. Today seems to have been somewhat difficult for him."

"Hmm. And, Lady Desmond?"

"In the drawing room, sir."

Thorneloe nodded. "Alone?"

"Indeed, sir."

"Excellent. Well, bring in a glass of something . . . port. No, make it a whiskey. I will have it in the drawing room."

He watched Barton's eyebrows fly up, two bushy, white arcs of surprise. "Very good, sir."

Thorneloe made his way into the drawing room, taking a modicum of pleasure in knowing that someday all of this would be his. *If Desmond would just hurry up and—*

"Ah, Richard, you are back."

"Yes, Aunt, I am." He forced a polite smile on his face and bowed to Lady Desmond.

Slimmer, grander, and by far more elegant than the condescending Lady Elwood, the Countess of Desmond looked up from her stitchery. "Do come in and sit down," she said coolly. "You are looking a trifle worse for the wear."

"I am. Done in. That beast will finish me yet."

Barton entered with a tray and bowed. "Your whiskey, sir."

Thorneloe accepted it with a nod, then waved Barton away.

Lady Desmond set aside her stitchery, folded her hands in her lap, and studied him for a moment, her expression neither approving nor disapproving.

"Strong drink so early in the afternoon?"

"Braces the blood, Aunt."

Thorneloe concealed a frown. He and Lady Desmond got on well enough, but it always seemed so odd to refer to her as "Aunt" when she was but a scant ten years older than he.

She and Desmond had married when she was quite young—an odd arrangement and an even odder set of circumstances surrounding their marriage. It was quite obvious that they did not love each other, but merely went on with their own separate lives and individual interests, having nothing in common except that they were married to each other. Thorneloe assumed this was the very reason why there had been no children. Elizabeth Thorneloe, Lady Desmond, always reminded him of a magnificent actress he had once admired: an ageless, elegant woman—poised, elusive, with an air of tragedy about her. And he could not help himself, he had always loved her.

"I understand my uncle has had a rather trying day."

"Yes. He retired about an hour ago."

Thorneloe tried not to sound eager. "How much longer . . . ?"

Elizabeth rose and moved toward the window to look out upon the terrace. "The doctors say not long. Perhaps a few weeks."

"I am terribly sorry."

She looked back at him, her expression cool and contained. "Are you? Forgive me, Richard, but circumstances force me to face the obvious: you are quite anxious for Desmond to die."

"Elizabeth! Really, you make me sound like a heartless blackguard."

She smiled ruefully. "No, you are not heartless, just penniless. If you are successful in winning the affections of the young American girl, then you should have nothing to worry about."

He flinched at her brutal frankness. "One must get along, mustn't one?" he asked softly.

"Indeed, but to what end, Richard? Desmond has quite given up on you. His patience is nearly exhausted. You have had ample time to marry. Can you not understand his reasons?"

"Yes, and as always, you are my conscience—a constant sharp reminder of my nefarious ways. I regret that I have not lived up to your expectations." He set the empty whiskey glass on the little table next to him and attempted a winning smile. But his charm never worked on her. She saw through him, completely.

She shook her head. "It is none of my concern. When Desmond dies, I shall be at the mercy of your good graces. You may turn me out in the cold for all I know. Dowagers can be something of a burden to one's lifestyle."

Thorneloe made a disparaging noise in his throat. "That is hardly likely. You will always have a home here, if you wish."

Elizabeth sighed. "We shall see, Richard." She returned to her chair and picked up her needlework. "Another package has come for you. From London, I believe."

She did not look up from her stitching. Thorneloe could never decide if she merely tolerated him or if she truly disliked him. Their relationship had always been civil, but never beyond courteous. It was as if she were a guest in his uncle's home, not a wife. In fact, as far as he knew, his aunt had no close friends— she rarely laughed or smiled, seldom held parties, and only attended two or three per year.

He did a mental shake of his head. When his uncle finally died, he would take delight in escorting Elizabeth to all the most fashionable parties. A scandalous thought, but he could not help himself. He loved her. She, on the other hand, loved no one. Except one.

Thorneloe's eyes narrowed. Oh, yes, he remembered him quite well—a stammering, long-limbed boy about his age, who often visited Greystone Priory with his father and mother. Nicholas had rarely taken part in the outdoor games, preferring to stay inside near the adults. Richard soon grew to resent "Nick," as Elizabeth was so fond of calling him. How could she? How dare she, his beloved, addressing that awkward boy in such an intimate fashion?

When Lady Sidney suddenly died, crushed under an overturned carriage, it was Lady Desmond to whom young Nicholas turned for solace—held in her arms while she murmured words of endearment, something Richard's own mother would never have done.

In his eleven-year-old mind, Elizabeth's actions were a cruel betrayal, particularly later when he had innocently stumbled into a room and witnessed something that changed his life forever. He saw a dark-haired man kneeling on the floor, his head in Elizabeth's lap, crying. His hands were twined in the folds of her skirts, while he wept like a child in racking, bitter sobs. Her hands stroked his hair while she murmured soft, loving words.

"There now, Edmund. Hush. It was not your fault."

Richard saw only a betrayal, to his uncle and to the honor of his family. To him. But he could not bring himself to hate her. He did, however, grow to hate the boy and his brokenhearted father.

When Sir Edmund finally drank himself to death, Richard was forced to attend the funeral. In his heart he was not sorry for Sir Edmund Sidney's death. He deserved to die for almost taking away the woman who now sat across from him, oblivious to his long-hidden feelings.

"Richard?" she said again. "Perhaps you did not hear me the first time. There is another package for you."

He snapped out of his reverie. "Ah, yes. Forgive me. You caught me daydreaming." He rose and bowed. "Pray, excuse me."

In the hallway he found the small, brown-paper-wrapped package addressed to him. He knew what it was: letters from London. He snapped the string and tore off the paper, then leafed through the bundle of letters. The courier was doing an excellent job.

He opened the latest letter first, scanning its contents. And smiled. His suspicions had been right. The identity of "E.A." was now positive and wonderfully convenient.

Watch for the empress.

Oh, yes, he would watch for her—a proud ship bearing his long-elusive contact . . . and much-needed gold.

All the more reason to double his efforts in winning the hand of the headstrong Miss Adams. She would see his way of things. Eventually.

Chapter Ten

Margaret and her budding romance with the young groom, Will Jackman, occupied Julianna's attention for the next two days. She kept Margaret's secret from Aunt Emily and particularly from Lady Elwood. To whom a poor girl from Portsmouth chose to give her heart was nobody else's business. Julianna supposed this opinion came from her father's rather eccentric notions about servants—their private lives were their own. And Margaret, all smiles and rosy with blushes, was only too eager to share the details of her romance. Either through boredom or worry, Julianna did not discourage her maid's prattling.

"He's ever so sweet to me, miss," Margaret said the next morning while setting a tray laden with breakfast on the small table near the window.

"I trust he is not unseemly in his attentions toward you?" Julianna clambered out of bed and slipped on her wrapper. She loved taking breakfast in her room, thus avoiding a tiresome hour of gossip with her aunt and Lady Elwood.

"Oh, no, miss. Not my Will." Margaret poured a cup of tea, then set it before her. "He's the perfect gen'leman. Brings me lovely things, he does."

"I see. Are his intentions honorable? Has he proposed?"

"Well, not yet, he hasn't, but I'm sure he will."

Julianna sipped her tea thoughtfully. "I shall miss you, Margaret. I am sure you will make him a wonderful wife."

The girl looked startled. "I'll not be leaving you, Miss Adams. Will hasn't spoken for me yet."

"He will. Then you must find yourself another position." She looked up at Margaret. "Do not worry. I shall write you an excellent recommendation."

"Oh, miss! I'll not be wantin' to leave you. We . . . that is to say, I was hoping that Will might change his situation, I mean, so's we could be stayin' together."

Julianna at once recognized what her maid was trying to say. If Margaret had hinted at such a thing in front of Lady Elwood or even her Aunt Emily, she would have been promptly dismissed.

"You mean, have your Will come along with you, to seek employment with me?"

Margaret blushed to the shade of a ripe strawberry. Julianna tried to sound understanding. "Dear Margaret, *my* future is as uncertain as yours. I could not guarantee you or your young Will a position."

"But I thought, well, that is to say, I thought you and that fine Mr. Thorneloe . . ." The maid bobbed a self-conscious curtsy. "I beg your pardon, miss. I misspoke."

Margaret *had* certainly overstepped her place by such an impudent assumption. Julianna knew she ought to be outraged, but she could not, she liked Margaret too well.

"I have no intention of marrying Mr. Thorneloe," she said tartly, hoping the sharpness in her tone would be enough of a rebuke.

"You'll forgive me for sayin' it, miss, but that's a relief."

Julianna took another sip of her tea, then reached for a slice of toast. "Oh? How so?"

"Well, I oughtn't to be sayin' this, but Will says he's talked to Lord Desmond's coachman and *he* says Mr. Thorneloe has a bit of a temper."

"Indeed? Do not all of us have a temper at times, Margaret?"

"Yes, miss, that's true, but Harry—that's the coachman's name—he don't trust him. Says Mr. Thorneloe can be mean-tempered if he don't get his way."

Julianna stopped eating to ponder what Margaret had said. A bit of tarnish now dulled Mr. Thorneloe's gentlemanly polish.

Unease filled her heart as she recalled how Mr. Thorneloe had been all smiles and easy charm during the day of their ride. He had even joked about her entering the Derby, but she also remembered the abrupt change in his demeanor when Sir Nicholas had galloped into the drive. The hatred between the captain and Mr. Thorneloe had been palpable and frightening.

Julianna chose to ignore Margaret's cheerful prattling while finishing her breakfast. She no longer cared to hear about the estimable Will Jackman. All she could think about was Nicholas and his hatred for Mr. Thorneloe.

A few days later, ensconced within the masculine confines of Brooks's, Nicholas found exactly the man he had hoped to find—Admiral Howard. The good admiral was deep in conversation with a young officer who Nicholas presumed was one of his squadron captains. He hoped he would find several naval officers who had decided to dine or linger long into the evening to play cards.

Admiral Howard looked up as Nicholas approached him. "Sidney! What brings you here, my good fellow? You know Captain Cathcart, I believe?"

"We have met a few times, Admiral." Nicholas bowed politely. "Captain Cathcart, an honor, sir."

Cathcart returned the greeting with a refined nod. "How d'ya do, Sidney? Understand you saved a pretty American gel from drowning, eh? Well done, man."

Nicholas flinched. So the news had made it through the fleet already. "The young lady nearly died from her ordeal. I was only doing my duty."

"Splendid," the admiral said approvingly. "Now sit down, Sidney, and have a splash of something." He indicated a brandy-filled decanter set on the table between their chairs.

"Thank you, sir, however, I cannot stay long. I have come in need of some information. I hope you might be able to help me."

He sat down in the chair next to the admiral, but refused the offered drink. Briefly, he outlined Julianna's situation and the possible fate of her father, particularly the two captains who could have impressed Adams into their service.

Both Captain Cathcart and the admiral listened attentively, occasionally responding with an astonished "Good God" or "Devilish bad luck."

Captain Cathcart sipped his brandy reflectively. "If it is Pittman, the poor chap has probably succumbed to the lash or worse. Pittman detests Americans."

"Aye, 'tis true," Admiral Howard agreed. "But I have observed that the Yankees make excellent sailors and fight like veritable tigers. I have had a few aboard my own ship. Brave lads—a bit too insubordinate for my tastes, but there it is."

Nicholas tactfully steered the conversation back to his original request. "Would either of you know who might be able to help me in locating this gentleman?"

The admiral pursed his lips. "Hmmm. I seem to recall Captain Dunning mentioning something about . . . He was here earlier. Billiards, I think. You had better ask him yourself, my dear fellow."

"Where might I find him?"

"I thought I heard him say he would be attending a ball tomorrow night. Viscount Greyly's, I believe," Cathcart said.

Nicholas rose and bowed again. "I thank you, Admiral . . . Captain. I shall speak with him directly."

"Oh, and Sidney," Captain Cathcart called out. "If

Adams *is* aboard the *Dagger,* I would prepare the young lady for the worst. The last I heard, Pittman was keelhauling Americans to set an example for the rest of his crew."

A cold knot of dread began forming in the pit of Nicholas's stomach. Keelhauling was by far the cruelest punishment inflicted on a man. To have a bound man thrown overboard and dragged under the water against the barnacle-encrusted hull of a ship, tearing him to pieces, was not the kind of discipline he approved of—he had never ordered it and never would. How could he begin to explain this monstrous form of punishment to Julianna, especially if her father had been forced to endure it?

The memory of her tears was all too vivid. It surprised him to think he did not actually feel pity for her, but rather a strong sense of admiration. There *was* something else. Nicholas could not bring himself to think it—dared not think it. He had long ago decided he was destined to remain a bachelor, but Julianna was beginning to change that notion. Kissing her under the willow tree only added to his dilemma. He had enjoyed kissing her, tasting her—inhaling the soft, intoxicating fragrance of lavender. He did not want to admit it to himself, but he liked the way she had clung to him. God help him, he had not wanted to let her go.

Damn and blast! This was not the time for any entanglements with females. Besides, it was quite plain that Julianna preferred Thorneloe. Well, so be it. All he wanted was to find Captain Dunning and get this business over with as soon as possible.

Nicholas left the club, heading straight for home. He had a lot of clever maneuvering to do in order to obtain an invitation to the Greyly ball on such short notice. Fortunately, he knew the viscount fairly well since they had attended Eton together. A well-worded note ought to do it. Once at the ball, he would find this Captain Dunning, obtain the information he sought, then leave.

* * *

Like almost all the fashionable routs he had ever attended, once Nicholas arrived, he could scarcely wait to leave. Too much noise, too many people, and nothing of any consequence to eat. Although, he *had* enjoyed Lady Elwood's ball at Malthorpe. Julianna had looked quite ravishing. . . . He stopped. Thinking such thoughts was too dangerous. If he were ever to discharge himself of this duty, he must eradicate any thoughts of Julianna and concentrate on finding Captain Dunning and getting the needed information.

After greeting his host and Lady Greyly, Nicholas elbowed his way through the throng of chattering guests, taking particular care not to step on delicate hems trailing behind their owners. Finding Dunning ought to be fairly simple. Except for himself, he spotted no other naval officers standing about or dancing in Lady Greyly's exquisite ballroom.

He felt about as comfortable as a hooked fish—no air to breathe in these hot, stifling rooms. The high collar of his uniform, combined with the stock about his throat, only added to his discomfort.

It was then he spotted Captain Dunning in one of the salons adjacent to the ballroom—an unremarkable-looking man except for the chestful of medals attesting to his bravery at Trafalgar. Upon closer observation, Nicholas realized he knew Dunning, a wild-haired, pompous lobcock. The fool did not know a mizzen from a mainsail.

As he entered the salon, Nicholas did not at first recognize the young lady standing next to Dunning, but as he drew closer, he felt his belly tighten with contempt. She turned so he could see her face. There was no mistaking the honey-colored hair, the pale, delicate brows, or the disdainful look in those lovely blue eyes.

Olivia Landon, in all her coldly gracious glory.

She spotted him first before Dunning could acknowledge his presence. "Why, Sir Nicholas, what an extraordinary surprise. I had no idea you were in London." She tapped her fan lightly on her companion's arm. "Surely you know Captain Dunning?"

Nicholas bowed slightly. "Miss Landon, Captain Dunning." He nodded to the others. "Indeed, an unexpected surprise."

"Egad, Sidney. I have not seen you since . . . By Jove, I believe it has been over a year. I thought you were out giving chase to the froggies, but the tattle is you managed to rescue some chit in buckskins—a rich Yankee gel. I say, Sidney, I hear she is a crack shot."

Dunning's circle of admirers tittered with amusement. Nicholas's jaw tightened. Cold rage added to his contempt. If it had been any other place but Lord Greyly's, Nicholas would have punched Dunning in the nose.

"Oh, but I met her at Lady Elwood's a few weeks ago," Olivia confided. "Quite common. Her manners were atrocious, but then, what *can* one expect from an American rustic? Gracious, she even avowed to shooting *bears,* or some such beast."

Nicholas fought the urge to respond with something highly impolite, salted with a few colorful and vulgar nautical terms. Olivia had not changed. Still beautiful, calculating, and ruthless—like a shark. Both she and Dunning were insufferable, but for Julianna's sake, he bit back the angry retort.

He chose to overlook Olivia's tactless opinion of Julianna and turned to Captain Dunning. "A word with you, sir, in private. I have urgent business and I must speak with you."

At once serious, Dunning dropped the foppish role. "Indeed, sir, I am at your disposal."

Nicholas nodded toward a private corner of the room. Once out of earshot he kept his voice low so no one, especially Olivia, would overhear him.

"I do not care for your ungentlemanly declarations toward someone you have never met, particularly when the one you are ridiculing is a lady. If this had been any other place, I would have called you out, but as it is, there are other matters more urgent that demand my attention."

Dunning's eyes widened. "Good God, sir, I meant no offense. Of course, you have my apology."

"Accepted . . . for now." In low terse tones, Nicholas explained the circumstances concerning the *Hart* and what he suspected had happened to Edward Adams. "I understand from Admiral Howard you might know which ship may have picked up the crew and passengers. Do you?"

Captain Dunning pondered the information for a moment. "Yes, I do. I saw Needham last week, just anchored in Portsmouth. He said he had picked up a few survivors from a shipwreck. Cargo vessel went aground off the coast of France. Lucky to get the crew off the wreck before the Frenchies spotted them."

"Any word about Americans?"

"Not certain, but he did say he was having to discipline a few troublemakers. Common problem with an impressed crew."

Nicholas nodded, acknowledging the same difficulties he had experienced in trying to train and discipline angry men who had been taken by force from their own ships—particularly the Americans. Nasty business, but there it was.

"Did you happen to see Pittman?"

Dunning blanched. "I did. Vile man—in high dudgeon as usual."

"Did he say anything about taking on board any Americans?"

"No. I believe, sir, you want the *Cassandra*. She sails within days. I would not worry about Captain Pittman. From what I could tell, his ship is in bad need of repairs. She will be in port for a long time. If I were you, I would make haste for Portsmouth before Needham weighs anchor."

Nicholas thanked Dunning, momentarily setting aside his personal dislike for the man. He had no time to lose. Word must get to Julianna immediately, then he would be off for Portsmouth.

Leaving the ball proved to be another difficulty.

Most all the guests had arrived, filling the already sti-fling rooms. He edged his way through the crush, occa-sionally greeting someone he knew, until his escape was blocked by a trio of beautifully attired ladies standing directly in front of the entrance to the ball-room. One of them was Lady Greyly, the second lady he did not know. The third was Olivia.

"L-ladies?"

"Sir Nicholas." Lady Greyly held out her gloved hand to him. "Miss Landon has been telling us about your splendid bravery. Lady Swindon, here, and I are eager to hear all the details."

He glanced at Olivia. It was obvious she had put the viscountess up to this little encounter.

"Well, madam, l-l-let us say it was a fortunate coin-cidence. My ship happened to be in the right place at the right time."

"Oh, fiddlesticks! Saving that poor creature from an untimely end. My dear Sir Nicholas, you are a posi-tive hero."

Nicholas made the determined effort not to grind his teeth in front of his hostess. "In truth, your lady-ship—"

"Sir Nicholas, I do believe this is our dance?" Olivia cut in smoothly.

"I—"

"But of course," Lady Greyly went on in her gush-ing tone, reminding him of Lady Elwood. "Pray, you simply must dance with Miss Landon." The viscount-ess moved aside to allow Olivia to step forward. Nich-olas had no choice but to take her outstretched hand and lead her to the dance floor.

"I trust you are enjoying your c-contrivance?" He made no effort to conceal his anger.

"Contrivance? You are too cruel, Captain. I would not dream of doing such a thing."

"Then why this charade, this d-d-dance?"

She executed a perfect little turn, then faced him. "It is necessary I speak with you for a moment. What better place than in front of the entire *ton*?"

"What better place, indeed? I seem to recall it was under the very same circumstances that you chose to announce your distaste for me."

"I was but a girl then, a featherbrain. In truth, I am sure I did not know what I was saying."

"I beg to differ, Miss Landon. You knew exactly what you were saying and I daresay knew what you wanted."

Miss Landon said nothing for a moment but continued in the dance, turning gracefully with each step.

Sharp memories flooded him, making him even more angry and impatient. "Well, what is it? Why do you wish to speak with me?" He was almost growling his words.

Unruffled, Miss Landon favored him with a condescending smile. "I have been corresponding with my brother, Richard. It seems he is quite taken with the American heiress, although I cannot imagine what he sees in her. She is so . . . common."

The lie was out of his mouth before he realized it. "I was not aware of this. I recently attended a ball at Lady Elwood's and Thorneloe seemed merely polite to Miss Adams."

"In all actuality, I care nothing for Richard's private *amours* but I am a devoted stepsister and always concerned about his well-being."

"Your point, Miss Landon?" Nicholas's impatience rose with the unbearable heat in the room. He wanted nothing better than to escape this awkward encounter and forget the unpleasantness of the past.

Miss Landon made another exquisitely performed turn. "I have not seen you since that regrettable day when we parted. I was perfectly beastly to you. You must allow me to make amends."

She smiled prettily at him, knowing she looked utterly ravishing. Her beauty had at one time ensnared him, but later had proved to be his downfall. He would not make that mistake again. Never again would he allow himself to be taken in by a pretty pair of blue eyes or a captivating smile.

He stopped abruptly in the middle of the next step, almost causing a collision with the couple behind them. "Your designs are well known, Miss Landon. I suggest you ply them on someone with fewer scruples."

Nicholas did not wait for Olivia's reply, but took her hand and firmly led her back to where Lady Greyly was standing with a cluster of guests. He made his good-byes—just short of being uncivil—then departed.

To make amends with that woman! Eighteen months had not diminished his contempt for Olivia Landon, nor his disgust with himself. To think he had almost offered for her. That conniving . . . just like her stepbrother, except Thorneloe had a modicum of charm to defray his desperate pursuit of money. Cards and horses had taken nearly all what he had inherited from his father and Nicholas knew Lord Desmond, Thorneloe's uncle, would not bequeath a penny until his nephew had changed his ways.

When the earl died and Thorneloe took the title, Olivia would be obliged to live under his generosity, at least until she married. Wycombe Hall had been an attractive lure, as had Nicholas's newly acquired wealth. It was also rather convenient that his own estate was not far from the earl's—a detail not lost to Olivia's scheming.

A kind fate had spared Nicholas the mistake of marrying her. It had been chance—a stroke of luck—that found him entering a room almost two years ago, just in time to overhear Olivia's conversation. Her cruelty still sent a chill through his heart.

". . . and when I become mistress of Wycombe Hall, I shall see to it that the renovations are more to my liking. Much will be accomplished as l-l-long as my s-s-sailor husband remains at s-s-sea!"

Nicholas could still hear the shrill feminine laughter until he had been noticed by Olivia and her friends. In a heartbeat it was over—all his schoolboy longing for such a beautiful, elegant creature had flown with those coldly calculated words. Never again would he surrender his heart so willingly, so foolishly. He had decided in that one terrible moment, he was not meant for a life with wife and children. The sea would be his life, and his ship, his mistress.

As Nicholas climbed into the coach, the thoughts of the sea suddenly reminded him of his purpose this evening—to find out which ship he should pursue to find Edward Adams. Which led him to Julianna. And Thorneloe.

A disturbing uneasiness settled over him. Nicholas had never admitted to it before, but now he was forced to face his growing jealously and an unaccountable sense of worry.

Thorneloe and Julianna. *Never!*

Chapter Eleven

"Pacing and worrying will do no good, my dear. Do sit down, Julianna. I cannot possibly continue with this stitchery. My nerves are in complete shreds."

Aunt Emily's pleas fell on deaf ears. Julianna could not stop her nervous circling—first to the window to stare out at the rain-soaked garden, then back to the pianoforte, only to start all over again.

Why had she not heard from the captain? He promised he would write the moment he had news.

"Why do you not play for us? It would soothe our nerves."

Julianna stopped pacing long enough to perch on the edge of a chair facing the entry to the drawing room. Her handkerchief had been worried into a crumpled ball clutched between her trembling fingers. Three days!

"I am sorry, Aunt, to be such a bother, but I cannot understand why Sir Nicholas has not written. He promised he would let me know the moment he had some news. Besides," she added, "I cannot play the pianoforte with any degree of skill."

Aunt Emily shook her head. "One can only assume he has no news, my dear. But come, child, he will let you know. Sir Nicholas is an honorable man."

Julianna nodded in mute misery. Her aunt was right. Captain Sidney had always done what he had promised. In fact, he had never let her down. Aunt Emily described him as stalwart and gallant. However, Lady Elwood's comments never went beyond "a steady, but fearfully dull man." Sir Nicholas was definitely not like Mr. Thorneloe, and Lady Elwood never missed an opportunity to persuade her to encourage *that* gentleman's attentions.

"When Lord Desmond dies, and I fear it cannot be too long now, Mr. Thorneloe will inherit the title. The earl and countess are childless, and Mr. Thorneloe's father, Lord Desmond's brother, had only the one son. So he will inherit. Lovely estate—Greystone Priory. We must drive by it sometime, my dear."

Somehow Julianna could not quite agree with Lady Elwood's high esteem for Mr. Thorneloe. Margaret's tidbit of gossip had cooled some of her former regard for him.

"Lady Elwood, I have no feelings for Mr. Thorneloe, nor his future estate."

"I am well aware of what you may say *now,* but you must think of the future. It would be an excellent match."

At this point in their conversation, Julianna always tried to turn Lady Elwood's attentions back to Sir Nicholas.

"He is a very fine man, but, Miss Julianna, he is an impoverished baronet, living in that great monstrosity of a house. And he is never at home—he is always away at sea."

"But he is not impoverished. Did you not say he made his fortune at sea?"

Lady Elwood smiled, but always there was a dismissive tone in her voice. "All the same, how much better for you to be aligned with one of the better families in England. Surely you recognize this fact?"

These conversations were never resolved to any satisfaction. Lady Elwood meant well, but Julianna could not help but feel there was something wrong in the argument. Why should she be expected to marry an earl? What made that title so much better than a baronet? Now she was sounding exactly like her father.

"Miss Julianna, you must try not to appear so distraught. Everything is being done that can be done," said Lady Elwood.

"I know, but I cannot seem to stop my worrying."

Lady Elwood settled herself near Aunt Emily. For once the grand lady was not her usual ebullient self. "When Sir Nicholas has discovered your father's whereabouts then you will know what is to be done. It will be as simple as that."

"I wish Mr. Fairchild had not returned to London so soon. I am beside myself as to who should escort you when the time comes." A pucker formed on Aunt Emily's round little mouth. "Perhaps, we could ask Mr. Thorneloe."

"An excellent idea, Emily, and I understand he did promise. I know he will be happy to oblige."

The faint sound of carriage wheels on the drive made Julianna jump to her feet. The post! A courier! She tried to calm her racing heart and forced herself to sit down near her aunt.

"Dear me, who could that be?" Aunt Emily set aside her embroidery and began to fuss with her lace. "Charlotte, had you any notion there would be any callers today?"

"Not that I recall."

Hughes entered and bowed. "Mr. Thorneloe, my lady."

"Mr. Thorneloe, what a delightful surprise! We were just speaking of you." The marchioness held out her hand to him.

Poised and elegant as usual, Mr. Thorneloe took Lady Elwood's hand and bowed over it. "Indeed. I hope I have not fallen out of your good graces, ma'am. To do so would cause me considerable grief."

"Rascal!"

He smiled then sat down next to Lady Elwood. "Ladies, you are looking exceedingly pretty today. A respite for the eyes on this gloomy, damp morning."

"Thank you for your compliments, but my niece is beside herself with worry. She has not heard from Sir Nicholas in three days. He is in London gathering information concerning Mr. Adams's whereabouts . . . on some ship, I am told."

"Ah, but gathering intelligence is time consuming, ma'am. I am sure everything is being done as quickly as possible."

He sounded sincere, but Julianna sensed a different tone in Mr. Thorneloe's voice, as if he were attempting to convince her instead of Aunt Emily.

"Exactly as I told her," Lady Elwood interjected. "We will learn soon enough. As soon as the message arrives, Miss Julianna must leave for London immediately. We were so hoping, Mr. Thorneloe, that you might consider escorting her there, since Mr. Fairchild has already returned to Town."

"I have already made that promise, madam. It would be my greatest pleasure."

Julianna avoided his pointed stare and resumed fretting the handkerchief in her hand. In spite of Lady Elwood's tactful request, she did not want Mr. Thorneloe to escort her to London.

"I *am* sorry to be so distracted, but I cannot help myself."

Mr. Thorneloe gazed at her thoughtfully, his expression turning serious. "Pray, Miss Adams, you have no reason to apologize. I daresay, if I were in your situation, I would be equally distressed. What you need is the reassurance that all will turn out well in the end."

"Such kind words," Lady Elwood said approvingly, then, without warning, sneezed. "Dear me! Your pardon. Perhaps I ought not to be in your company."

She rose, upon which Mr. Thorneloe promptly stood.

"Dear lady, are you ill?"

" 'Tis nothing but a cold, a trifling. I shall retire for the remainder of the day. Emily, would you be so good as to attend me for a moment?"

Aunt Emily again set aside her needlework. "Gracious, Charlotte, such botheration over a little sneeze." But she rose and obediently followed Lady Elwood to the door.

Julianna watched the proceedings with a growing sense that some connivance was afoot. Lady Elwood did not look *quite* as ill as she professed—in fact, her expression was positively smug.

Mr. Thorneloe bowed. "My condolences, Lady Elwood. I pray for your speedy recovery."

"You are so thoughtful, as always. And allow me to extend my best wishes to Lord and Lady Desmond."

"I shall do so, ma'am. My aunt will appreciate your kindness. I fear my uncle is quite frail."

"Hmmm. A great pity. Good day, Mr. Thorneloe."

Lady Elwood left the room, trailing Aunt Emily in her wake. Julianna rose and moved toward the window, suddenly realizing she was quite alone with Mr. Thorneloe. He wasted no time with additional pleasantries but hastened to her side.

"An advantageous moment, Miss Adams. I can scarcely believe my good fortune."

He was so close, she could see the thickness of his dark lashes, the perfection of his beautifully shaped mouth. Her heart began to hammer in impossibly large beats.

"You will forgive my forwardness, but I fear I have but a few moments."

"A . . . a few moments for what?"

"Surely you must know of my feelings for you, Miss Julianna—if you will allow me to call you by your given name. I am quite undone. Ever since that moment at Mrs. Heldon's card party when you so thoroughly trounced dear Olivia."

"Indeed?" She backed away from him a step.

He laughed softly. "Yes, she deserved such a resounding set-down. Oh, she and I get along tolerably well, but she can be quite a handful at times. You will be amused to know she once held a *tendre* for your captain."

"Your stepsister and Captain Sidney?" Julianna

could scarcely believe what she was hearing. Sir Nicholas and Miss Landon? Impossible.

"In point of fact, they were to be married, but regretfully, things did not resolve as one would have hoped."

"What happened?"

"You must understand that Sir Nicholas's life is the sea. He's hardly the kind of man who would tie himself to the joys of domesticity. I am afraid he quite broke Olivia's heart."

"That cannot be true. You are mistaken."

He shook his head. "Regretfully, it is all true."

"Is that why you despise him?"

Mr. Thorneloe looked surprised. "Despise him? Why would you think that?"

"Because when the two of you meet, one can almost feel the animosity."

A rueful smile quirked his fine mouth. "I daresay you are correct. He and I have never gotten along so well over the years. Sir Nicholas knows nothing else but the navy. He has devoted his life to it. He ofttimes pays scant attention to the feelings of others, as he did to my sister."

Julianna pressed her palm to her brow. "But my father . . . ? The captain promised to find him for me."

"And so he shall. He is a man of honor and high principles, but I fear of little else. He has no heart."

Mr. Thorneloe suddenly caught Julianna by her upper arms, forcing her to face him. "Come, Miss Julianna, I cannot bandy with words much longer. Your aunt will return momentarily. Sir Nicholas will find your father, of that I am certain. When you receive word, I will escort you to London to be rejoined with him. Then . . . dearest Julianna, forgive me for my forward manner. You must know my heart is quite lost to you. In truth, I am convinced I have been bewitched."

Before she could collect her wits, Mr. Thorneloe bent closer to her, not allowing her to escape. His eyes were enormous, consuming her. He was going to kiss her and there would be nothing she could do about it. At the first touch of his mouth on hers, Julianna fought a sudden weakness in her limbs, then felt revulsion rush through her—a betrayal—not to Michael, but to Nicholas. She now understood the cold, hurt look in his eyes when he had arrived in such a rush at Malthorpe and had seen Mr. Thorneloe helping her down from her horse.

Julianna found her wits and placed her hands on Mr. Thorneloe's shoulders—and *pushed*. "No. Please, you must stop." She was almost gasping. "I cannot—"

"Of course you cannot," he murmured, still dangerously close. "I will leave you for now, Miss Julianna, but I expect more than just one kiss from you."

He took her hands and lifted them to his lips. "I will call tomorrow."

At that moment, they both heard the door open and Aunt Emily bustled into the room. "Dear me! Oh!"

Julianna hastily stepped away from Mr. Thorneloe. The heat of her embarrassment burned her cheeks.

"Ah, Mrs. Fairchild. I was just reassuring Miss Adams that the captain will, of course, find her father in good time. She must not worry herself too excessively. Do you not agree?"

Aunt Emily blinked, befuddled. "Oh, yes. I mean, of course. To be sure. Dearest Julianna, Mr. Thorneloe is correct. We are all most concerned for your well-being."

Unruffled, Mr. Thorneloe bowed politely to both of them.

"Ladies, I must away. I have recalled an urgent matter which I must attend to immediately. I bid you good day."

He strode from the room in bold, confident strides leaving Julianna still standing by the window.

"Good day, Mr. Thorneloe." Aunt Emily watched as he left the room then turned back, noticing her. "Dear child, you are shaking. Whatever is the matter? You must sit down. Now everything will turn out splendidly. Your father will be found and all will be well. Mark my words."

Julianna's trembling increased—not from confusion or even any feelings of attachment, but from disgust. Allowing Mr. Thorneloe to kiss her had been shockingly improper and she was glad Aunt Emily had not seen it. She would have preferred if it had been Nicholas who had kissed her instead—in front of Aunt Emily *and* Lady Elwood.

"Miss, wake up! Please, wake up!"

Julianna stirred, reluctant to give up a sound sleep. She turned toward the sound of that frantic voice and realized with a start it was Margaret. She bolted upright, awake.

"What is it?"

"The courier has come from London."

Heedless of propriety Julianna jumped out of bed and reached for her wrapper. She raced out of the bedroom and down the hallway with Margaret leading the way, carrying a candlestick.

In the entry hall, an alarmed-looking Hughes, periwig askew, wearing his liveried coat over his nightshirt, held a candelabra high over the head of the courier. The young man, covered in muddy water and exhausted from his late-night ride, handed Julianna the thick cream-colored paper.

She cracked the seal and scanned Nicholas's bold handwriting:

Dear Miss Adams:
I have discovered the exact ship on which your father has been serving—HMS Cassandra. *She sails within the week. You must come to London immediately. There is still the possibility we might have to appeal to the American consul. Do not delay.*
          Yours etc.,
          Sidney

"Margaret, please pack at once!"

The house became a flurry of activity for the next hour. A messenger was sent off to fetch Mr. Thorneloe; Julianna even managed to dress without Margaret's aid while the maid hastily packed a small traveling trunk. All the while, Aunt Emily stood in the middle of the room, anxiously wringing her hands.

"I promise I shall send a letter to Mr. Fairchild in the morning. Dear child, I feel I should go with you, but Charlotte's cold has taken a turn for the worse."

Julianna snapped the lock shut on her trunk. "Do not worry yourself, Aunt Emily. You must stay and look after Lady Elwood."

"Yes, but I still feel I should come with you."

"I will be quite fine. Margaret will be with me. You must not worry." Julianna stopped packing and embraced her aunt. "Please do not distress yourself. As you said, all is going to be well. I know it. Once everything is settled, I will get word to you at once."

A servant rapped softly on the door and announced the arrival of Mr. Thorneloe's carriage. With Margaret on her heels, Julianna flew down the stairs. In spite of the short notice, Mr. Thorneloe looked as if he were on his way to some evening party. Every hair was in place, his linen was immaculate, and not a wrinkle or speck dared to spoil the image of the perfectly turned-out gentleman. He held a gold watch in his gloved palm.

"It is four A.M., Miss Adams. We must make haste. Where is Lady Elwood?"

"Lady Elwood is quite ill, I am sorry to say."

"Ah, I am sorry to hear that, however, we have no time to dally. We must hurry."

Once outside, she caught herself in time from gaping at the carriage drawn by four handsome bays, their coats gleaming from the light of the torches held by the attending servants. It took her a moment to realize that it was the earl's carriage.

She felt Mr. Thorneloe's hand on her elbow. "There is no time to lose."

Shrugging off the unsettled feeling, Julianna climbed inside. Margaret, now yawning after all the activity, followed her and promptly curled up in the corner, using her small bundle as a pillow, and went to sleep.

Mr. Thorneloe settled himself more comfortably in the seat across from them. "You are not too cold, Miss Adams? There is bound to be some fog and dampness this early in the morning."

She shook her head. Although she could not see him too clearly in the gloom, Julianna detected a certain eagerness in his voice. The unsettled feeling returned. While he made no reference to the previous morning, or that he had kissed her, she knew it was on his mind and he would eventually mention it.

Leaning back against the squabs, she became determined not to recall that disturbing event, but rather turn her attention to her father . . . and Nicholas.

Surely Mr. Thorneloe was wrong about his sister and her feelings for the captain. Julianna knew she had no right to question the captain on such a private matter, and yet she could not bear the idea of knowing that Nicholas had at one time held strong feelings for Olivia Landon—strong enough to offer for her. She could not imagine it any more than she could imagine herself becoming Richard Thorneloe's wife.

It did not matter that she might become a countess, or that she would live in a great house, or even ride in a beautiful carriage. She did not want Richard Thorneloe, even if he was handsome and elegant. What Julianna wanted was the tall, serious man who had rescued her from the sea.

Chapter Twelve

By the time the sky was just turning pale, Julianna knew they were not heading for London. Fog hung heavily over the countryside, obscuring any landmarks, but she knew instinctively they were heading in the wrong direction.

She first realized something was amiss when Margaret awoke. The young maid said nothing but Julianna could see something was bothering her.

"Margaret, are you ill?"

"No, miss, just . . . nothing."

"Something upsets you. What is it?" she insisted.

"Well, I was just wondering why we're going east?"

Mr. Thorneloe cleared his throat. "I can resolve that mystery. We are taking a slightly longer, but safer route."

Alarm flared within Julianna. "I thought you said we did not have a moment to spare, that we must make all speed to London."

Mr. Thorneloe's smile was cool and knowing. "I did, but I was concerned for your safety, Miss Adams. Not to worry, we will arrive at our destination in plenty of time."

His words did nothing to dispel her fears. East was not the direction in which they should be traveling, but having no knowledge of where they were, exactly, Julianna remained silent and tense until late in the afternoon, when the carriage stopped in front a large coaching inn.

Stiff and weary, she and Margaret entered the smoke-filled inn and waited while Mr. Thorneloe arranged for rooms. Julianna had no notion how he managed to devise an explanation as to their improbable relationship, but allowed herself to be led to a large comfortable room with a clean bed and a cheery fire burning in the hearth.

Mr. Thorneloe stood outside the doorway, smiling. "I shall have a tray sent up directly. I have spoken to the innkeeper's wife, Mrs. Dobson. She is to see to your every need." He bent closer so only she would hear him. "I bid you goodnight, Miss Julianna. Until the morning . . ."

She shut the door and turned toward Margaret, who was huddling near the fire, trying to warm her chilled hands.

"Margaret, you know more about this than I. Where do you think Mr. Thorneloe is taking us?" she asked.

"In truth, miss, I've had my suspicions. I think he's headin' for the coast, then takin' a ship up north to Scotland."

"Scotland? For what purpose? What business can he possibly have in Scotland? He knows we are to be in London tomorrow."

Margaret gulped, clearly too frightened to tell her. "To marry you, miss. In Scotland, you need no banns. A parson says the words and yer married straightaway."

"Married!" So that was it. She vaguely remembered Aunt Emily whispering about one of those "scandalous marriages." Julianna had no idea what she was talking about since she had no interest in Scotland or doing anything so shocking as running away to get married.

She paced the confines of the room, struggling for an answer. One thing was clear: she had no intention of marrying Mr. Thorneloe in Scotland or anywhere else. And then there was the matter of her father.

"Margaret, I must know for certain. Can you find out where we are going?"

"I think I can, miss. I'll go down and have a chat wi' the mistress. She'd know. Mayhap she's spoken to the coachman."

"Yes, good. Say that you need to fetch me some linens."

Margaret slipped out of the room, leaving Julianna again to pace in front of the fire.

Odious man! To think she thought him so *kind*! Julianna clenched her fists. She would rather marry a . . . a toad. How dare he play her the fool. The little flatteries and compliments. His pretty words to Lady Elwood and Aunt Emily. His lies—for they must be lies—about the captain and Olivia Landon. Remembering Miss Landon and her vicious character made Julianna wonder if it was not Nicholas who had been treated so badly.

She scarcely heard the door open when Margaret returned.

"Well?"

"I found out, miss. Mistress Dobson likes to talk."

"Where are we going, Margaret?"

"Ramsgate, miss. 'Tis on the coast, east of London. Lots of ships. I've got an uncle what lives there."

"Then we must get word to Sir Nicholas."

"I know, miss, but how?"

Julianna stopped her pacing. "I have some money. . . ."

Money. That was it—the real reason Mr. Thorneloe was so "infatuated" with her. The thought of his deception almost made her ill. She chastised herself again for thinking him so handsome, so charming— Lady Elwood and Aunt Emily had almost convinced her he would have been the perfect match, much more suitable than encouraging someone like Sir Nicholas.

What a little fool she had been! Once she was married to Mr. Thorneloe, he would gain control over her inheritance—the property in Maryland and a portion of the income from her father's lands in Virginia. Since she was the only one in England who really knew what Edward Adams looked like, Mr. Thorneloe could simply forbid her to continue her search. In time, because there was no clear record or proof where Edward Adams was, exactly, it would be assumed that he had perished at sea. It horrified her to think Mr. Thorneloe would do something so reprehensible, but she now knew him for what he was: a bounder and a cad.

Grim determination replaced her fear. "Margaret, I think I know what we must do. How is your play-acting?"

In the morning, Julianna heard a polite knock at the door. Standing at the entrance was a short, red-faced woman who peered up at her anxiously.

"Mr. Thorneloe sent me up to see if everything was all right. He says the carriage is ready."

"Mrs. Dobson, is it? Be so kind as to tell Mr. Thorneloe that Margaret, my abigail, is quite ill. She must have eaten something that was not quite right or gone sour. She is dreadfully unwell and I promised I would stay with her."

"She's not got something catchin', does she?"

"Oh, I hope not, but I think it is. Tell Mr. Thorneloe I will send word when Margaret is feeling better. In the meantime, would you be so good as to send up fresh linens and some tea?"

Mrs. Dobson bobbed a hasty curtsy. "Yes, miss. Of course, miss. I'll see to it."

Julianna shut the door and turned to a white-faced Margaret.

"All right, the way is clear. Do you have the money and the note for Sir Nicholas?"

"Yes, miss."

Julianna placed comforting hands on Margaret's shoulders. "It is a very simple task, Margaret. All you have to do is slip downstairs and catch the next mail coach back to London. You have plenty of money. Once you give the note to Sir Nicholas, he will see that you get home to Uncle Fairchild." She shook the girl's shoulders a little. "Please, Margaret, if you do not do this, then Mr. Thorneloe will carry out his plan and my father may be lost forever. No one will ever find him, not even Sir Nicholas."

Margaret nodded. "I promise, miss. I won't let you down."

Once the girl had left, Julianna strode to the bed and rearranged the pillow and coverlets to make it look like someone was asleep. She knew it was a weak ploy, but she had to forestall Mr. Thorneloe as long as possible. She also knew he was already fuming over the delay, but all she had to do was wait long enough to make sure Margaret got away, so that Mr. Thorneloe would be unable to stop her.

By the time a dinner tray was sent up, Julianna knew Mr. Thorneloe had lost his patience. Mrs. Dobson had knocked several times on her door to inquire about her maid's health—assuredly at Mr. Thorneloe's instruction. Julianna finally sent word that she would be ready in the morning, although she would have to leave Margaret in the care of Mrs. Dobson.

Promptly at eight the next morning Julianna made her appearance. The scowl on Mr. Thorneloe's face indicated his displeasure.

"I hope your maid has improved?" His sarcasm was impossible to ignore. "Tell me, Miss Adams, what did you hope to gain by this little charade? Your maid is no more ill than I am."

He took her elbow and sharply pushed her toward the carriage. "Get in," he snarled.

Julianna hesitated, wishing fervently that she had escaped with Margaret earlier, until she saw the wink of a pistol butt in Thorneloe's other hand.

She climbed into the carriage and stalled by creating a great show of making herself comfortable. He joined her, but said nothing.

"Charade, Mr. Thorneloe?" She managed to find

the courage to look at him directly. "It was *you* who began this ghastly charade. You realize, of course, I have no intention of marrying you. Ever."

"And you must realize you will have little choice." Exasperation marred his handsome features. "Come, Julianna, I am not a beast. You will not be ill treated. You will be a countess and want for nothing. You will be admired by everyone."

"I do not want to be admired nor do I want to be a countess. I shall never consent to this. You will have to find someone else to deceive."

"We shall see," he said grimly.

Nicholas was beside himself with worry. Where was she? Hand-delivered messages to and from Mr. Fairchild failed to yield any information—Mr. Fairchild had heard nothing since receiving a hasty note from his wife advising that Julianna was on her way, escorted by Mr. Thorneloe.

Of course. Thorneloe. Lady Elwood's *paragon*. Nicholas should have guessed. There was no telling what lies Thorneloe had concocted or if Julianna had believed him.

Time was running out and Julianna was a day late. Nicholas had no choice but to send word on ahead to Mr. Smythe to ready the *Gallant*. There had been some fast finagling to get permission from the Admiralty for him to pursue the *Cassandra*, but Nicholas had also received a fortuitous piece of luck in that the Admiralty needed urgent dispatches delivered to Captain Needham. However, should Nicholas miss boarding the *Cassandra* while she was still in port, he knew his own ship would be fit to sail at the appropriate time.

To his relief, it would not be necessary to involve the American consul, but he did need Julianna's description of Edward Adams, and, as he had promised, to deliver her personal message to him once he was found.

By midday, Nicholas could not keep still any longer.

He had to do something soon or go wild with frustra-
tion. Without quite realizing what he was doing, he
ordered Peters to bring him something to drink. In
moments his valet entered the sitting room carrying a
tray bearing a decanter of brandy and a single glass.

"Your brandy, sir—to calm one's nerves." Peters
poured a small amount into the glass and handed it
to him.

"Excellent, Peters. Thank you." He tossed down a
mouthful then set the glass back on the tray. "Difficult
day." He eyed Peters. Good man. Peters had been
with him since his father died and had guided him, a
heartbroken lad, into manhood with discretion and
wisdom.

"Indeed, sir. If I may say so, ladies tend to compli-
cate one's life."

"They do." He gestured to the tray. "I will have
another."

Nicholas accepted a second glass, filled to the brim,
but this time he sipped it, savoring the brandy's excellent flavor.

"If I may be so bold as to offer a suggestion, sir?"

"Of course, man. I am open to anything at this
point."

"I understand you have recently received word from
Mr. Fairchild that the young lady is on her way to
London, escorted by Mr. Thorneloe."

"Yes, I did."

"And she should have arrived yesterday some time?"

"Yes."

Peters poured him a third glass, somewhat smaller
than the second. Nicholas downed it quickly.

"Well, sir, perhaps they were 'blown off course,' as
it were—heading on a different tack, for one reason
or another. Perhaps someone *else* may know of their
whereabouts?"

He stared at Peters for a moment, absorbing his
startling suggestion. "Of course." He set the empty
glass back on the tray with a careless rattle. "Peters,
you are devilish clever."

Peters bowed respectfully. "Very good, sir."

The brandy made Nicholas a bit reckless—not like the half-seas over when he had been newly promoted to lieutenant, with shore leave in Lisbon, swaggering drunk and looking for a fight—but with just enough edge to make him do or say almost anything. His brain was clear—so was his intent.

He knocked on Olivia's door. When the butler answered it, Nicholas made a point of speaking in his most condescending voice of command. "Captain Sir Nicholas Sidney, to see Miss Landon, if you please."

He flicked the butler his card, daring the poor man to defy him with some lie about Olivia not being at home to receive him.

She did make him wait, but eventually he was ushered into the drawing room. As always, she was perfection—exquisite in pale pink-and-cream lace.

"Sir Nicholas, this is indeed a surprise and pleasure."

He bowed. "A surprise, yes, but I am not here on pleasure."

"Oh? Pity . . ."

"I shall not trifle with words, but come straight to the point: Where are they?"

Olivia blinked. "Who? I have not the slightest idea of what you are talking about."

"You know perfectly well what I am talking about. Where has your brother taken Miss Adams?"

"I am sure I do not know."

"Yes, you do. You told me yourself that you have been corresponding with Thorneloe and knew of his interest in Miss Adams."

She must have gotten a whiff of the brandy because she rose from her chair and moved gracefully toward the window, smiling.

"You are foxed, Captain," she said merrily.

He glowered at her. "Not foxed enough. Where are they? I warn you, Miss Landon, a man's life is at stake as well as the reputation of a young woman who does not deserve to be ruined by your brother's greed." He paused, making sure she understood the import of his words. "If he has done anything . . . I warn you, I will call him out."

Genuine fear crossed her delicate features. "You would not do that."

"You think not?"

Olivia swallowed nervously. "You realize Richard is in serious straits. You and I both have known that Desmond will not advance him any more funds. Not unless he marries."

"I see." Everything fell neatly into place—Thorneloe wanted Julianna's money. "He has been living on his expectations for too long. He will, by God, not use Miss Adams to pay his gambling debts. Now where has he taken her? Scotland?"

She said nothing, but looked away, not daring to meet his intense gaze.

"Good God. And you would let him do it?"

"Richard is desperate," she pleaded. "He will not harm the girl. He even cares for her in his way. Gracious, she will be a countess! What more could she want?"

"To find her father," he said grimly. "Miss Adams may lose him if he is not found soon."

"Oh, I do not think that will happen. Richard has every intention of helping Miss Adams find her father. Why, only the other day he wrote to me that he intends to spend their honeymoon on the Continent to look for Mr. Adams. Belgium? Or was it Portugal?" She waved a dismissive hand. "I can never remember such things."

"He is going to the Continent with Miss Adams?"

"Why, yes. After they are married, of course. Special license, I presume." She sniffed. "He has some other business in Europe. Political business—at least that is what Mama told me."

Nicholas stared at her, thunderstruck. "Lysette Corbeil. Your mother is Lysette Corbeil?"

Olivia laughed lightly. "Mama? Do not be ridiculous. Lysette is Mama's lady's maid, her abigail." She frowned delicately. "I do not see what Mama's maid has to do with Richard's state of affairs."

Nicholas felt his belly tighten into a sick knot. Lysette Corbeil was Thorneloe's courier. Thorneloe was the English contact, the spy receiving information from the infamous Marquis d'Avergne. Except that Thorneloe had never met the marquis, but knew him only by his initials on carefully worded letters. For all Thorneloe knew, Edward Adams was his French counterpart. Of course he would help Julianna find her father, and no doubt he would receive a handsome payment for passing certain military secrets. Together with Julianna's dowry and inheritance, Thorneloe would do quite well—pay off his debts and inherit Greystone after Desmond died.

Nicholas looked at Olivia's bewildered, pretty face. It was obvious she knew nothing of her brother's traitorous activities. Olivia Landon was exactly as she seemed, a beautiful, vain woman whose scheming went no farther then destroying a man's heart.

"You cannot expect him to live as an earl in poverty," she went on petulantly. "It would be unconscionable. He is a gentleman and deserves the best."

"By *any* means possible, I imagine. Even if it means compromising a lady. I wonder if that was not the strategy for your renewed interest in me?"

Her blue eyes flashed her anger. "How dare you, sir!"

Nicholas bowed with exaggerated courtesy. "I dare much, Miss Landon, because I am only . . . how did you put it? A common sailor. Good day."

He turned and strode out of the room, down the stairs, and out the door to his waiting horse. It was only then did he realize that he had not stammered at all. Not once.

The effects of the brandy had worn off by the time he hurried home to find Peters looking somewhat out of sorts.

"There is a young *person* waiting to see you, sir. She says she knows you from Portsmouth."

"Did she give you her name?"

"Indeed, sir. She says her name is Miss Chetley, quite common—a serving girl. She claims she is Miss Adams's abigail. She has been *most* insistent she see you and will not leave."

"Margaret? Send her up, at once."

Peters obliged and in moments brought a very frightened-looking Margaret into the sitting room. She was pale and tired and gratefully accepted Nicolas's invitation to sit down.

"What has happened, Margaret? Where is Miss Julianna?"

In a voice cracking with tears and emotion, Margaret explained the events leading up to her early morning escape on the mail coach.

"You are certain Mr. Thorneloe is taking Miss Julianna to Ramsgate?"

She nodded. "Oh, yes, sir. I'm sure of it."

"Then there is no time to lose." He rang for Peters. "See that Mrs. Thompson finds Margaret something to eat, then get word to Mr. Fairchild. I will be leaving shortly and will be needing my saddle horse *and* the carriage. And find Mr. Dain, too."

Nicholas left Margaret in Peters's good care and hurried to prepare for the long ride ahead. He hoped he would not need it, but he packed a pistol. Two, in fact.

Chapter Thirteen

Her mother would have never approved of her sulking, but Julianna made no attempt to feign forbearance or ladylike composure. Sailing to Scotland against her will, with a man whose only ambition was to secure her inheritance, was reason enough for her insolent manner. She refused to converse with him and stared out the carriage window to avoid his gaze.

"I can understand your anger, Miss Julianna. You feel you have been misled. In truth, had there been any other way, I would have striven to use it, but as it is—"

"You mean, you could find no other heiress who would succumb to your flattery—except by force?"

He smiled. "Touché. You are as quick-witted as ever."

"Evidently, not quick-witted enough. I have been naive in the extreme. To think I once believed . . . Well, I am ashamed to think of *what* I believed." She resumed staring out the window.

"Do try to cheer up. It will not be so bad as you think. Once we are married, I shall continue to help you find Mr. Adams."

"And should I refuse?"

"To marry me? Then I am afraid there will be nothing I can do." He smiled cruelly.

Julianna shook her head. "Despicable."

"Actually, no. You will be my wife and quite comfortable. As I said, you will have everything you could desire."

"With my money," she said bluntly. "I care nothing for your offer, Mr. Thorneloe. My only concern is for my father."

To this, Mr. Thorneloe said nothing.

As the day wore on, they changed horses twice. With each mile the air grew a bit chiller, the sky, grayer. Julianna had no idea how long it would take them to reach Ramsgate, but felt certain they were getting very close. She refused to speak to Mr. Thorneloe and instead absorbed her time trying to think of a way to escape.

If only Margaret reached Nicholas in time! Julianna bit her lip, trying to keep down the rising panic. Perhaps he had given up waiting for her, dismissing her as capricious, thinking her more interested in Mr. Thorneloe than finding her father. What could she do? She knew no one. If she tried to ask for help, she would probably be dismissed as a hysterical new bride—or worse, a foreigner, a "Yankee girl" not to be trusted. She took small consolation knowing that her aunt and uncle would be worried about her and would, no doubt, engage the aid of Lady Elwood to help find her. But by then, it would be too late.

And the captain? Would he abandon all effort to help her? If he received new orders to go to sea, what then? The thought of losing Nicholas's good opinion of her cut deeply. She could not bear it.

In the darkening gloom, Julianna noted that Mr. Thorneloe had dozed off, his head nodding to the jolt and sway of the carriage. She swallowed hard. Now was not the time to cry. She *must* think of a way to get help.

At dusk, they changed horses one more time at a small posting inn and Mr. Thorneloe allowed fifteen minutes for a hasty meal. Then they were off again. Scarcely ten words had since passed between her and Mr. Thorneloe, and she was determined to keep it that way, until the carriage began to slow and finally came to a complete stop. She could smell the sea and hear the faint screeching cry of seagulls.

The sound of horses impatiently snorting, bits and harness jingling caused Mr. Thorneloe to open the window and lean out.

"What is it, Fleming?"

"We have arrived, sir."

"Excellent."

A groom opened the carriage door and let down the steps. Mr. Thorneloe stepped out, turned, and helped Julianna descend. In the distance she could just make out a bleak, forgotten shoreline and a dilapidated dock extending out onto the water. A small sloop of some kind tugged and bobbed against its moorings.

Julianna trembled within the folds of her cloak. Even though it was summer, the air was sharp and raw, heightening her growing terror. She felt a sudden urge to run, but not knowing where she was or where she could go, decided against the idea.

From the gloom, a tall, rough-looking man with a rag tied around his head like a pirate and an old-fashioned tricorne pulled low over his eyes approached them carrying a lantern. He held it up high so he could see their faces.

"You are theese Engleesh milor', T'orneloe?" the man asked.

"I am. And who the devil are you?"

"Capitaine Lejeune. I take you and the lady to Calais."

"Calais? But that is in France!" Julianna backed away from Mr. Thorneloe. "I thought you were sailing for Scotland."

A cruel smile twisted his handsome features. "I was, but unfortunately, my plans have changed. We sail for France, as I have more pressing business. Later, after we are married, we *may* visit Scotland, but I am afraid you will simply have to do with a French wedding, my dear."

"No! You cannot do this. How dare you abduct me like some common . . . !" So enraged, she could not even bring herself to say the word.

"Calm yourself, my dear. Nothing is going to happen to you. We are simply going to take a short boat ride. By tomorrow, you will be right as rain."

Thorneloe signaled to the coachman and grooms. "Bring the baggage. And now, Captain Lejeune, please lead the way."

He took Julianna's elbow and led her toward the dock. Panic rose within her. Where was Nicholas? Oh, dear God, where was he?

Thorneloe wasted no time with niceties, but simply picked her up and lifted her from the dock over the side of the boat onto the deck. The French captain followed, along with six tough-looking sailors. Yellow lamplight cast weak shadows over the tattered rigging and grimy furled sails. The ship stank of fish and bilge water.

"You take 'er below, monsieur, to my cabin." Captain Lejeune jerked his head toward the hatchway leading down to the lower deck. "I show you, eh?"

Thorneloe shoved her toward the hatchway, forcing her to follow Lejeune. Julianna's heart beat in huge, agonizing beats. She could not believe any of this was happening to her. She followed the Frenchman down the narrow, steep steps to the lower deck. No light filtered through the ship, except from the single lantern.

Lejeune reached the end of a dank, cramped corridor and ducked through an open door that led into a cabin not much bigger than a large cupboard. Inside, Julianna could make out a pile of filthy clothes or rags on the floor, and a table littered with tattered nautical charts, a compass, and sextant. A dirty hammock had been strung across the width of the cabin.

"She stay here, *non*?"

Thorneloe made a disparaging noise in his throat.

"Beastly place, but it will be only for a short while, my dear. Pity there is only room for one in that hammock."

Julianna stared at him, furious, her fists clenched at her sides. "I have no intention of staying in this hideous boat. You will take me away from here at once, Mr. Thorneloe!"

"You have no choice, m'dear. You are vital to my plans."

"I shall not—"

Without warning, the French captain grabbed Julianna's arm and pulled her into the cabin, then shoved the lantern into her hands. From the folds of his ragged coat she caught the gleam of a pistol. Looking down, she noticed that the French captain wore riding boots and spurs. Her heart caught in her throat.

The captain's arm whipped up and around and aimed the pistol directly into Thorneloe's face. In clear, precise English the pirate said, "In the name of the king, I arrest you, Richard Thorneloe, for high treason and for the abduction of this lady."

"Good God! Sidney!"

"Aye, laddie, that I am. Mr. Dain!"

From above deck, Julianna heard the young lieutenant call back. "Sir!"

"Mr. Dain, bring the local constabulary and take Mr. Thorneloe into custody."

"Aye, sir."

Nicholas glanced over his shoulder at her and winked. "And, Mr. Dain?"

"Captain?"

"Bring the manacles. I'll have this lubber in irons."

"Aye, aye, sir!"

"You cannot do this, Sidney!" Thorneloe snarled.

"Can't I now, matey? What's to be stopping me? You? How about E.A.? You *do* know who he is?"

Thorneloe swallowed nervously, eyeing the unwavering pistol barrel aimed directly at his forehead. "Not precisely. I was to meet with him in France. He is Miss Adams's relation, her father."

Julianna gasped.

"Ah, you should be knownin' yer spies, matey. Mr. Adams is not yer man. Edmund Rameau, the Marquis d'Avergne—now there's a spy if I ever laid me eyes to one."

Even in the sallow light of the lantern, Julianna saw Thorneloe grow sickly pale.

The distinct rattle of iron announced Mr. Dain had returned. Behind him, Julianna could make out the dark shapes of the local constables.

"You will pay for this, Sidney! I'll see you hang!"

"Will I now? I think it's you who'll be payin'. His Majesty don't take kindly to traitors."

Julianna heard the ominous sound of a cocked pistol. Thorneloe turned a shade whiter.

Nicholas grinned wickedly, his voice soft and menacing. "And if you was on me own ship, matey, I'd have you swingin' from the t'gallant yard."

"You're mad! I've done nothing—!"

"Mr. Dain, take the prisoner ashore."

Later, after Thorneloe had been taken away and the "crew" had removed their disguises, Nicholas removed the coat and pulled the rag off his head. He tossed them onto the dock.

"I am afraid you will have to ride with me for a short way. My carriage awaits about a mile down the road. We must hurry if we are to arrive in Portsmouth in time."

Julianna shook her head. "I do not mind. Anything to get away from this dreadful place." She shook her head. "How could he have done such a thing?"

"Money, Julianna. Thorneloe was desperate for money. He lost nearly all of his own inheritance to cards and horses. Lord Desmond has cut him off. When the earl dies, Thorneloe will get the title, but no money unless he marries. You were almost a godsend, an American heiress who just happened to be the daughter of the man with whom he has been in contact. Or so he thought."

"And he was taking me to France to meet him, because—"

"You are the only one who knows what he looks like."

She nodded. Seeing Nicholas had almost made her weep. Again he had come to her rescue, and she could see by his expression the irony of the situation was not lost to him either.

He took Julianna's arm and led her to his horse, held by Lieutenant Dain. The lieutenant surrendered the reins and awkwardly mounted his own horse. In an instant, Nicholas's hands were to her waist, lifting her onto the saddle—then he was behind her, an arm about her to keep her steady.

Spinning the horse around, he set spurs to sensitive flanks, and they were off, galloping back down the road, Lieutenant Dain right behind them. Julianna felt Nicholas bend close to her, a brush of stubble against her cheek.

"My dear Miss Adams, can you not find a way to stay out of harm's way? I declare, ma'am, I shall be obliged to confine you to quarters."

Exhausted but happy, Julianna arrived in London eager to be off to Portsmouth, but her uncle and Sir Nicholas had other ideas. After a few hours of sleep, she confronted Uncle Fairchild and the captain in the drawing room, for both had decided she was not to leave London.

"But I must go. Who else will be able to identify him?"

"Miss Adams," Nicholas said sternly, "it is impossible for you to be aboard my ship."

"Why? I was on your ship before."

"That was different. You were ill."

"There is no difference. I will . . . take Margaret along, if you are concerned about proprieties."

Her uncle interrupted her tirade. "Child, it is not only the proprieties, but the situation. We are at war with France. If the *Gallant* were to encounter a French warship, well, it could be quite another thing. You would be in terrible danger."

Julianna thrust out her chin a little. "I am willing to risk that for my father."

"It is an unnecessary risk." The captain, who had been standing next to the hearth, moved toward her, arms crossed over his chest. There was no mistaking his unyielding position on the matter. "If we encounter the French, we would undoubtedly have to fight them. A battle aboard a ship is no place for a woman. There is the distinct possibility you could be injured or killed."

An ominous silence filled the Fairchild drawing room. Julianna had no words to reason against him. She clasped her hands firmly in her lap. Tears and pleading would not change his mind, only a sensible reason—and she had none.

"Captain Sidney." She looked up at him. "Sir Nicholas, please let me go with you. If I am to die, then I will die, but so could my father. I cannot remain here knowing that I might have missed the chance to see him simply because of my gender. I beg you, sir, please let me go."

Another long silence. She caught his unwavering gaze, severe and uncompromising, like an officer sizing up a disobedient sailor. She also saw respect and admiration. Her heart did a curious little bump in her chest.

At once she recalled their night ride back to his awaiting carriage, his arm tightly about her waist, his lips just brushing her ear. The sharp memory of Mr. Thorneloe's unwanted kiss made her look involuntarily at Nicholas's mouth—a firm, serious mouth not meant for saying deceitful things or curling in foolish laughter. Julianna suddenly wanted to kiss him again and persuade him to say more of the soft, delightful words he had murmured the other night.

"Very well, you may go, but you must take Margaret along with you. I must also warn you that this time will be much different. You must obey every word for your own safety's sake and for Margaret's."

Julianna made herself not cry. "Thank you, Captain," she whispered. There was no doubt in her mind that she would see her father again, and somewhere along the way she would satisfy her newly discovered secret wish.

Once again, Julianna found herself frantically preparing for a long journey in the early hours of the morning. Margaret was just as frantic and excited at the prospect of going home to Portsmouth. She kept folding and refolding items of clothing into Julianna's traveling trunk.

"Goodness, I've packed this trunk three times and it still isn't right!"

"Margaret, go do something else. I will pack the trunk."

"Oh, no, miss, that wouldn't be right. I'll finish it properly."

"Only a few things will be needed, Margaret—the gray merino, my heaviest cloak, warm stockings, and gloves."

Julianna took a moment to sit down at the writing desk and compose a letter to her brother Benjamin. It surprised her to think that she had been in England for several weeks and had not bothered to write him. Perhaps she had not written to spare him the news of the shipwreck and the anguish of losing their father. She tried to make her letter sound cheerful and full of hope, but in her heart she realized this could be the last letter he would ever receive from her.

Dear Benjamin. Ben. So like their father—tall and proud with a mane of dark hair and piercing blue eyes. How would he manage if she were killed, or if their father were truly dead?

The final question was the most sobering. If her father had died aboard a ship or had been captured by the French, what would she do? Aunt Emily would undoubtedly urge her to stay in England, but she could not impose on her hospitality forever. She would have to return home to Baltimore without ever knowing what had happened to her father. How long should she continue her search? What would Benjamin do? Certainly her uncle would offer good advice, too, but as she turned these thoughts over in her mind, Julianna realized that it would be Nicholas who would have the most sound advice. She smiled a little sadly as she finished writing. Her brave pirate . . .

Julianna folded and sealed the letter, then rose, gathering her cloak and bonnet. The morning air was chill. The captain would undoubtedly remark about it and insist she dress properly. She heard Margaret let in the footman to take her trunk downstairs. Taking one last look about the room, a sense of foreboding filled her heart. Julianna knew she might never see this room again.

The dashing pirate was gone. Only the captain waited downstairs, looking imposing in his blue uniform with the deep cuffs and the spotless lapels. Each button had been polished to a high gleam—the white waistcoat, immaculate.

"Good morning, Miss Adams." He bowed slightly. "Are you ready?"

"Good morning, Captain. Yes, I am."

She turned to her uncle, who was standing off to one side with Toby tucked under one arm. Julianna decided to make her good-byes brief. She pressed a light kiss to Uncle Fairchild's cheek.

"Good-bye, Uncle. Be sure to convey my love and gratitude to Aunt Emily and my thanks to Lady Elwood."

"I shall, child. Now you must hurry. The captain has told me his ship and crew are at the ready and they must sail the moment you arrive in Portsmouth." He placed a fond kiss on her forehead. Toby managed a good-bye lick on her chin.

Julianna tickled Toby's ear. "You be a good fellow, Toby." Remembering her letter, she pressed it into Uncle Fairchild's free hand. "Please be so kind as to post this to Benjamin. I have tried to explain everything. If I should not return . . ."

Her uncle's look stopped her. She nodded and turned back to Nicholas.

"I am ready."

A curious sense of history being relived engulfed her as she climbed into the coach: Captain Sidney, Margaret, and another long, unknown journey ahead.

Chapter Fourteen

She had forgotten about the creaking sway of the ship and the queasiness while acquiring one's sea legs, but going through the motions of unpacking soon made Julianna forget her discomfort. Margaret, however, did not fare so well. Once they had been settled in the captain's sleeping cabin, she promptly collapsed onto the cot prepared for her, too ill to move or eat anything. Julianna was obliged to stay and help Margaret get over her seasickness, grateful that her own bout had lasted such a short time.

Only once did the captain look in and ask how they were doing. Upon seeing Margaret's suffering, he beat a hasty retreat to the upper decks. Finally Margaret fell into an exhausted sleep and Julianna felt it safe to go up onto the deck to get some fresh air.

Sir Nicholas had made it clear that she and Margaret were not to go wandering into those places that were strictly off-limits: the gun room below, where the officers ate and slept; the gun deck, where the rest of the crew lived; the lower decks, where the stores were kept; and particularly the powder room, where the casks of gunpowder were stored. There were few places where two women could go except the main deck, the cabin, and the chart room.

With Margaret settled, Julianna made her way to the main deck, mindful to keep her bonnet ribbons firmly tied under her chin. The wind was fresh and quite cool in spite of the fact that it was July. Respectful sailors tugged at their forelocks when they spotted her—not one of them cast her a roguish look or the slightest suggestion of disrespect. She knew they dared not, especially with so many keen-eyed lieutenants on duty.

Young Lieutenant Dain greeted her and touched the edge of his hat. "Good day, ma'am. You are looking well."

"I am feeling much better, now that I can get some fresh air. Would you mind telling me where Captain Sidney is?"

Dain pointed over her head and behind her. "He is on the quarterdeck, aft."

Julianna spun around and noted he was indeed on the quarterdeck standing near the rail. "May I speak with him?"

"Of course. Allow me to assist you."

With Lieutenant Dain's hand on her elbow, she managed to negotiate the narrow, ladderlike steps to the upper deck.

Nicholas noticed her and smiled. "You do not look quite as pale or as green as poor Margaret."

"Well, she confided in me that in spite of having lived all her life next to the sea, she has never been on board a ship—fishing boats, but not a warship like this."

"Not many women have." He clasped his hands firmly behind his back. "So you are settled comfortably?"

"Yes, and I think Margaret will come round soon. She is a hardy girl and I do not believe she wants to miss any of the excitement."

"Hmmm. Let us hope we do not have too much 'excitement.' "

Julianna looked up, marveling at the intricacy of the masts, sails, and complicated rigging. Truly a remarkable creation, she thought. How long it must have taken to build such a ship and then have all these men learn how to control and sail it.

Out of the corner of her eye she noticed Nicholas snap open a telescope and study the horizon.

"Do you see anything?" she asked.

"Not yet, but I imagine we will see plenty of ships, soon. The French are quite busy and this is a trade route. There will be many cargo ships and the like. For instance, look over there." He pointed over the left side of the ship at a tiny white speck in the distance.

Julianna squinted. "Is that a ship?"

"Here." He handed her the glass. She took it and held it clumsily against her eye, seeing nothing but blue sky and the sea careening wildly at impossible angles.

A large ocean swell caused the deck to suddenly dip and tilt, forcing Julianna to step back in order to keep her balance, only she backed directly into Nicholas. His hands caught her elbows in a firm grasp.

"Steady on, sailor," he murmured. He reached around her and adjusted the glass so she could see the faraway ship.

"Oh! Oh, now I see it. What flag is that?"

"She is a Dutch brig, filled with cargo." He looked down at her and grinned wickedly. "I'll let 'er go—this time."

"Why, Captain Sidney, you really are a pirate!"

"Aye, that I am, and that be true. Cap'n Nick of the high seas, at yer service, ma'am." He winked.

"I have never seen you quite so lighthearted, Captain. Is this what happens when you go to sea? You become a pirate?"

"Let us say, a *part* of me becomes a pirate. In truth, prize money from captured ships is eagerly sought after, since the Admiralty chooses to pay their captains so poorly. Even the crew partakes of a share."

"Even the American crewmen?" She could have

bitten her tongue for that last remark, but it came unbidden.

"Yes, even the American sailors receive their share."

"I see. And how many Americans do you have on board?"

A long uncomfortable silence hung between them; the former bantering mood vanished.

"Miss Adams, I do not *like* taking men against their will, but a ship such as this demands many men to sail her and to man her guns. The Admiralty does not care how I do this, but *does* expect me to do my duty. It is the ugly business of war. I make no apologies for it." He again clasped his hands behind his back.

"I am sincerely sorry, Captain. I did not mean—"

"I know what you did not mean." He looked upward at the rigging creaking and humming above them. "If it is any consolation to you, I do not force the Americans on my ship to fight against their own countrymen."

"I am thankful to hear that." She looked down, too embarrassed to say another word.

A polite cough from Mr. Smythe interrupted the awkward moment. "Captain, I beg your pardon, but I have recharted our course. I thought perhaps you would care to discuss it."

"Very good, Mr. Smythe."

Realizing she was now in the way, Julianna hastily made her excuses. "I must get back to Margaret. She has probably awakened now." She sketched a curtsy to the captain and Mr. Smythe.

"Miss Adams?" the captain called to her.

She turned back. "Yes?"

"There are only four of your countrymen aboard the *Gallant*."

Scatterbrained little pea goose! How could she have said something so stupid, so thoughtless? What must he think of her now after he had done so much for her? He was risking everything: his ship, his men, even his own life to find her father—an American, who, for all intents and purposes was an enemy of England. She was so ashamed of herself she hardly noticed where she was going and she almost stumbled down the ladder to the main deck. She wanted to put that dreadful conversation behind her as soon as possible. Margaret would have to wait.

Julianna stood next to the railing and gazed upward at the masses of white sail filled with wind, like great wings carrying the ship over the water. The *Gallant* felt alive, a living being straining to catch the slightest breath of wind and with each wave, she rose and fell, her masts and lines all creaking in an effort to sustain as much speed as possible.

All this effort, this great endeavor . . . for her. Julianna almost wept. Captain Sidney did not deserve her derision for doing his duty for his king and country.

Somehow she must find a way to make it up to him. There had to be a way to apologize. The idea of losing his respect was almost too painful to contemplate. At that moment, Julianna suddenly realized she loved Nicholas—more than Michael, more than her father and her single-minded determination to find him.

Dearest Nicholas, can you ever forgive me?

Julianna gathered her cloak tightly across her shoulders and made her way forward. The breeze over the water was quite cool and she shivered a little. Close to the bow, she spotted a sailor coiling a line of rope on the deck. It took her a moment to realize who he was.

"Why, Mr. Jacko, what a surprise."

The old salt looked up at her and grinned. He had not changed much. He still resembled a gnarled tree— skin as tough as bark. His thatch of white hair had been tied back in a queue and his blue eyes shone with delight.

Jacko tugged at his forelock and bobbed his head. "It be a right pleasure to see you again, miss."

"Thank you. I see it has been arranged for you to stay on board the *Gallant*."

"Truth be known, I cut me teeth aboard a frigate."

"So you are familiar with this kind of ship?"

"Aye. Forty-two guns she has. Fast, fine ship. If the luck be with me, I might be seein' a bit o' the prize money now and again."

"I hope so. If I did not say it before, I should like to thank you for saving my life."

"Well now, that be just fine. Glad yer farin' so well."

"Is this sailor bothering you, Miss Adams?" Lieutenant Dain's voice cut sharply, causing Jacko to look down and hastily resume his task.

"Oh, no, Mr. Dain. Mr. Jacko saved my life when we were cast adrift from the *Hart*. He is just being kind."

"I see."

"I promise I will not keep him from his work for long."

"Very well." The lieutenant touched his hat and moved away.

She turned back to Jacko. "Well, I must not keep you from your duties. It was good to see you again. I hope all will be well with you."

"Thankee, miss. And if I may be so bold as to wish you the same." He again tugged his forelock and returned to his work.

Julianna slowly made her way back to the cabin. She did not want to nurse Margaret. What she really wanted was to seek out the captain and tell him what was in her heart—and maybe he would find a way to forgive her for her hurtful remarks.

In a few days, Margaret recovered but chose to remain in the cabin. Julianna stayed with her and amused herself by playing cards or doing a bit of needlework. It seemed wiser to keep out of the way of the crew; she would find a more suitable time to speak with Nicholas later.

The ship teemed with activity. It seemed no one ever rested. Only very late at night did the crew settle down. Sometimes she could hear the low murmur of conversation, or the faint sound of a sailor playing a fiddle—a sad, melancholy sound that made her think of her home in Maryland.

However, boredom led Julianna to take several walks around the main deck, mindful of coiled ropes and other equipment. Occasionally, Mr. Smythe would join her, or Mr. Dain. Either by circumstances or perhaps by his design, she rarely saw Nicholas, which only added to her despair. She did not dare venture onto the quarterdeck to find him, but she hoped their paths would cross eventually.

Nicholas demanded every inch of sail unfurled to catch every breath of wind—and they were in luck. The *Gallant* leaped over the water, sailing before a brisk, strong wind. By his reckoning, they would sight the *Cassandra* any day. She could not be that far ahead.

With the wind right aft, they made excellent time. Nicholas eased up on his crew, permitting a few hours of relaxation. He even allowed himself and his officers a respite by arranging a pleasant dinner party one evening, followed by cards.

Julianna looked as lovely as ever wearing a gown of deep violet that complemented her dark hair and eyes. She was the only woman at the table and without using feminine tricks or allures had all his officers fairly eating out of her hand.

She said little, but occasionally he would catch her looking at him. Nicholas was not blessed with the ability to determine exactly what her gaze meant, but he suspected it had something to do with their conversation on the quarterdeck. He regretted his sharp words when explaining the consequences of impressing American seamen. He had not meant to hurt her, but he could not lie or give her the false impression that life aboard a navy ship was easy or pleasant. Julianna did not deserve to be spoken to so harshly, but she needed to know the truth.

The *Gallant* had been at sea only a few days; stores were still fresh, and Nicholas made sure a proper dinner was served, including a fine claret he had been saving for a special occasion.

Second Lieutenant Lawrence, who sometimes fancied himself a "gentleman with the ladies" kept the conversation lively. "I say, Miss Adams, I have a good acquaintance who is from America—Mr. Nathaniel Blake of Virginia. Perhaps you know him? Delightful chap. Raises blooded horses."

"I am afraid not, Mr. Lawrence. Virginia is quite large and there are several gentlemen who raise horses. However, my father might know of him since he owns some crop land in Virginia."

"Ah." Mr. Lawrence nodded knowingly. "A gentleman. Landed gentry."

Nicholas decided to enter the conversation before things turned political and got out of hand. "Miss Adams is from Maryland. I understand it is quite beautiful there."

Julianna smiled at him from across the table. "Yes, it is, and very like England in some places. However, it does not have quite the rain that England endures."

"You must miss it very much," Lieutenant Dain said softly.

"Why, yes, I do. I am looking forward to going home, except I shall miss England in some ways."

She was looking at Nicholas almost as if the others were not in the cabin. "I shall miss not seeing some of the places I had wanted to visit and also not having the opportunity to properly thank those who have been so kind to me. I owe many people a great debt of gratitude, particularly those who have risked so much."

Nicholas was uncertain if his officers realized that Julianna was referring to him, but Mr. Lawrence broke the awkward silence by raising his glass. "Well, here's to those who have risked so much for one so fair," he said grandly.

A chorus of "here, here's" followed, saving Nicholas any further discomposure. Thank God for Lawrence's excellent timing, or lack of perception.

There was no more talk of Maryland, or England, for that matter. After the remains of the meal had been taken way, Smythe suggested a game of whist, which Julianna accepted, although admitting she was not the best player. Out of courtesy, Nicholas was paired with her; Smythe partnered Lawrence, while the others looked on.

After several rubbers, they trounced Smythe and Lawrence—although Nicholas could not be certain if his officers had merely been polite and allowed them to win. No matter.

It was getting quite late, the lanterns and candles filling the cabin with a soft, warm light. Nicholas found it increasingly difficult to keep from staring at Julianna. Candlelight suited her. It accentuated the rich color of her hair and the lustrous depths of her dark eyes. For a moment, there was a mutual silence, no one spoke. The only sound was the creak of the ship and the faint rush of water against the hull. The silence only lasted a few seconds, but in those moments, Nicholas envisioned another room and another dining table with Julianna seated across from him, presiding over the meal and guests—*their* guests. Lovely Julianna, mistress of Wycombe Hall. It seemed perfectly natural to him.

Nicholas caught himself in time and abruptly turned his attention to the fascinating contents of his wineglass. He felt himself redden, glad for the subdued light. Clearing his throat, Mr. Smythe took the cue.

"It is getting late, Captain, and Mr. Lawrence has the next watch." He gestured toward Lawrence, who nodded.

Taking Smythe's hint, Julianna prepared to rise, prompting all the officers to push back their chairs and stand, including Nicholas.

"Captain Sidney. Gentlemen. It has been a lovely evening. Thank you. I enjoyed our game." She looked at him and smiled. "It was a delicious dinner, and the company delightful. But I am afraid it has been a long day. I bid you all good night."

His officers murmured their "good nights" and remained standing until the door between the dining cabin and the sleeping cabin closed with a decisive click.

"Lovely gel," Lawrence said quietly.

"Indeed," Smythe agreed. "Such a shame about her family."

"I hope we find her father in time," young Dain added.

Nicholas found his voice. "We shall, gentlemen. The *Cassandra* cannot be that far ahead of us. I have made my own calculations and I believe we will catch up to her within a day, maybe two."

"Do you think Captain Needham will discharge Adams into our custody?" Smythe asked.

"I feel reasonably confident he will, however, I am taking no chances. Gentlemen, we will need a volunteer, a good able-bodied seaman to take Mr. Adams's place. Captain Needham is as hard-pressed as any of us to keep a full company of crew. I would not presume he would readily give up a man without some kind of exchange." Nicholas looked at each of his officers in turn, expecting an answer.

"We will get our volunteer, Captain," Lawrence stated firmly. "If not, we shall do some convincing."

Nicholas knew Julianna would not like Lawrence's tone or the implication, but she would have no say in the matter. One of the crew would have to go in exchange for her father. The *Cassandra* was no nimble frigate, but a ship of the line with an enormous crew able to man three full gun decks. Captain Needham was well-off and known to be a good captain who was fairly generous, oftentimes supplementing his crews' pay with his own money. A seaman serving on the *Cassandra* could hardly ask for better.

"Very well, gentlemen. I bid you good night."

One by one they bowed and filed out, leaving Nicholas alone. He moved about the cabin slowly, ducking to avoid bumping into the hanging lanterns. He was not ready for sleep yet, but too edgy to sit down to write in his log or engage in other duties.

"Excuse me, Captain, but I think I forgot my fan."

Nicholas whirled. Julianna stood in the doorway, still attired in her violet-hued gown, but the light from the inner cabin cast a pale aura around her dark hair that now fell around her shoulders—an exquisite vision. He could not take his eyes from her, and for a few hushed moments, he dared not breathe.

"I . . . that is, I believe you left it at your place."

Julianna moved to the table and picked up her fan. "I am so forgetful at times." She paused. "Does it not seem odd to you, Captain, that we have come full circle? It was only a short while ago I was the nearly drowned, sunburned creature you pulled out of the sea. And now, here I am again."

"An extraordinary circumstance, to be sure," he agreed, cursing himself for such an inane answer.

She flicked open the fan, ran her hand over the edge, then closed it. "You know I owe you more than I can possibly repay. My gratitude is boundless."

"I have only been doing my—"

"No, do not say it. Please do not say you have done all this for me because you were doing your duty. You have risked everything: your ship, your crew, your officers—even your own reputation—for my sake and for a man you do not even know."

"I do not feel I have risked anything. You misjudge my motives."

Her gaze met his. "Then why are you doing this, Nicholas?" she whispered.

The sound of his name on her lips gave him immeasurable pleasure. He took a step toward her, now close enough to see the tears forming in her eyes and catch the fragrant hint of lavender.

"Perhaps," he said softly, "because I want to, or perhaps because helping you is more gratifying than fighting the French or anything else I have ever done."

Somehow his palm caught her cheek, his fingertips traced her warm tears.

"Julianna," he breathed.

He bent to her, catching her hair in his other hand. His lips just brushed hers, a light, tentative kiss. She started to pull back, but he caught her by the upper arm, not allowing her to escape. Emboldened, Nicholas deepened his kiss; the taste of her mouth against his was infinitely sweet, like something long-forbidden to him.

He felt her rise on her toes, and her arms went about his neck, pulling herself closer to him. Julianna returned the kiss with unashamed eagerness, her mouth warm and pliant beneath his—a delicious and unexpected surprise.

Good God, how he wanted her! It would have been so easy to lift her into his arms and carry her into the inner cabin, but a soft rap on the outer door startled them both, making Julianna jump away from him.

Her face was aflame with embarrassment. She hastily smoothed the edge of her gown and ran a hand over her tousled hair. Unable to look at him, she turned and hurried back to her cabin, shutting the door just as young Clarke entered, stammering and apologizing for the intrusion.

"I'll be just a moment, Captain, sir. I'll just take these things. . . . Oh, Miss Adams must have dropped her fan." Clarke stooped and picked it up from the deck. "Would you like me to give it to her, sir?"

Nicholas glared at him and held out his hand. "Indeed not."

Clarke handed him the fan, then resumed his duties, clearing away the cards and glasses.

The fan would be returned, but for now Nicholas would keep it locked in his sea chest. Tomorrow he would give it back to her and he would finish what he had begun only moments ago.

Chapter Fifteen

It was late morning when Julianna finally woke up, exhausted. She had stayed awake for hours reliving the events of the previous evening, particularly Nicholas's kiss. Her wish had come true and its realization had left her shaken. She tried not to compare him to Michael, but found it impossible. Nothing, in all her brief experiences with men, had left her feeling quite so helpless or uncertain.

She stood on trembling limbs and realized she had slept in the very place where Nicholas slept, just as she had the first time on board the *Gallant*. This time, she felt his presence surround her, filling her senses— a dangerous, provocative feeling—almost shameless, decidedly disturbing.

Margaret rose and helped Julianna dress in her plainest gown of paisley cambric then brought in her breakfast tray. Julianna scarcely noticed the food and ate quickly.

"How are you feeling?" she asked Margaret.

"Much better, miss. I might even take a bit of a turn about the deck."

"Good. I know you will enjoy it—most invigorating."

Having Margaret join her would help keep her from thinking about the captain and what had happened last night.

After breakfast, Julianna convinced Margaret to take the shortened tour of the ship. Once on the quarterdeck, the breeze caught the hems of their skirts and whipped them about their ankles. Margaret shivered and clutched at her bonnet.

"Oh, miss, I fear we will be blown off the ship."

"Nonsense, it is a good healthy wind. Much better than being cooped up in that cabin. You will feel much bet—"

"Ladies, good morning." Mr. Smythe touched his hat and bowed slightly. "We have a fair wind today and will make good time. We shall overtake the *Cassandra* in a trice. I have spoken with the captain and— Ah, Captain, I was just explaining to the ladies that we should be seeing our quarry in no time."

Julianna could not meet Nicholas's gaze, but he appeared completely unaffected by what had transpired between them the previous night. It had been only a frivolous moment of wild abandonment—two people caught up in uncontrollable passion, it seemed, to him. Her heart sank. Now she was certain he had no further interest in her. Thank goodness no one had seen them, particularly one of his officers.

Hands clasped firmly behind his back, Nicholas looked every inch the austere captain of the ship. "Good morning, ladies. Indeed, I believe we should see the *Cassandra* today. She is a second-rater and much larger than the *Gallant*."

Julianna managed to find her voice. "That is good news indeed. What will happen once we catch up to her?"

"I will see Captain Needham and ask to have your father discharged into my custody."

"Captain Needham is a good man, Miss Adams," Mr. Smythe interjected. "He will readily comply with the captain's request."

"I have known Captain Needham for many years. We fought at Trafalgar together," Nicholas added. "I do not anticipate any difficulty."

A sudden cry from above made them all look up. "Sail, ho!"

The *Cassandra*! Julianna's heart leaped within her. Papa, at last.

"Where is she, Mr. Smythe?" Nicholas asked.

"Astern, sir, off the starboard rail. She's coming on fast."

Julianna watched as Mr. Smythe and Nicholas each trained their own glass on the ship coming toward them—a huge ship, under full sail.

"Good God. Captain, it is the *Josephine*," she heard Smythe mutter ominously.

"Beat to quarters, Mr. Smythe," Nicholas ordered crisply, then turned and headed for the starboard rail.

"Aye, aye, sir."

A flurry of shouted orders, the rattle of a drum, and running seamen made Julianna follow Nicholas to the railing.

"Captain, what is it? What is happening?"

He turned to her, his expression grim. "I will not mince words, Miss Adams. We are being pursued by the French and she is bearing down hard upon us. You recall the letter from Rameau and the particular line referring to the 'empress'?" He jerked his head toward the oncoming vessel. "There she is, the French ship *Empress Josephine*, and she will have us for supper if we do not act quickly."

Nicholas took her arm and led her away from the rail.

"You and Margaret must go below to the orlop, the deepest part of the ship. It is unpleasant there but it is the safest place. I will see that you are escorted."

He looked over her head and around at the frantic crew preparing the *Gallant* for battle.

"Mr. Dain! Find Mr. Shaw. Have him take the ladies to the cable tier."

"Aye, sir."

"Miss Adams, this is precisely what I tried to warn you about in London. I do not wish to frighten you, but our situation is quite grave. The *Josephine* outguns us by at least three to one. It will be all I can do to outrun her."

"But—"

"Please do not debate this with me. You *must* go below." He gently took her arm, turning her toward the eager young midshipman standing nearby. "This is a direct order. Go with Mr. Shaw. I will let you know when it is safe to come up."

He nodded toward the red-faced crew member. "Mr. Shaw, you will escort the ladies below. Find a crate or something. Throw a tarp over it for them to sit upon. And a lantern—see that they have a lantern."

The officer gestured toward the hatchway. "Aye, aye, sir. Ladies, if you will follow me? We must go, now."

Julianna moved reluctantly, loath to leave Nicholas. As she looked back at him standing resolute and unafraid, it struck her that there was a very real chance she might lose him.

Not again. Not another. Not him.

She suddenly wanted the ship turned around and headed back toward England. It did not matter now. They would find her father by other means, perhaps through diplomatic sources.

A loud booming noise made her involuntarily duck, as it did Margaret and Mr. Shaw. A moment later, a huge spray of water cascaded over the deck.

"She's firing on us, Captain!" Julianna heard one of the seaman call out.

The able Mr. Shaw needed no more encouragement. He nudged Margaret to the hatchway and motioned for Julianna to follow him.

"Hurry, miss!"

Julianna followed him and Margaret down into the deepest part of the ship. The cable tier was not merely unpleasant, but disgustingly filthy and dark, and it stank of bilge water. Slimy anchor cable lay coiled in the deepest part of the hull like huge decaying snakes.

Mr. Shaw shoved a lantern into Margaret's hands. "I'll find a canvas and be right back."

Margaret's eyes were huge with terror. "I don't like this miss. It's terrible. And—" A sudden movement near their feet made Margaret jump and shriek. "Merciful heavens! Rats!"

Julianna took the lantern and held it out so she could see for herself. Mud-encrusted cable and a few battered casks lay piled about the hold partially submerged in the bilge water. Holding the lantern higher, she could just make out the glow from dozens of tiny eyes looking at them. She shuddered.

At that moment, Shaw reappeared with a large length of canvas. Next to the bulkhead he found a large crate and dragged it closer to them, then draped the heavy cloth over it.

"It's not much, ma'am, but you won't get so dirty or wet."

"How long will we have to say here?" Julianna asked, her voice quavering.

" 'Til the captain gives the order. Sorry, ma'am, but you'll be safer here. The orlop's below the waterline. Cannonballs rarely hit below the waterline."

Small reassurance, but Julianna only nodded.

Shaw hurried away, leaving them alone in the gloom. There was nothing to do but sit on the crate and wait.

Then it came, a deafening series of explosions as the ship's guns were fired. Margaret screamed and covered her ears.

Another explosion caused the entire ship to reel and shudder from the impact. The cries of the wounded and loud crashing noises all added to their terror. Margaret clutched at her, sobbing hysterically. It was all Julianna could do to keep herself from succumbing to the same.

Again and again, they heard the *Gallant*'s guns being fired, a thundering roar reverberating through the entire length of the ship. At one point, Julianna felt certain the sound would blow them to pieces.

Margaret was beyond consolation. Too frightened to move, she huddled on the crate, hands over her ears, eyes squeezed shut. Above their heads, they could hear dozens of running feet, the rumble of gun carriages being rolled across the deck, and always the deafening cacophony of cannon fire, muskets, and shouting.

Another hit pounded against the side of the *Gallant*, but this time it made Julianna look up. A neat hole the size of a dinner plate had been knocked through the side of the ship—sea water poured through the opening at an alarming rate. An impossible, lucky shot.

She grabbed Margaret's shoulders and shook her. "Stop crying! We must get out of here and go to the top deck. The ship is filling up with water. We will sink!"

Julianna knew Margaret did not hear her, but she took her hand and half pulled, half dragged the girl to the ladder that led to the upper decks. Climbing was slow and awkward, hampered by their long skirts and the constant pitching and heaving of the ship.

Chaos reigned on the upper decks. Boys, the powder monkeys, ran like wild things, barefoot, filthy, carrying leather canisters of gunpowder. Officers bellowed at the crew, who frantically loaded, fired and reloaded the guns amidst a choking cloud of stinking smoke. Red-coated marines lining the side of the rail fired at the enemy ship, which at first glance appeared to be almost on top of them.

Julianna gazed up in horror. The French ship was enormous and towered over the *Gallant*. All of its gun ports were open and every cannon firing directly at the British crew.

She shoved Margaret back down into the hatchway, not caring where she went, then forced herself to climb onto the deck. At a second look, she realized the *Josephine* was farther away than she had thought, but still she could clearly discern the French sailors hanging from the shrouds, firing their muskets on the crew of the *Gallant*.

In spite of the tremendous size difference, the *Gallant* had done serious damage to the French man-o-war. A huge yardarm had been shot from the mast and lay crossways on the deck in a tangle of rope and sail. French sailors lay pinned beneath it, dead or dying.

Julianna turned, desperate to find Nicholas, but he was nowhere to be seen. The deck was littered with the dead, blood everywhere. She almost gagged in horror when she saw Mr. Lawrence, the charming second lieutenant, lying in a widening pool of red-black blood, his right leg shot away.

A shirtless, sweaty sailor nearly collided with her. "Miss, you must get below! 'Tis not safe for ye here!"

"Where is the captain?" she shouted.

"Aft, miss, with Mr. Smythe."

Julianna thanked him and scurried across the deck, trying to avoid stepping on any of the poor sailors left wounded or dying. Near the great ship's wheel she saw Nicholas shouting at Mr. Smythe over the roar of the guns. Except for a dark smudge on his sleeve and a streak of blood on his cheek, Nicholas was still perfectly attired and in control of his ship and crew. When he looked up and scowled, she knew he was furious with her for disobeying his orders.

"What the devil are you doing here? I told you not to come up on deck until it was safe to do so. Go down this instant. You will do so at once, madam!"

"Nicholas . . . Captain, a cannonball has made a great hole in the ship. The water is pouring in!"

"What?"

"There is hole in the side of the ship down there. Please, someone must see to it or we will sink!"

Nicholas turned to Smythe. "Find Dain, no, Lawrence—"

"Lawrence is dead, sir."

"Very well, get Dain to take four men down to the orlop."

"We may need Mr. Dain on deck, sir. Allow me to send Mr. Cox."

"Very good, Mr. Smythe. See to it." He looked at Julianna. "You have saved my ship, Miss Adams, and my crew. Perhaps I should promote you." A tired smile touched his mouth.

She shook her head. "No, Captain, I would make a dreadful pirate, besides, I cannot bear the sight of rats!"

Nicholas looked up as a high-pitched whirr sounded above. He grabbed her arm and shoved her to the deck. "Get down!"

Grapeshot flew over their heads, spattering across the deck, ripping through anything in its path. Nicholas groaned, then rolled away from her to sit up. Flat on her stomach, Julianna managed to push herself up to an awkward sitting position. She glanced at Nicholas.

"Oh, Nicholas, no!"

Blood oozed through the fingers of his right hand as he clutched at the upper part of his left arm. Through gritted teeth he managed to convey a terse order. "Get below, Julianna!"

She scrambled on her knees next to him, trying to think of how she could help. With his heels, he pushed himself backward along the deck until his back was against the bulkhead. He glanced down at the blood pouring over his hand.

"It is nothing, a flesh wound."

"I do not believe you, Captain. You are bleeding badly."

She grabbed for the hem of her gown and, taking it in her fists, pulled and tore it into long, wide strips. Ignoring his protests, she pressed the cloth to his arm, then wound the ends around in a firm, tight bandage.

Nicholas examined the paisley-patterned bandage. "My dear Miss Adams, I must amend my decision and make you our new ship's surgeon. The loveliest ship's surgeon in the fleet."

Even amidst the confusion and noise all about them,

Julianna felt her cheeks grow warm. He was smiling at her now, in spite of a frenzied sea battle waging on all around them. There was no question about her love for him—her dearest brave captain, as gallant as the ship he commanded.

"Come, Miss Julianna. I must get up."

All humor vanished as he got to his feet and offered his free hand to help her stand—only she never quite made it.

A sharp report from a musket came just as she started to stand. The blur of a red-coated marine flew past her, landing heavily, his shoulder catching the flounced hem of her petticoat and pinning her to the deck. The man was dead and Julianna did not have the strength to push him over.

Nicholas bent to help her and was unable to see what was behind him—but Julianna saw. High in the shrouds of the *Josephine,* a French sailor aimed a musket directly at her, then she realized that Nicholas's broad back was his target.

No. Not him. She would not lose another—not to a fire, the sea, or to a musket ball. First her mother and Michael, then her father, but not Nicholas.

At her feet lay the dead marine's musket, still loaded and unfired. Julianna had not shot a musket in a long time, but did not hesitate. She lifted it to her shoulder. It was so heavy she could barely support it. The long barrel wavered as she aimed over Nicholas's shoulder at the grinning Frenchman. She blinked rapidly, trying to dispel the thick smoke blinding her vision.

All of Papa's lessons came back. She took a deep breath, held it, sighted down the barrel, and squeezed the trigger. A snap, a puff of acrid smoke, and a deafening report as the musket fired. It slammed into her shoulder, the recoil so powerful it threw her back to the deck. Through the smoke she saw the French sailor clutch at his chest and fall from the rigging into the sea.

A horrified streak of guilt shot though her. *I have committed murder.*

Julianna tried to get up again, but another sound stopped her and a sharp, blinding pain streaked across the side of her head. The pain became excruciating and she was so dizzy she could barely stand. Her knees buckled. She felt hands clutch at her. The sound of running feet and shouts. Nicholas barking orders. A loud, victorious hurrah, then many.

". . . Captain! It's the *Cassandra*. She's come to our aid. She's alongside and firing on the French. The *Josephine*'s striking her colors!"

". . . Mr. Cox, fetch Mr. Philips. . . ."

". . . will she die, sir . . . ?"

". . . grapeshot . . . her head . . . looks bad. . . ."

". . . I shall try to stop the bleeding, sir. . . ."

"Oh, God . . . my darling Julianna, please not you. . . ."

Chapter Sixteen

Nicholas paced the confines of his dining cabin, into the chart room and back, making a poor show at trying to conceal his worry. It was unseemly for him to be so visibly upset, but it could not be helped. Julianna lay just beyond the door with Mr. Philips and Margaret attending to her.

From the pocket of his waistcoat he pulled out his watch and studied the time. One hour, twenty-three minutes. Philips had been with Julianna for almost an hour and a half. What, in heaven's name, was he doing to her?

Nicholas returned the watch with his good hand and adjusted the sling cradling his left arm. The musket ball had just creased him—a messy superficial wound, but thanks to Julianna's prompt bandaging, he had not lost too much blood. It would heal quickly.

A polite rap on the door made him stop his pacing. "Enter." Nicholas acknowledged Mr. Smythe with a nod. "Well, sir, what is the butcher's bill?"

"Fourteen dead including Mr. Lawrence and two midshipmen, Mr. Croft and Mr. Reed. There are twenty-two wounded including Miss Adams and yourself, and one seaman who is quite seriously wounded—it is doubtful he will make it, sir."

"And the ship?"

"The *Cassandra*'s intervention was most timely as our damage was minimal. We lost the fore topgallant yard, rigging and sail—the damage belowdecks is being attended to as we speak. The pumps have nearly cleared away all the water in the orlop. All in all, Captain, we fared rather well.

"The *Josephine,* however, is badly crippled. Her mainmast and top yards are gone and *Cassandra* hit her broadside several times. We estimate she's lost about two hundred men."

"Now she is a prize of war, Mr. Smythe. See to it that she holds together long enough so the prize crew can sail her home in one piece."

"Aye, sir."

Nicholas absorbed Mr. Smythe's report, deciding what he should do next. Duty reminded him that he must attend to the dead by reading a short service. However, the most urgent business demanded he confer with Captain Needham as to the disposition of the French officers and crew.

The *Josephine* would be an entirely different matter. She would be sailed back to Portsmouth or Plymouth and be refitted as an English ship. The French man-o'-war was a handsome prize, a rich cake to be shared by many.

"Very good, Mr. Smythe, carry on. Oh, and, Mr. Smythe?"

"Sir?"

"Any word from Captain Needham? Has he sent over his compliments?"

"No, sir, not yet."

"Hmmm. Perhaps I should. . . ." he muttered absently.

These little niceties always troubled him. While Captain Needham had the bigger ship, Nicholas had more seniority. It was a bit of a muddle. He decided to forgo any overtures to Needham for the present, at least until his own ship was order.

As he glanced at the door leading to the inner cabin

where Julianna lay, he also knew he would not leave until he was certain she would survive her wound. A severely injured woman was something one rarely saw, especially aboard a naval ship, and it was deeply unsettling. The grapeshot had creased her left temple, not hitting her directly, but enough to cause an alarming amount of blood to stream down her face and neck. Fortunately, Mr. Philips had been close at hand and managed to bind her head before she had lost too much blood.

The door finally opened and Mr. Philips emerged looking tired. He wiped his hands on a bloodstained towel and Nicholas realized that the blood was Julianna's.

"Well, how is she?"

"I believe she will be fine, sir. Head wounds sometimes appear more alarming than they actually are. Miss Adams is still unconscious, but I feel she will come round soon."

"I see. Then you believe her prognosis is favorable?"

"Indeed, sir, I would not fear too much. However, I will keep an eye on her."

"Good, thank you, Mr. Philips. Can she be left alone with Margaret?"

The surgeon nodded. "She will be in good hands. Now, if you will excuse me, sir, I will see to the other wounded."

"Yes, that will be all."

Nicholas dismissed the surgeon then resumed his pacing. He must find some useful activity or go mad. The only real remedy was for him to see Julianna and be reassured that she would recover.

He stopped pacing and gazed at the door separating the two of them. If he could just see her, even if it was for only a moment, and tell her . . . What would he tell her? Perhaps he could thank her for saving his life. Or that she must recover so he could escort her to the *Cassandra* in order to find her father.

What rubbish. There was only one thing he wanted

to tell her. He loved her. It was that simple. Julianna filled his heart. He needed her like he needed to draw breath. All those months he had wasted convincing himself he was not meant for marriage because one spoiled, arrogant girl had hurt him and made him angry for succumbing to his outraged vanity and wounded pride.

As soon as Julianna was strong enough, he would tell her what he knew he had always wanted to tell her—how he needed her to be by his side and share his life. As he pondered his course of action, he realized that the only thing to do was to offer her marriage. Then he would take her home to Wycombe.

Even with all his orderly planning, Nicholas suddenly realized Julianna might refuse him. He still had not completed what he had promised to do: find Edward Adams—and there were other matters to consider. What if Adams had died of injuries sustained from the shipwreck? What if he had somehow made it to the Continent? Could he be found?

Julianna's primary purpose had been to find her father, and Nicholas had willingly obliged her. If he failed to locate Adams, then all his plans would be for nothing. He would lose her. She would return to Baltimore, and that would be the end to it.

Except a part of him refused to believe such an argument. The way Julianna had kissed him the night before proved the depth of her feelings for him. No woman could kiss a man like that and hide her passion.

Nicholas collected his hat and sword, reminding himself he would have to find Clarke—he could not possibly manage to buckle on the sword one-handed.

He hurried to the door. The sooner he found Adams, the sooner he would speak to Julianna. His beautiful, sweet Julianna.

The wreckage on the *Cassandra* looked much like his own ship—a tangle of rigging and torn sail, splintered wood, the lingering stench of gunpowder, and dark blood staining the decks. The crew raced to restore the ship while laboring under the barrage of orders from the lieutenants and warrant officers.

Captain Needham invited Nicholas below to his cabin, a much larger and more luxurious accommodation than on the *Gallant*. A young midshipman hastily rolled up a sheaf of nautical charts littering the dining table, then bowed and left the cabin.

"You will have a glass of wine, sir?" Needham offered, reaching for a handsome cut glass decanter and two glasses from a mahogany sideboard.

Nicholas accepted the wine and the invitation to sit down. He glanced at Needham, noting the careworn lines and signs of exhaustion creasing his face. He had always liked Charles Needham—a reliable, forthright man, and a damned good sailor.

"Well, we have bloodied the Little Corporal's nose a bit, eh, Nick?"

Nicholas had to smile. Needham always called him "Nick" in private, a familiarity left over from their Trafalgar days as lieutenants aboard the *Agamemnon*.

"To be sure, sir. I daresay the Admiralty will be pleased." Nicholas paused, then removed the dispatches tucked inside his uniform coat. "Before I forget, these are for you."

Needham took the papers and cracked open the seals. He scanned the writing and smiled then tossed the papers across the table to Nicholas. "It seems we have been following orders without realizing it. The Admiralty's orders were to hunt down and engage the *Josephine*. She has been a damned nuisance for several months, taking out supply ships and the like."

"Aye, sir. If I may ask, did the orders include finding and apprehending a certain Edmund Rameau, Marquis d'Avergne?"

Needham's eyebrows shot up. "Indeed they did." He gestured to the paper on the table. "Read it for yourself."

Nicholas picked up the paper and read the orders

directing Captain Needham not only to seize the *Josephine,* but also to take the marquis into custody.

"Do you know this man, Nick?"

"Only by reputation. He is a spy, passing and receiving information from an English contact." Briefly, Nicholas explained the circumstances surrounding Thorneloe and his subsequent capture.

"Despicable bastard," Needham muttered. "But it seems we have quite a feather in our cap."

If he and Needham struck an equitable arrangement in dividing the spoils, then they would both return to England rich men. Wycombe Hall would be restored and become a proper home for a wife. He did not doubt Needham would be fair.

As if having read his mind, Captain Needham continued, "I believe dividing our prize equally in half would be the best arrangement. Would you agree to this, Captain?"

Nicholas demurred politely. "Most generous, sir, but it was the *Cassandra* that came to our rescue in such a timely manner."

"You are too modest, Sidney." Needham poured himself a second glass of wine, then took a reflective swallow. "If you will recall, it was the *Gallant*'s last broadside that forced the French to strike their colors."

"Indeed, sir."

In actuality, Nicholas had not seen it—the final broadside had been fired from the *Gallant*'s guns forcing the *Josephine* to surrender just as he had been desperately trying to save Julianna's life.

Needham tossed back the last of his wine. "I will see that you get your share, and the estimable First Lord of the Admiralty with his precious rules, can go to the devil."

That transaction done, Captain Needham went on to discuss the exact disposition of the *Josephine*'s officers and crew. Later, another meeting would be arranged between both Nicholas's officers and Captain

Needham's to decide who would command the prize crew to sail the French ship to England for repairs.

Their business nearly concluded, Nicholas directed the conversation to Julianna and her father. "Captain, I have one other request, of a somewhat personal nature."

Captain Needham nodded. "Indeed, sir? What might that be? I would venture to say that we have covered all subjects pertinent to the occasion. The French ship is ours. Captain Montblanc has surrendered his sword and I have this marquis fellow in irons. What else is there to discuss?"

"Captain, it concerns a lady."

His interest clearly piqued, Needham settled back into his chair and folded his arms across his chest. "Continue, sir. I am at your disposal."

As succinctly as possible, Nicholas explained Julianna's situation and the presumed fate of her father. He avoided any embellishments, but held to the facts—it would not be wise to imply that he also had strong personal feelings for Julianna.

Needham listened, offering a sympathetic "tragic" from time to time. When Nicholas concluded, Captain Needham remained silent for a moment, palms together, fingers steepled at his chin, tapping his lower lip.

Nicholas pressed on. "I am perfectly willing to offer a trade, Captain—one of the *Gallant*'s crew in exchange for Adams."

"That is not what concerns me. I have a large crew, Captain Sidney, over seven hundred men, but I will be bound if I can recall any American seaman by the name of Edward Adams. I do have Yankees on board, about forty, but none from the *Hart*."

"Then you did not encounter her in the storm I mentioned?"

"No, sir, I did not. We just managed to miss that storm. However, a day or two later, we did rescue a handful of survivors, crewmen clinging to wreckage, but they were all British seamen."

Nicholas's heart sank. "No sign of the *Hart* or her passengers?"

"None. We must presume that all were lost. I regret I cannot help you, but there it is. If you would like, I can look into it thoroughly, see if there *is* anyone on board by that name."

"No, sir, that will not be necessary. I will take your word on it. I only regret what I must tell Miss Adams. I fear she will be devastated by this news." Nicholas rose and picked up his hat. "I thank you, Captain, for your assistance and your forthright manner. Perhaps you will excuse me; I have much to do aboard the *Gallant*. I must see to my crew, the repairs, and then bury the dead."

"I, too, am so engaged." Needham bowed. "Good day, Captain Sidney."

Nicholas returned the bow. "Good day, sir."

The short boat trip from the *Cassandra* back to the *Gallant* gave Nicholas scant time to prepare for what he was going to say to Julianna. He dreaded telling her. All her hopes, *their* hopes, had been pinned on the assumption that Edward Adams had been impressed into service aboard Captain Needham's ship.

Except for delivering those urgent dispatches from the Admiralty, the mission to find Adams had been a wasted effort. He took small consolation in knowing Edward Adams had *not* been impressed aboard the *Cassandra* as he had originally surmised. So where was he? While Nicholas now felt Adams had indeed been lost at sea, it did not explain the letter to Mr. Fairchild. Who wrote it? Was the letter a forgery? By whom and why?

More puzzling questions, all of them unanswerable—and he knew for certain these were the very questions Julianna would ask him.

Julianna awoke to a monstrous headache and an empty stomach. These two discomforts did nothing to improve her disposition. She snapped at Margaret, then immediately regretted it. Margaret never indi-

cated she was hurt or offended. She cheerfully went
about her business, fetching her breakfast tray, but the
smell of breakfast almost made Julianna retch and she
waved it away.

The ship's surgeon had given her a few drops of
laudanum to ease the pain in her head, but now the
effects had worn off and her skull felt as if it had been
filled with thick mud and then baked dry. Even the
bandages felt too heavy. She watched, in mute misery,
while Margaret bustled about tidying up the cabin.

"Margaret, do stop fussing. It is making my head
hurt."

"Oh, I'm ever so sorry, miss. Please forgive me. Can
I get you something? Perhaps some tea?"

"No, thank you."

Margaret pressed a gentle hand to her brow. "Shall
I fetch Mr. Philips? You are so pale, miss."

"No, Margaret, thank you. It is just my head—I
have a thundering headache. Perhaps you could help
me sit up."

Margaret obliged her and patted the coverlet in
place. "I'll fetch him anyway. I'll be back in moment."

"No, Margaret—"

It was too late. Margaret was gone and there was
no telling how long it would take before she found
the surgeon. Julianna knew Mr. Philips would be very
busy taking care of the wounded and it might be hours
before he could be coaxed back to the captain's cabin
to attend to one snappish, out-of-sorts Yankee invalid.

She tried to distract herself by attempting a bit of
needlework, but soon abandoned the effort since it
only exacerbated her headache. The minutes dragged
on and on. Where was Margaret? And, yes, she really
did want to see Mr. Philips.

A soft knock startled her. Julianna tugged the coverlet a little higher to her chin. The surgeon had come
much sooner than she expected. "Come in."

Only it was not Mr. Philips, but Nicholas. Pain and
fatigue etched his face, a weariness brought on by too

many duties and too little sleep. Julianna's heart ached for him. Helplessly, she watched as he entered the cabin and attempted a stiff bow.

"Please excuse this intrusion, Miss Julianna, but I have just come from Captain Needham and I have news that cannot wait."

By his expression, she knew the news would not be good. Her dearest papa was dead, but for some mysterious reason Julianna did not feel grief yet, only concern for Nicholas. Nicholas needed her now. He did not need her tears, but her courage.

She touched the bandage at her brow, knowing she looked dreadful, but somehow none of that seemed to matter. He, too, had been wounded—a sling cradled his left arm and she spotted a still-healing cut on his right cheek.

"Very well, Captain. What is your news?"

"Your father is not aboard the *Cassandra*. He was never rescued. Captain Needham only managed to save a handful of the ship's crew. He never even saw the *Hart*, just the wreckage."

Nicholas looked down. "I am sorry, but it appears your father *did* go down with the ship. I wish I had better news."

Julianna swallowed, fighting back the need to cry. She nodded. "I understand, Captain." Her attempt at sounding brave rang shallow even in her ears. "However, there is still the letter. . . ."

Nicholas passed a tired hand across his brow. "I do not know. Perhaps it was a hoax, or some kind of cruel joke. I am at a loss. I will try to think on it later. There must be some explanation." He looked at her, eyes hollow with remorse. "You will excuse me, but I must see to my ship."

"Yes, of course," she answered in a small voice.

Ignoring the pain in her head, Julianna rose from the bunk. Somehow she knew he needed her. Before they both realized what was happening, Nicholas caught her awkwardly in his good arm, holding her close, the fingers of his bandaged hand clutching the fabric of her dressing gown. She felt his lips pressed against her neck, stirring her hair.

"I am so very sorry, Julianna," he whispered.

Her arms went around his neck, the gold braid on his collar roughening her cheek. "I am sorry, too, but you must not blame yourself."

She could feel him nod, then gently, he let her go. He stepped back, turned, and moved out of the cabin without looking at her again.

Once the door was shut Julianna allowed for the tears she would not shed in front of him. Her bitter sobs were not only for her father, but for Nicholas, and ultimately for her loss. Once back in England, she would never see him again. His responsibility, his duty to her had ended when he had discovered the truth about her father.

By the time Margaret returned with Mr. Philips, Julianna was past caring about her head, only the dreadful, aching pain in her heart.

Chapter Seventeen

The voyage home, as Mr. Smythe explained over dinner one evening, would take less time than when they sailed out. Julianna hoped he was not inventing tales just to impress her—she could not wait for the voyage to end.

Once she arrived in London, she would begin making plans for her return to Baltimore. There was no reason for her to stay in England as she could no longer cling to the thin thread of hope that her father might still be alive. Benjamin would decide if they should pursue the search. He would know and he would make the proper inquires.

For the moment, she was simply too tired, too distraught to continue by herself. And Nicholas had certainly done enough. After risking so much, she could not ask him to do more. His duty was done. As soon as they anchored in Portsmouth, she would formally discharge the captain of any other responsibilities on her behalf. She would then take the post chaise to London and explain to her aunt and uncle that it was time for her to go home to America.

Her head wound healed quickly, and wearing a bonnet covered most of the dry scabbing on her temple. Except for an occasional dizzy spell, Julianna improved every day. Brisk walks about the deck were all the more satisfying since the entire crew knew she had saved the captain's life by shooting the French sailor. She saw warm respect in their eyes, sincere deference in the way they tugged their forelocks when she passed by.

To her delight, Jacko had survived the battle. His creased face broke into a broad grin when he saw her. "All the angels in heaven be smilin' on you, miss. 'Twas a brave thing ye did. A young lady like yerself shootin' down that frog, savin' the cap'n's life." He chuckled and nodded toward the red-coated marines patrolling the deck. "A crack shot—better'n them jollies."

Julianna laughed. "Well, I am not so sure I could outshoot a Royal Marine. Let us say it was a lucky shot."

As the convoy sailed back to Portsmouth, Julianna passed much of the time reading or finishing her needlework. In the evening, one of the men would rig a small hammocklike chair on the main deck, where she could sit and enjoy the pleasant night air while taking a cup of tea. It was during one of those times she spotted Nicholas standing at the stern of the ship, his good arm firmly behind his back as he gazed out at sea.

Remorse welled up in her. When the voyage was over, there would be only their cordial good-byes. Eventually she would write to him and formally thank him—a dry, polite show of gratitude for all that he had done.

No more tears, she told herself firmly. Not one more tear.

At last the cry "Land, ho!" came one bright morning. Julianna rushed to the rail along with Margaret to gaze at the distant shoreline. England, at last. She sensed someone at her elbow and looked up. Her heart did a little bump in her chest. It was Nicholas.

Margaret bobbed a hasty curtsy and slipped away, leaving them alone to look out across the water toward the faint outline of England rising in the distance.

"We should be anchoring by this afternoon, Miss Adams. I trust you will be ready?"

"Yes, of course. I see you have decided not to address me by my given name anymore," she said sadly.

Nicholas cleared his throat. "I, um, that is to say, it would not be proper, under the circumstances."

"But I hope we will always be friends."

"Always." Nicholas studied the horizon for a long moment, then spoke in a low voice. "I regret that I have failed in finding your father."

"You must not blame yourself. You did everything you could and risked much. My only regret is that I cannot make up to you for all that you have done—your ship and crew, your reputation as an officer." She shook her head. "No, it will be impossible to repay you."

"I have considered it a privilege."

They continued to gaze out upon the water in silence. Julianna struggled to find the right words to say. It was on her lips to profess to him all that was in her heart—an indecorous, immodest display of emotion. Soon it would be too late for any unladylike confessions.

Nicholas turned from the rail to face her. "What will you do when you return to London?"

"I will make arrangements to go home to Maryland. My aunt and uncle have been most kind to me and I cannot impose on them any longer."

A sudden gust caught the edge of her bonnet, tugging the ribbons loose. She fumbled with them as they fluttered about wildly in the breeze until Nicholas caught one in his good right hand and held it steady. Her fingers lightly brushed his as she took the ribbon and retied the bonnet more firmly to her head.

"Thank you. What will you do, Captain?"

"Well, I shall become a pirate of leisure." He grinned a bit wickedly. "With my share of the prize money from the *Josephine,* I shall be able to restore

Wycombe Hall completely. However, I do not believe Lady Elwood will like having a retired buccaneer for a neighbor."

Julianna laughed at his little joke. "Captain Nick, the Pirate of Wycombe. I am certain Lady Elwood will have a great deal of trouble introducing you to her friends at dinner parties and balls." She feigned a horrified shudder. "Shocking!"

The lighthearted moment did not last long. Two of Nicholas's officers stood off to the side at a discreet distance, waiting patiently to gain his attention. Noticing them, he bowed to her.

"Duty calls, Miss Adams. Please excuse me."

"Yes, of course."

A hollow, tired feeling welled up in Julianna. She watched him walk away, knowing this was probably the last time she would ever speak with him alone.

All three ships anchored in Portsmouth at exactly six bells, three o'clock in the afternoon. Julianna made certain she was ready. Her trunks had already been placed on deck, awaiting transport to shore.

At the captain's order, she and Margaret were hoisted up in a bosun's chair, a swinglike contraption, and, one at a time, lowered over the side of the ship into the waiting launch below.

A sharp breeze blew over the water as they headed in to shore, making the trim cutter buck and pitch over the choppy waves. While Mr. Dain barked orders, the crewmen strained at their oars. Julianna huddled next to Margaret, clutching her cloak together, feeling desolate. Nicholas remained on the *Gallant* with Captain Needham to make the final arrangements for the *Josephine* and her officers and crew. Later, he would join them in Portsmouth, where Julianna would see him one last time.

Once ashore, two stout sailors helped her and Margaret out of the swaying boat onto the quay. Happy to be standing on terra firma once again, Julianna shaded her eyes from the afternoon sun and scanned across the harbor to the three anchored ships. She could detect no activity from the *Cassandra,* but several boats were being rowed away from the *Josephine,* filled with seamen.

Lieutenant Dain joined her after crisply ordering the launch crew to return to the *Gallant* and bring the captain ashore.

"Who are they, Lieutenant?" She nodded toward the small flotilla of boats heading in to the harbor.

"Those are the prisoners, ma'am—the French crew and their officers."

A faint thread of guilt tugged at her heart. Prisoners of war. Julianna could not eliminate the disturbing feeling that the only reason those Frenchmen were being rowed into an English port and eventually taken to a prison was because of her. If she had not been so insistent on coming with the captain . . . but it was too late now for regrets.

She gazed back at the *Gallant* in time to see the white launch come against the hull of the ship. She heard the faint shrill sound of the bosun's pipe announcing that the captain was leaving the ship.

"Dearest Julianna! Dear child, we are here!"

Julianna spun around. To her astonishment, she saw the door of a familiar carriage fling open. An excited little dog came bounding out onto the cobblestones and raced up to greet her.

"Toby!"

Toby jumped and barked happily, scurrying about her feet, tail wagging madly.

Julianna hurried over to the carriage just as her aunt was being helped down, followed by Uncle Fairchild.

"Oh, gracious, dear child. What an opportune moment. We had heard the *Gallant* would be in port today and came as fast as we could."

Julianna embraced her aunt and uncle, fighting fresh tears of joy and regret. It was wonderful to see them again—her family. Except for Benjamin, they were all the family she had left.

"I did not know you would be here."

Aunt Emily patted her arm. "Of course you did not,

but we simply could not keep away. We wrote the Admiralty and *demanded* to know what was happening. They, of course, avowed to nothing, but we decided to come to Portsmouth and wait. We have the most charming rooms."

"Dearest Aunt, Uncle Fairchild. I cannot believe you have gone to all this trouble."

Uncle Fairchild chuckled. "It was no trouble, my girl. In point of fact, it was a splendid excuse to leave London for a time. I have even had the opportunity to enjoy a little fishing, while your aunt has bought out all the shops!"

"Mr. Fairchild, you are a scoundrel!"

Julianna smiled at both of them. "I am so pleased to see you again."

Recalling her manners, she introduced Lieutenant Dain. The young officer bowed and touched his hat.

Aunt Emily acknowledged the lieutenant, but looked around him anxiously.

"And where is Sir Nicholas? Is there any news of Miss Adams's father?"

"Captain Sidney is on his way, ma'am."

Mr. Dain turned and pointed to the approaching boat cutting through the rough water. Nicholas sat in the stern, looking appropriately severe. Julianna knew each sailor in that boat was pulling for all he was worth, but it appeared it was not enough to satisfy their captain.

"Gracious, he has been wounded," Aunt Emily remarked, noticing the sling supporting his left arm.

"There was a battle and—"

"Julianna, you mean to tell me you were engaged in a sea *battle*?" Uncle Fairchild gaped at her in astonishment.

"Yes, Uncle. We were attacked by the French ship the *Josephine,* however, the *Cassandra* helped the *Gallant* defeat her. That is why there are the three ships in the harbor."

She was not able to finish her story as the launch had come alongside the dock. Almost before the sailors lifted their oars, Nicholas had climbed ashore. He spotted them standing near the Fairchild carriage and immediately headed in their direction.

Julianna's heart leaped in erratic, wild beats as he approached her, but as Nicholas drew closer she could see by his expression he was not in a congenial mood. He sketched a short bow to her aunt and uncle, then turned to her.

"Miss Adams, I have news of the utmost importance."

"What is it?" Julianna asked, puzzled.

"I have just come from a meeting with Captain Needham. He has informed me that while he was making terms with Captain Montblanc of the *Josephine,* he discovered there are some Americans among the French crew."

"Oh, dear heavens!" Aunt Emily exclaimed.

Julianna felt herself turn pale, her limbs suddenly went weak. "You mean, he is *here,* in Portsmouth?"

"Yes, but I fear he is among the other prisoners." Nicholas took a step closer to her and placed a steadying hand on her arm. "It appears he *was* rescued by the French and not the English."

"Good God, man," Uncle Fairchild interjected. "How is that possible?"

"I can only surmise that it was the *Josephine* and not the *Cassandra* that got caught in the storm along with the *Hart.* It was the *Josephine* that rescued Mr. Adams."

The full import of what Nicholas was telling her finally sank in—Papa was alive. The wound at her temple suddenly made her faint. She swayed. Nicholas's grip tightened on her arm.

"Perhaps you should sit down, Miss Adams?" he said solicitously.

"No, I—"

"You must sit down at once, Julianna. I insist!" Aunt Emily took her other arm and began guiding her toward the carriage.

"Please, I will be fine." Julianna forced her aunt to

stop. She looked up at Nicholas, whose firm mouth was pressed in a tight, grim line. "Tell me what I must do, Captain."

"We have no time to lose. The prisoners will not remain in Portsmouth for long."

"Where will they be taken, Sir Nicholas?" Uncle Fairchild asked.

"French naval prisoners of war are taken to prison hulks, sir—old, decommissioned ships that have been anchored offshore for that specific purpose. These men will be going on to Plymouth as the hulks here in Portsmouth are full."

"But surely they will release him to us?" Julianna asked in a small voice.

"Hopefully, but we must act soon."

Julianna rallied. Her chin went up. "Very well, give us orders, Captain. Tell us what we must do. Anything."

"But, dearest, you are not well," Aunt Emily protested.

"For Papa's sake, I must do what I can. Besides, you know I am the only one who can identify him."

Nicholas turned to her aunt and uncle. "Are you staying nearby?"

"Yes, we have rooms on Lombard Street," Uncle Fairchild advised.

"Good. See if you can procure another room or two for Miss Adams and for Mr. Adams."

Aunt Emily rose to the occasion like a seasoned veteran.

"But of course, Captain. We shall see to it at once. Come, Mr. Fairchild, let us away and speak to Mr. Crenshaw—estimable man and so obliging. And we shall take the girl. Into the carriage, Margaret."

Just as she was about to ascend into the carriage, Aunt Emily turned and spoke to Julianna in an admonishing voice. "We shall expect to hear from you the moment you have any news, either good or bad."

"Yes, Aunt, you shall."

As the Fairchild carriage departed, Nicholas again

took Julianna's arm and began briskly leading her down the quay, his long strides forcing her to take rapid little trotting steps to keep up with him. Even Mr. Dain had to move quickly to keep abreast with the captain.

She grabbed for her bonnet, pressing it firmly to her head. "Where are we going?"

"A place no lady should have to see."

A warehouse served as a temporary prison for the crew of the *Josephine*—a grim, dirty building at the edge of Portsmouth's Royal Dockyard.

Nicholas led Julianna through the dockyard, a place teeming with activity. Hundreds of men, shipwrights and craftsmen, were busy building ships for the Royal Navy. The place smelled of raw wood, damp hemp, and the sea. Seagulls soared and screeched above as if directing the entire operation.

Nicholas spoke to no one, although if any of the men saw him they readily acknowledged him as a superior officer by tugging at their forelock or presenting a smart salute.

The afternoon seemed to turn grayer, more dismal, as they approached the stone building guarded by red-coated Royal Marines, each armed with a loaded and primed musket.

A serious young officer commanded the company guarding the warehouse. Upon seeing Nicholas, he strode up to meet him, snapped to attention, and saluted. "Marine Captain Thomas Jordan, at your service, sir." He eyed Julianna uneasily, as if uncertain how to address her.

"Stand easy, Captain. Do you know who I am?"

"Yes, sir. You are Captain Sir Nicholas Sidney of the *Gallant*."

"We have met before?"

"I once served aboard the *Meteor* several years ago as a sergeant. You were the first lieutenant then, sir."

"You have an excellent memory, Captain."

"Thank you, sir."

Julianna could no longer keep silent. "We have come to find my father. He is being held here as a prisoner, but he is an American. Please allow me to look for him."

The young marine frowned. "That is quite impossible, ma'am. No one is allowed to see the prisoners. Orders from the port admiral. Besides, I cannot let a lady in there. It would not be proper, I mean . . . I am sorry, ma'am, but no women are allowed inside."

"Captain Jordan, perhaps if *I* were to go inside— the lady may wait out here with Mr. Dain."

The marine hesitated—duty and sympathy warred across his sharp features. "I am not sure, sir. I should speak with the admiral, first."

Julianna lost her composure. She was tired of worrying and waiting for others to make decisions for her.

"Captain you *must* allow us to search for him. Perhaps he is ill or injured. He is an *American* citizen. He should not be sent to a prison ship with the others."

"I am sorry, ma'am, but—"

"Do not force me to issue a direct order, sir," Nicholas snapped, a thread of menace creeping into his voice. "The crew of the *Josephine* came under the direct authority of Captain Needham and me."

"I know that, Captain Sidney, but Admiral Barrett has issued orders that no one is to see the French prisoners, except by his personal approval."

The marine captain looked as unhappy as any young man with a conscience—he clearly did not want to refuse Julianna her request, nor could he disobey his orders.

"I believe I will have a word with the admiral." Nicholas turned to her. "Come, Miss Adams. We have not lost this battle yet."

Chapter Eighteen

As darkness settled over Portsmouth, the atmosphere in the Gull, where Julianna and her relatives were staying, became increasingly melancholy. A small sitting room had been provided where the family could read, take tea, or simply wait.

Nicholas had been invited to join the Fairchilds and Julianna for a late supper—a somber meal, taken at the end of a disheartening day. Julianna said nothing. And he, the man who had always struggled to speak coherently to a lady, found himself attempting to draw her into a conversation.

After supper, Julianna excused herself to sit by the small bay window and gaze out over the harbor. It broke his heart to see her so silent. It occurred to him that she had been grieving her entire lifetime: first for her mother, then for her fiancé, and now for her father. Too much grief for one so young. Yet there was a courage about her that he admired. Perhaps it had to do with the fact that she was an American—a girl made of sterner stuff—someone who had survived unimaginable ordeals and still managed to retain her poise and sweetness.

He knew he loved her, and he yearned to tell her so and to take her home to Wycombe.

Nicholas knew he ought to leave. He had rooms, a small house actually, waiting for him at the 'Yard, special quarters meant for officers. Needham was there, awaiting further orders. Nicholas knew he should be expecting new orders, too. Until that moment came, he would not relinquish his efforts in trying to save Edward Adams—the task had almost become a quest. If it was the only thing he did to keep Julianna in England, he knew he had to find a way to free Adams.

The need for action forced Nicholas to his feet. "Mr. Fairchild, Mrs. Fairchild, I must bid you good night." He bowed to them. "Miss Adams."

She acknowledged him with a cheerless smile. "Once again, Captain, thank you for all you have done in trying to find my father."

"It has been a pleasure. However, the game is not up yet. Tomorrow I intend to speak with the admiral. We shall find a way to obtain Mr. Adams's freedom."

"I am grateful you have not given up hope," she said, her eyes infinitely sad. "If the admiral will listen to you . . ."

Nicholas could not bear another moment watching Julianna suffer. He left quickly, striding through the quiet streets of Portsmouth back to the Royal Dockyard.

Damn and blast! Would nothing resolve easily? He would have to see Admiral Barrett in the morning. "Old Barnacles" Barrett, as he was referred to by many of the higher-ranking officers in His Majesty's navy—tough, irascible, and autocratic—was a man who lived by the Articles of War as if they were Scripture. Nicholas would never get Adams out.

There had to be another way. Perhaps an Act of Parliament.

Or piracy.

Nicholas stopped and smiled. Captain Sidney might not get the American set free, but Cap'n Nick could.

It had grown increasingly silent within the sitting room as the evening wore on. The shadows from the few remaining candles and the glow from the fire cast deepening shadows into every corner. Aunt Emily and Uncle Fairchild had long since retired to their chamber. Still, Julianna would not leave the window seat. She had too much to think about and she was not at all sleepy.

The extraordinary events aboard the *Gallant* kept repeating over and over in her mind: the horrors of the battle and finally the disappointment in not finding her father. Nicholas had tried so diligently to find him, and even this night he had not given up. No one, not even her dearest Michael, would have been so conscientious and steadfast.

She heard the soft rustle of fabric brushing against the carpet but did not bother to look to see who had entered the sitting room.

"My dear, I know it is late, but since you are still awake I thought this might be a good a time to speak with you."

Aunt Emily touched Julianna's shoulder, forcing her to turn from her dismal staring out the window. She had scarcely heard the captain leave when he had departed earlier that evening and knew she would probably be chastised for her bad manners.

"Yes, Aunt, I am sorry you are cross with me. I should have spoken to Sir Nicholas before he left."

"Oh, no, my dear. I am not cross with you at all. The good captain understands completely. He knows you are distraught over recent events."

"Still that is no excuse for bad manners."

"Oh, fiddlesticks! We are all excessively overset by this wretched business. Dear me, to think your father has been imprisoned on a French ship, living under the most dreadful conditions. I dare not think of it. It is too upsetting."

Her aunt patted her arm encouragingly. "Oh, my dear, I have distressed you again but I have brought you a letter that arrived just after you left London."

Julianna took the slightly dirtied letter bearing American postage. "Great heavens, it is from Ben!"

Dearest Ben, he had written to her! She had to

remind herself that this was not a letter in response to the one she had sent to him just before she left London with the captain, but a letter that had crossed in the mails—a letter Ben had no doubt sent weeks ago.

She cracked the battered-looking seals and opened the thick paper.

> *Dearest Sister:*
>
> *I have not heard from you or Papa for some time now and have become worried about your safe arrival in England. Before I continue my letter, I beg you to write immediately to let me know you did, indeed, arrive safely. I pray all is well.*
>
> *Life continues as usual here. We'll have a fine harvest this fall. I have just returned from Virginia with four new horses: a team of draft animals for plowing, a handsome stallion for breeding, and a sweet little saddle mare for you.*

Julianna touched away a threatening tear. So like Benjamin to be thinking of her. The letter continued with all the ordinary, everyday happenings—who had married and who among their acquaintances were expecting new additions to the family. Ben concluded by hoping she and Papa were enjoying their stay in England, but looked forward to their return.

When she finished the letter she again found herself staring gloomily out the window to the darkened harbor. She knew she would be returning home soon—Ben needed her. Without Papa it would be difficult for him to manage, even with the servants.

Without Papa.

The words rang within her like a cheerless bell.

"I do hope it was not an upsetting letter," Aunt Emily said.

"Oh, no, it was a delightful letter, but he misses us and worries if we are well."

"Well, that is a relief."

"He also wonders when we will be returning home.

Oh, Aunt, what if Sir Nicholas is unsuccessful? What must I do?"

Aunt Emily settled on the window seat next to her and placed a comforting arm around her shoulders. "There now, all will be well. Your uncle has many connections and we are not destitute of influential friends. I daresay Charlotte will have a say in the matter."

Julianna nodded. She had heard of Lady Elwood's outrage over the news concerning Mr. Thorneloe's deception. However, the shock had been too much for Lord Desmond. Knowing that his nephew was involved in treasonous activities had hastened the earl's death.

Her aunt rose from the window seat, still holding her hand.

"Now, my dear, off to bed with you. In the morning, you must write Benjamin and explain to him that you will be home, but not until this matter with your father has been settled. If you like, I shall have Mr. Fairchild send an accompanying letter to explain this dreadful impressment business."

Julianna reluctantly allowed herself to be led to her room. Aunt Emily had resolved the most pressing problem, but it did not ease the heavy ache in her heart that had nothing to do with her father.

If God had ever decided to create a hell on earth, the Almighty would have chosen either the belly of a stinking prison vessel, or this place.

The earnest Captain Jordan was not on duty by the time Nicholas reached the prison warehouse. Only four marines stood guard: two at the back and two at the main entrance, one of whom was a sly-faced sergeant who smelled suspiciously of rum.

After returning to his quarters, Nicholas had changed from his uniform into rough civilian clothes, the clothes of a common dockworker or a shipwright. He had obtained the old clothing years ago for walking his estate at Wycombe, unrecognized and unconcerned about spoiling fine clothing. For this venture he wanted no one to recognize him.

Reluctantly he removed the sling from his arm. The wound still hurt, but he would manage. Underneath a long, shabby coat, he tucked his pistols into his belt.

It had been relatively easy to make his way through the dockyard, past the dry berths and the mast ponds where great logs floated waiting to be shaped into masts. At the farthest perimeter of the yard, he spotted the stone building where the prisoners were being held. The sergeant approached him, scowling, and held up a lantern to Nicholas's face.

" 'Oo might you be? Get off wiff ya."

Nicholas tugged the large, floppy-brimmed hat over his eyes. "Nick Thorne, at yer service, sir."

"Is that so? An' what are you doin' 'ere, Nick Thorne?"

"I've a bit o' business to transact, you might say." He jerked his head in the direction of the warehouse. "One of them prisoners you got in there."

He stepped closer to the surly-faced sergeant and smelled the rum. The marine had not just been tippling, he was three sheets to the wind. Nicholas reminded himself to speak with the conscientious Captain Jordan in the morning.

"Oh? And what business might that be?" the sergeant asked.

Nicholas leaned closer. "There's a Yank in there—rich as a lord. He got taken by mistake, y'see, in the fightin'. The Frenchies don't want 'im, but . . ." He paused dramatically. " 'Is family do. Willin' to pay handsomely for him."

The sergeant looked suspicious. "So what's in it for me? It's against the rules to be meddlin' with prisoners. It's a court martialin' offense."

"Aye, but who's to be the wiser?" Nicholas opened his palm so the sergeant could see the bright wink of gold in the pale light of the lantern. "It's five quid, sergeant. Half now and half when I get the Yank out—and yer silence, mate."

The marine gaped at the gold in Nicholas's hand—a half year's pay. "Five quid?"

"Aye. Enough for you and yer mates to buy all the rum you can drink. All you have to do is let me inside and I'll be gettin' the American. Half in yer pocket now and half when I get 'im out. You'll not be sayin' a word. Who's to know? No one will miss one Yank from a crew of frogs."

The sergeant licked his lips. "Just the Yank, eh?"

"Just the Yank and I'll be gone like a will-o'-the-wisp."

"All right, then. This way."

The sergeant led Nicholas to the entrance of the warehouse. He nodded to the marine guarding the door. "Open the door, Corporal."

The corporal hesitated. "Open the door, sir?"

"Now, Corporal!"

"Aye, aye, sir."

The befuddled marine obeyed, fumbling with the key. Once the heavy bar was raised, Nicholas stepped past him, turned, and palmed the gold into the sergeant's hand.

"I'll be needin' the lantern."

The sergeant gave him the lantern, then jerked his thumb at the corporal. "Go on wiff ya. I'll be watchin' this gen'leman."

Once the bewildered corporal was out of sight, Nicholas winked at the sergeant, then entered the warehouse.

He had seen a lot of misery during his years serving in His Majesty's navy, but he had forgotten the ghastly plight of prisoners of war. Exhausted, beaten men filled the warehouse. Some amenities, several dozen cots and a few tables and chairs, offered scant comfort to the imprisoned Frenchmen. The place stank with foul odors. Some of the prisoners were wounded or sick. He heard an occasional ragged, wet cough and knew a few of these prisoners did not have long to live.

Nicholas held the lantern up higher. The men eyed

him suspiciously. In rough French, he tried to reassure
them he was only looking for an American.

Silence. Their hostility grew. For a frightening moment, it occurred to him that they might ambush him
and try to escape.

"I am looking for an American, Edward Adams!"
he said in English. He held the lantern up and slowly
scanned it over a sea of dirty faces.

Nicholas tried again. "Are any of you Americans?
I am looking for Edward Adams."

From the back of the room, Nicholas saw a man
slowly rise to his feet. He was tall and lean. His once
fine-looking clothes were in rags. Dark hair, flecked
with gray, hung in long, dirty locks. However, there
was no mistaking what kind of man he was.

This was no beaten prisoner of war, but a proud
patriot, a defiant man who had at one time fought
hard for his new country. Nicholas had seen that look
many times from the American sailors on board the
Gallant—angry, rebellious men, and not the least bit
intimidated by him or any other British officer.

"I'm Adams," he said flatly. "Who the devil are
you?"

He motioned for Adams to come closer. "I am Captain Sir Nicholas Sidney of the HMS *Gallant*."

Adams's eyes widened. "The *Gallant*?"

"Aye, sir, and I have come here on behalf of someone who has been trying to locate you for several
months. Someone who was nearly killed in the
attempt."

Adams's brows came together. "Who?" he
demanded.

"Your daughter, sir. Julianna."

Being awakened in the middle of the night was becoming a routine. Julianna gave in to the overwhelming desire to sleep and snuggled deeper under the
quilts, but Margaret would not let her.

"Hurry, miss. Wake up!"

"Why? I am sleeping, Margaret. Go away."

"No, you can't, miss. You must get up."

Julianna sat up and pushed back a lock of hair from her cheek. "Very well, I am awake. What is the matter?"

Margaret was now tugging her arm, pulling her from the bed. Julianna stood, groggily. What on earth was the matter with Margaret? Was the house afire? The sobering thought forced her to come fully awake.

"Is something wrong?"

Margaret forced Julianna's arms into the sleeves of her wrapper then scurried across the room and snatched the hairbrush from the dressing table. In short rapid strokes, she yanked the brush through Julianna's hair.

Patience lost, she snapped, "What is the matter with you?"

"You must come now. Please, miss," Margaret pleaded.

"Oh, all right. I am coming," she murmured. She was too weary to find her slippers and hurried across the damp floor to the doorway.

Margaret hastily led her into the little sitting room that adjoined the Fairchilds' private chamber.

Julianna stopped. There were two tall men standing in the room. One she knew to be Captain Sidney, but why he was dressed so oddly was a complete mystery. The other man—

Her hand went to her throat. Her breathing nearly stopped.

"Papa?"

The man smiled and opened his arms. He was thin and unkempt, his hair long and dirty, but he *was* her father.

With a cry, Julianna crossed the room and threw herself into his arms. She did not care if it was all shockingly improper. This was her father and Aunt Emily's notions about propriety could go to . . . Halifax.

After she had shed the last happy tear and had heard every detail of Papa's ordeal with the French,

Uncle Fairchild led him away for a hasty meal and a comfortable bed. Julianna remained in the sitting room, too excited to go to sleep. Margaret had been allowed to go back to bed, and Aunt Emily sat near the small hearth, dozing.

Nicholas had removed the long coat and battered hat. Underneath, he wore the clothes of a working man, clean but shabby. It was a startling change from his splendid uniform, but that certainly did not matter. He still looked every inch the captain of a British war vessel.

In the subdued light of the candles, deep shadows etched the tired lines of his face—it was quite late, or early, depending upon how one viewed the hour. It was only then Julianna realized she was still wearing her dressing gown and was glad for the low light that hid her embarrassed blush.

"However did you manage it, Nicholas?" she asked in a soft voice so as not to disturb her aunt.

A wry grin touched his mouth. "Let us say, I had a bit of help."

"Indeed. Who helped you?"

"A pirate."

Julianna could not contain a burst of happy laughter, then immediately clamped her hand over her mouth. Her aunt stirred, snorted, and resettled herself into the chair.

"I assume you mean that rogue, Captain Nick?"

Still grinning, Nicholas winked. "Aye, that I do. A sly fellow he is, to be sure."

"Well, please thank him for me."

"I shall. He will be pleased he was able to help."

"In all the excitement, I forgot to ask Papa how he managed to send Uncle Fairchild the letter."

"Your father informed me earlier that when he was first taken on board the *Josephine,* a young *ensign* took pity on him and permitted him to write a letter, on the condition he would not reveal their location or that he was on a French ship. I believe Mr. Adams said that the *Josephine* came in contact with one of their supply ships, thus allowing for letters to be exchanged and posted."

"Of course, that would make perfect sense. And all that time, we thought he was on a British ship."

"*I* was the one who came to that conclusion," Nicholas admitted.

"Well, it is all done now. My father is free and we shall be able to return home."

An awkward silence ensued. Nicholas rose and reached for his hat and coat. "I should be leaving. It is nearly dawn."

"Then, this is truly good-bye?"

"I believe so." He paused. "What will you do now?"

"As soon as Papa is recovered, we shall return home. I have just received a letter from my brother. He needs us."

Nicholas nodded soberly. "I know whereof he speaks. A large estate needs the assistance of many people to make it prosper."

She bit her lip, holding back another urge to cry.

"Good-bye, Nicholas. It has been an honor knowing you. My thanks for your generosity and for all you have done for me and my family."

Julianna felt her heart wrench within her chest. She did not want him to go. After all this, she would only be allowed a courteous good-bye and another tedious avowal of gratitude. It was not nearly enough. He must know that she loved him.

"You know it was my pleasure. Perhaps we shall meet again. I hope so. Good-bye . . . Julianna."

She saw the pain in his eyes and the lines of bitter regret bracketing his mouth. He reached for her hand, placing a light kiss on her wrist, then turned and headed for the door. It opened and clicked shut. In a heartbeat, he was gone.

Julianna stared at the door. No. Not like this. He could not be gone so soon. "No. Oh, no."

What had she done? She hurried to the door. It would be highly indecent—wearing only her dressing gown and no shoes—but she did not care. Julianna pulled open the door and raced down the stairs to the outer door leading to the street.

Once outside, she stopped, looking frantically for Nicholas. The air was chill and damp in the milky predawn light. Not a soul stirred on the street. A pair of noisy gulls flapped overhead, screeched, and disappeared behind a row of houses.

Julianna suddenly spotted him, striding purposefully down the street toward the harbor. She could hear the sound of his footsteps beating against the wet cobblestones.

"Nicholas!" A hushed cry, like a muted sob. "Wait!"

She saw him stop and turn. Delight replaced his astonished expression. Heedless of all that was decent, Julianna snatched up the hem of her dressing gown and ran toward him. He waited for her, legs braced, and caught her, one-armed. Her arms went tight around his neck as her toes left the ground.

"My darling Julianna," he whispered. "Tell me you will stay because I will not let you go."

"Yes, I love you, Nicholas. I will never leave your side."

"And I love you."

He began placing frantic kisses on her cheeks, her eyes, her forehead, and finally her lips—a long, possessive kiss, sweeter than their first or even the second, because Julianna knew she was his and he would forever be hers. Her dearest pirate. Her brave, gallant captain.

And no one saw them. Not even the gulls.

Now available from
REGENCY ROMANCE

The Rake and the Redhead and
Lord Dancy's Delight
by Emily Hendrickson

A fiery young lass places herself in a lord's path of
conquest and a lord thrice saves a young woman's life
and now she's returning the favor—with passion.
0-451-21587-7

The Whispering Rocks
by Sandra Heath

Fate has granted once-poor Sarah Jane a fortune. But
scandal has sent her to a far-off land where evil seems
to lurk in every corner—and a handsome local man is
filling her with desire.
0-451-21560-5